Born to Fight

The Born Trilogy
Book Two

Tara Brown

ISBN: 10::0991841158
ISBN-13::978-0991841158

This book is dedicated to the believers, and my Dad.

ACKNOWLEDGMENTS

Thank you to my family and friends for supporting me and believing in me. Thank you to my fans, you are the reason. Thank you to Steph at Once Upon a Time Covers for making my vision come to life. Thanks to my editor for taking this journey with me, love you Andrea Burns!! Special thanks to my kids and my amazing husband. In the short time this has all been going on, you have been very supportive, even when it all consumed me and you had to eat from the freezer. I am sorry about that. To the fans and the bloggers and reviewers, I bow before you.
Lastly, thank you to my Nators!!!!! Best Street team/friends ever!!!
Thanks Dad for all the weird survival things you know!!!!

It's us and them, there ain't no normal people anymore. Everyone's sick, in some way.

Chapter One

The music doesn't make the dream better. Everything in my dream is grey, except the blood. The blood is red and running throughout. I don't know the song playing, but it makes me feel like I should be dreaming about children playing or couples dancing, like in the old movies I watched with Granny. It's a happy song.

I hear a whine through the music and look around for Leo. I smile when I see him next to me, until I see he has his worried look in his eyes. I want to tell him everything is going to be okay, but I'm not sure.

Seeing him, I know it's all a dream. That realization hurts. It makes me miss his sloppy-wolf face. The dream starts to hurt more when his wet nose is against my arm, shocking me. But when I reach for him, the dream won't let us touch anymore. It's keeping us apart. The blood flows on the ground like rivers do. I don't want to cross it. I'm scared for some reason.

I hear my dad calling me.

I turn and look back at him; he's standing next to the bunker lid in the yard, where we hid when everything ended.

"Em, I told you, it's us and them. I told you not to trust anyone." His words sound funny, like he's under water.

My eyes open. The light blinds me momentarily.

I glance around the room, as the memories of it start to fill in the blanks I have.

I hate that things have changed.

I hate that my rules have changed… that I have changed.

Months spent living with others, have aged me more than the years I've spent alone. More than the years I spent with my dad. The memories of everything still feel so new and fresh. They hurt, like it all happened yesterday, which scares me.

How long will everything else hurt, if my childhood still pains me?

I look around the stark room and feel darkness settle in. I knew I would feel it eventually. You can't spend as many years alone as I have, and not expect the feeling would come for you. I have spent too much time alone in my head, to not know I would be able to sense it, like I am now.

The feeling that has finally arrived, makes my hollow insides tremble a bit. Almost a decade alone, and it has chosen now to come. Perhaps, because things don't seem like they can get worse.

The feeling is my impending death.

I'm going to die today. I feel it. I sense it in the air, like a pig smelling its final moments before being taken to the slaughterhouse.

It burns inside. It's desperation to change the way my life will end. I hate that he isn't with me. I hate that I'm here. I hate that I am focusing on every detail, as if the next one will truly be my last moment. I wish I had one of those balls, the gypsy lady at the fair had. The one she could see the future in. I wish I knew which moment would be my last.

I sigh and look for a solution. It's not like I haven't already spent hours investigating every detail of my time spent in this room. Some of it has been tied to the cold, metal table, like I am now. All of it has been spent in this lonely, cold room, with a man I am planning to kill.

If I had to guess, I'd say he has the same intentions as I do. It feels like an unspoken race between us, to be the one to live through the unspoken battle.

There are things I am certain of.

Firstly, I know I am going to die escaping. I am too exhausted for it to be a perfect escape. I know I will die today. I can feel it in the air. I will escape today and die trying, and that is a better outcome than remaining tied to this table with this man. I've been too lucky. Way too lucky. I have no lives left. As long as I die free, with the wind in my face, I don't care about the other details. But I will not die strapped to this table.

Secondly, Leo is near me. I can sense him. He is looking for me. He is pacing. I can feel the cold of the floor on his paws. Maybe it's the drugs they've been putting in me. They make me feel funny, thick, and foggy. Maybe, it's the fact I have nothing to do but stare at the ceiling and the nineteen pinholes in the plaster directly above my head. They form a constellation. I don't know which one; but when I've camped out in the summer, I know I've seen it in the sky. I don't know the names of the constellations, but I know when I will see them, and what they remind me of. This one is the donkey. He reminds me of Will. Will the ass.

Will, who has a nice ass, as Meg always says. Damned kid. I grin, weakly. My chapped lips bleed when I do it. The blood trickles down into my mouth. It's the first thing I've tasted in a while.

Lastly, I know the devilish doctor will slip up. Today is the day. Just as I sense my death, I feel his exhaustion. I can see it. He seems more tense than normal. He's upset about something. He's human, after all. I have spent a lifetime watching humans. We make mistakes. When he does, I will kill him with whatever means I can.

He moves about the room in a white coat and a light-blue mask. He touches my arms and pokes me. He likes his job. I can see that, in his squinty eyes behind his mask. He squeezes my flesh to tighten it and stabs extra hard. I cried out the first time, but it made smile creases around his eyes. I don't scream for him anymore.

I plot.

The minute he unties me, I am going to be stabbing that needle into his eyeball. His pale-blue eyeball, that I think is the coldest thing I have ever seen… colder than a winter in the mountains.

I can't help but wonder about the other kids who have been in his care, and the stabbing of the needle. It fuels my fire—my anger.

I don't know how many days/weeks I have been here. I haven't left the room. I woke, tied to the bed. The first doctor was nice to me. He called me sweetie and had sad eyes. He let me be untied more often, drugged and mellow, but free to roam the room and use the toilet. He left one day, and this guy came the next time the door was opened. I have spent more time tied to the table with him here.

No one else has been inside my room.

I'm disappointed Marshall hasn't been to see me. I am going to skin him, probably alive. My Granny's skinning knife is the best. I can imagine peeling him. I can imagine the screaming. It makes me happy, which I assume makes me no better than the man torturing me with needles. I am comfortable with that comparison.

I look back at the doctor; there is no way he is alone here. We are not alone. There have to be others. My skin crawls imagining what is down the halls. What horrors could there be awaiting me?

He pats my arm and grins, "You're a special girl. A very special girl." His voice is gravelly and weird, like he doesn't talk much so it gets bogged up.

I don't respond. He has no idea, just how special I am.

I am waiting for it, my moment to show him.

My eyes flutter when he injects something into my arm. I fight it, but I'm out before I even realize what's happening.

I don't dream but I hear voices, "Emma. I need you to wake up, Em."

The voices make tears flood my closed eyes. The wetness of them on my cheeks feels real. The voices have been my constant for the past weeks. I have imagined the voices so often. If only they knew where I was. If only they could come and save me. If

4

only they were real. My exhaustion is too great to escape alone. It's why I'm going to die.

The drugs fade slightly and I open my eyes to a surprise. They flutter again, but this time it's the flickering of the inconstant light that gets them. I hate the inconstant light.

The voices have become a hallucination. The face behind the mask smiles, but it's not him, it's her. It's her eyes and her face and I feel my lips split into a grin when she talks again. "We gotta be fast, Em. You okay?" she says softly. She touches my arm and I swear it's real.

I shake my head, as my hands reach towards her, regardless of not being able to move from the restraints. My fingers twitch and strain themselves; they want to touch her back. They want the confirmation it's not a dream. But the door opens and the evil doctor comes back in. I close my eyes and pretend I'm sleeping, in case she is just a dream, and he's here to torture me some more.

"What are you doing in here?" his voice is grumbled and cold.

She speaks again and my heartbeat picks up on the monitor, "I was asked to come and get some samples of her tissues."

"I told them, I'm not ready. I'm injecting her with it soon. Now get out of here," he says here like he has an accent.

Her voice is still singing inside of my head. I'm freaking out. I don't want her to leave me. I peek through my lashes as she walks from the room. My heart sinks. I press my eyes shut and let him think I'm sleeping. She was real. She is here for me. They came.

I can't focus on them coming for me. I have to focus on the fact she's gone again, and when he came back in the room, he had a tray of things in his hands. I peek through my lashes when I hear him doing things. I see the tray and shiver. The things on it look shiny and new. Tools of his cruel trade. I can imagine the feel of them in my fingers. I have to block out the thoughts of them in my skin.

His cold fingers brush against my arm, as he unties one of the leather cuffs that's around my wrist, and starts to change the IV needle in me. I'm not sure if I believe in God and miracles, but this moment feels like one. I act like I am falling back to sleep. He takes the rubber tube off and turns his back. He is humming a creepy song. It might not have been creepy if someone else was humming it, but he is creepy in general.

I peek at him through my lashes. His pulse in his neck is slow. His breathing is steady. His back is to me. He doesn't know that the girl who was just here, is my way out. She'll be back for me and I am praying she isn't alone.

The adrenaline mixes with the hope she brought me, and the rush of anger and fury come in a wicked flash.

Moving fast, like lightning, I grab his back and tip his balance. I pull his lab coat by the collar, until his neck is low enough, that I can wrap my skinny arm around his throat and hold him tightly to my chest. He is flailing about and kicking with his feet. Something sharp stabs into me. I feel a cold rush of something, but I don't let go of my grip on his neck with my arm. His body is fighting hard. He is panicking. He scratches me with his needle. I scream out for the first time in days of stabbing and pain. His throat makes a crunching noise. The tray is smashed and his worktable is kicked over, before he stops thrashing about.

He doesn't go limp. He scratches and digs his fingers into my arm. He reaches around, grabbing at me, but I lean back. My boney arm is perfect for making the sound that comes next. The crunching sound in his throat turns to a snapping noise and I feel him leave his body. I let him go. My arm is cramping up. It hurts to straighten. It's bleeding and scraped up.

I take my first, big breath since he came back into the room. My heart monitor is going wild. I pull the tabs off my chest, making the beeps turn into a constant hum. I untie my other arm and push myself to sit up. Something instantly pulls between my legs. Terrified of what I'll find, I slowly put my fingers between my legs where the nightgown I'm wearing is open. I don't have any underwear on, they must have taken them off. Fear and disgust start taking turns at being bigger in my heart, as I feel the tube that's running in me down there. My fingers shake. My arm, where he put the needle is going numb. I gag and feel woozy when I feel the whole apparatus. The tube hurts when I move it. I pull slowly and try not to let my hands shake. It doesn't hurt to take out, but it scares me, more than killing the man by crushing his windpipe. I pee all over the bed and floor when the tube is out completely. The warm urine is running between my legs. I look at the door and pray this isn't the moment that she comes back.

I untie my feet and swing my legs to the edge of the bed. My pee drips from the bed onto the floor. The single splashes and the constant sound of the heart monitor, make the room smaller. I'm panicking. It stings between my legs. I don't want to know what that was, or what they've done to me.

I push myself off the bed, but my arm is weak and fuzzy. My vision is getting hazy. The floor is cold against my toes. My legs feel weak like a baby deer's. My first steps are awkward and uncoordinated.

I lick my lips and whisper, "Anna." Warmth washes over me and I shudder, staring at the door weakly.

I stumble to the wall and bend to unplug the heart monitor. I have to slide down the wall to get the cord. I jerk it and the sound stops. I want to cry, but I can't. I can't stand up again. Whatever he shot into my arm, is making me feel sick. I crawl along the wall to the tray of things. I pull out some alcohol and pour it over my arm. I wince and almost cry out. It stings. The scrapes are red and angry. I wrap a long, thin, white bandage around my arm and tape it there.

Then I drag myself to where his dead body lies. I slide my smelly nightgown off and tug off his pants and his coat. I dress myself painfully and slowly. I tuck my hair into the back of the lab coat. His shoes are ridiculous on me, like the clown at the circus I saw once with Granny.

I put on his socks. He lies there in his underwear and undershirt.

He is pudgy. I look at his meaty body. Compared to the skin and bone I am used to seeing, he is huge.

I crawl to the door and prepare myself for the effort, I am about to use.

"Anna," I whisper again. She doesn't come back. Did she not hear the commotion? Is she okay? Was she taken captive too? I don't have time to ponder. I need to run, but like the feeling I had earlier, I fear I won't live through it. I'm too tired and too sick.

I use the handle of the door to pull myself up to my feet. Exhaustion is not the right word.

I stand and steady myself. I feel inside his coat pockets. I need an inventory of what he has and what I need. The sliding card in his right pocket looks exactly like the one from the farm.

I wish Anna, and even Will, would come. I feel sick and my arm probably needs stitches. I can feel it's still bleeding, soaking the bandage. I look around the tiny room and try to fight the feeling that everything is hopeless, before it's even started. Maybe she wasn't real.

"She was there, Em. Get a grip. Anna was here. The doctor is dead." I whisper to myself. "You did one thing today." The words make a tiny smile cross my lips.

Granny always had lists. She would check things off all the time.

I glance back at him and see the check mark in my mind. Sometimes she would put 'Watch Days of our Lives' on the list. We would watch it and eat popcorn or chips. Everyday was Days. My favorite character was Sami. When I turned eight, I was allowed to start watching it with her.

I hold the cold, metal handle and force my mind back around to my own list. Die free with the wind on my face, is pretty high on it. I need to be more positive.

"Try not to die... not yet," I say hoarsely and turn the knob of the door. As I hear the handle hit the end of its rotation, I stop.

I should have waited an extra second. The drugs are making me crazy. I'm talking to myself and making mistakes.

I look around. Memories and skills are flooding my mind, as I try to formulate a plan.

Do I stay in the room and wait for Anna to come back? I need weapons. I glance back at the dead doctor and turn the knob closed again. I stumble over to where his tools are splayed across the floor. I bend as best as I can and pick up a couple of the silver knives from the floor. The cold metal in my fingers feels just as amazing, as I imagined it would. There are bags of water and other things. I grab them and stuff a couple in my pockets and stagger back to the door. I put my hand back on the door and grip the cold knife with the other. I take a breath and imagine how the forest is going feel when I'm in it again. His fur and the cold air of the woods; my daydreams consist of so little.

The cold metal and stark white of the room make me feel exposed and naked. The door handle turns again with ease. I open it a crack and peak out. The hallway doesn't look the way I thought it would. Anna is nowhere to be found; no one is. It isn't like the breeder farms.

The lights are muted and flicker. They make me painfully aware of the fact that she probably wasn't real. She wasn't really there. I am still alone.

The old fluorescents flicker like they're running on something unstable. Brian's generator was like that. The lights would flicker. Granny's generator was too. I never ran it much, but when I did, it freaked me out the way the power felt half on.

The light in the hallway looks the same.

But the hallway itself isn't immaculate and stark like the room I'm in. It's dingy and empty of life. I look down one end of the hallway. Nothing stirs. I can see papers on the floor and closed doors. It looks like people fled in a panic, like all the other buildings I've seen. I look down the other side of the hallway to find it looks the same. Nothing is the way I think it will be. It's not clean like the breeder farms or organized. Where am I? How could this be the place Marshall would bring me?

I have a bad feeling. What if Anna was real? Is she safe? Is she alone? I gag as my vision blurs. I don't have the strength to help her.

I whistle softly in case he's with her. Nothing moves or makes a sound. I look up to see if there are cameras or anything. Dad always hated the video cameras that recorded everywhere you went and what you bought. He hated being recorded. He had weird theories about the cameras and the information they gathered. I smile faintly when I think about how crazy I thought he was. He would have loved this place. It would have confirmed so many things for him.

My first steps feel forced, like I'm wading through water. I can't listen to the nothingness surrounding me. I don't know if I hear everything correctly. The flickering lights are working against me. They're trying to drive me crazy. I twitch and shiver and know it's too late; I already am crazy.

There is too much suspense and empty space in the hallway. Sweat is trickling down the sides of my face, making me twitch and wipe it away. The flickering lights make it impossible to get a good view of everything. I see nothing but me, the papers, and doorways, but the flashes won't guarantee I am alone.

I try every doorknob along the hall, but they're locked. The cold of the metal against my fingers is shocking. I think I have a fever. He has injected me with poison and now I'm dying.

I put a hand on the bumpy wall to steady myself. I lick my lips. Everything feels slow and pronounced.

The lights flash at the same rate my heart beats.

I peek around the corner at the end of the hall. Again, I find myself alone in a long corridor with papers and debris on the floor.

A sharp pain hits me in the stomach. I break a rule, not that it matters—I think I've broken them all at this point.

I bend and cry out. I can't stop myself. The pain is agonizing. It feels as if my insides move. I drop to my knees and slide myself along the floor. I ride a piece of paper like it's a magic carpet and grip my stomach with my left hand.

The flashing lights are inside my eyes now. When I close them, I can see the flashing and the hallway. Even in my mind, nothing about this hallway makes sense. Except maybe, the flashing lights. The uneven power supply makes sense.

I move forward on my knees, until I feel like I can stand again. I grip a door handle and pull myself up. My legs shake and attempt to buckle. I refuse to fall.

The wall is holding me up completely.

"Leo," I whisper his name. I need his fur in my fingers. I always imagined it would be the last thing I touched. Tears are streaming down my cheeks. I'm going to die alone in a hallway with nothing in my fingers and no wind on my face.

The pain is unbearable.

I lean on a doorknob for a breath, but instead I fall inside. The handle was unlocked. I hit the floor and cry out again. I wait for the room's occupants to attack me. I wait for the sound of my own tearing.

Nothing happens.

I look up and in the flashes of light from the hallway, I see something I never expected. Jesus is looking down on me with huge wide-open arms. He is smiling and telling me that everything is going to be okay. I drag myself into the room and kick the door shut. As the door closes, the light leaves us. Me and Jesus, perfect strangers, sit alone in the dark. I don't introduce myself. He will know me soon enough.

Chapter Two

In the darkness of the closed-up room, flashes of images pass in front of my eyes—memories of the beginning.

In the flashes and fever, I see the TV at Brian's. It's old and small. When we got there, I didn't even know how to turn it on. I hadn't seen a TV like it before. Gramps had a huge flat screen. I miss Gramps and Granny.

My dad had his face plastered to the rounded screen, the entire time we were at Brian's hiding out. We barely made it there. I remember the panic and pandemonium. I remember the way he dragged me through the woods, yelling at me to hurry up; we needed to get to Brian's. We had left it too late. A tidal wave was coming and we needed to get to high ground and cut through the woods to Brian's. He screamed and I tried to run, but my legs hurt.

Once we made it to the bunker, no matter how hard I tried, I couldn't fight the urge to watch the news. It was so scary, and yet, my eyes wouldn't leave it.

The same news lady was on everyday. I knew her voice better than my own. "We have passed the point of needing blood donations. The public is safer to stay inside and wait it out. Rations and remaining inside, are your best bet at this point. Right now, on the Western Seaboard, we believe there to be at least one million cases of the Dengue fever that is sweeping across America. That number is reported cases. We do not know the exact number, as many people are trying to stay home and fight it out." Her face was tired, and the makeup didn't hide the pain in her eyes. Her perfect brown bob was shiny and clean. She was the last clean person I remembered, before the breeder farms.

I was already dirty when I watched her on the news in Brian's bunker. I glanced back at Dad. I didn't like the way he nodded, like he was part of the conversation with the news lady. He looked crazy when he turned to me and said, "We leave soon, kid. When the panic is over."

I nodded and hugged my knees in tighter to my body. I looked back at the news lady. Her dark-blue eyes were glassy. I imagined she knew something, but couldn't tell the rest of us, like how bad it all really was.

She swallowed hard and continued. "In other news, Japan has again been hit by several strong earthquakes. They are ranging between 4.3 and 7.5. As we all know, the Dengue fever is considerably worse in Asia, so this couldn't come at a worse time for them. Several small tidal waves have already hit Alaska and Northwestern Canada. Power outages and flooding have been bad along the Northwest Coast. Canada is suffering through its own earthquakes. The famous Hot Springs Island in British Columbia is dry. The hot springs are gone. In other news, New York and New Jersey are still underwater from the mass flooding that's left over from the hurricanes this season." My stomach sunk.

Brian turned the TV off and we sat in the bunker in silence. Dad had been saying it would happen. He had been saying it for as long as I could remember. All the names I'd called him inside my mind, started to make me feel bad. I remember thinking bad things about him as he dragged me along the hillside, yelling at me that we needed to get to high ground. The highway was blocked and another tidal wave was coming.

Brian left the bunker a lot. He turned the handle and opened the sealed door in the ceiling. It made a noise like Granny's Tupperware did. I could imagine the outside world. The news images were horrifying, but I would still see it the way it was when we came into the bunker. Only Brian and my dad got to leave. The only fresh air I got, was when they cracked the door open to leave. The cold wind shot down the ladder. I would get goose bumps and feel excitement every time.

I hated the bunker. We ate canned and dried food and watched the small TV. The panic was all just the way Dad said it would be. The news footage was scary—looting, bombing and countries at war. Everyone blamed each other for the Dengue fever. Then they all started bombing areas to kill the sick, who weren't dying from the fever. It seemed like it would never end.

But then it did, when the TV stopped working. When the power and the water turned off, we sat in the candlelight and spent the days wondering and imagining. What was it like out there?

The day we left the bunker was a bad day. The TV hadn't been on for two weeks. The last thing I saw was the President making a speech and crying. I missed half of it. I was sleeping. That's all there had been to do in the bunker. I woke to Dad packing the jeep and the bunker door opening.

When we got into the jeep, Dad told me and Brian his plan, again.

He was as impassioned telling it the hundredth time, as he had been the first time. "So we'll cross the freeway at the Green Mountain exit and take the backroad till we get to the base of the mountain range, where the cabin is. It's a day's hike up then. There is an old farmhouse there at the base of the mountain that the cabin is on."

I was so tired of the plan. I was so tired of his voice. I could scream with frustration. The only thing getting me by, was a copy of a book I found, called *Twilight*. I'd read it three times in the bunker, always wondering if she ever got what she wanted.

I gripped the thick book to me in the jeep and held back the screams that clogged my throat and left me breathless.

Dad looked back at me, "When the people who live at the farmhouse die off, we can go and see what they have. Farmhouses always have the best stuff. Canning and dried foods, and not to mention, the best survival supplies. Ropes and shovels and extras of everything. Remember that, Em. It's us and them now." I had heard it so many times, I could have choked him. There were moments I hated him.

Brian looked back at me and tried to smile like he always did, trying to make me feel better. Dad never sugarcoated anything. He wanted me to know the worst. He always wanted me ready.

Brian disagreed. He wanted me to be a little kid. But I had never been a kid. I'd always been more.

Sometimes they fought about me, like a mom and dad would. More than my mom and dad ever did.

I would never forget Brian's face, as he tucked my hair out of my face, and gave me a small sucker. He always had candy. It was red. I didn't really like red, but I took it anyway.

He grinned, "It'll be fun at the cabin, kid. Lots of things to do there."

I rolled my eyes, "Fun? My iPad, iPod, DSI, Xbox, and even that stupid eReader, Granny gave me, are all dead. What fun is there? I've been to wilderness camp every summer for five years. I know what there is to do at a cabin. It's never been fun."

Brian laughed.

My dad eyed me up in the rearview window, "Em, you know those things are part of a world that doesn't exist anymore. Your generation is soft—weak. One day you'll thank me for all that camp. I can tell you now, no other girl your age has been going to camp since she was five."

I scowled, "I know." And I did. The other girls at camp always thought I was weird. They had been sent because the other summer camps had filled up and their parents just needed somewhere for them to go for a few weeks. I, however, was almost able to teach the stupid courses. Shooting with a bow and a rifle, setting traps, first aid, and everything else. My favorite thing was when we learned how to make a bow and arrows.

Dad went over the map one last time before we drove away from the bunker. I looked back once and missed it instantly. The place I hated all those weeks was gone, and in its place was the unknown.

The jeep could drive over everything... logs, broken roads where the bombs had dropped, bumps Brian told me not to look at, everything. I covered my eyes and peeked through my fingers.

There were cars, trucks, vans, and people everywhere when we got to the freeway. People had been hiding out in the beginning, but when the food and supplies started to run out, they fled the cities. Everyone ran.

The panic was over by the time we left the bunker. What was left, was unimaginable. The road was broken everywhere and lined with burned-out vehicles. A huge, burned-out jet plane sat in a field next to an old house. It looked like a skeleton but burned badly. I couldn't help but wonder, if anyone had lived.

Fortunately, we didn't have to drive through the city. The freeway was bad enough. I couldn't imagine the city. Brian lived in the country, in a small town on the outskirts of a city. He bought the house because it had an already-built bunker from the Cuban Missile Crisis.

As we drove, we passed people straggling along the roads in small clusters. They looked broken and half dead. It looked like a movie.

"Every one of those people probably has the fever, Em. You gotta remember that. Every one has the potential to kill you now. It's us and them, Em." The more things we saw, the less annoying his voice got. I gripped the book to my chest. His voice was calm and haunting. Like a narration to the things I was seeing.

"The water is going to be sick for a long time where the bombs were dropped. The fields too."

The tear-stained and filthy faces of the people we passed, made me feel scared and sick. I'd never felt smaller. I wanted to curl into myself, and hug my knees and rock, but I couldn't stop looking at them. Cars turned over. Burned-out old trucks. People carrying children and bags. People dragging suitcases on wheels. People holding hands and pulling each other along. People.

"Look at them. They're fools. They still group up," he pointed at a small group.

I saw a man with blood-shot eyes, and I knew from the pictures Dad had shown me, that he had the fever.

The man looked at me. His blood-shot eyes seemed like they saw everything inside of me, all my fear.

A little girl, who looked like she was my age, was walking alone. For a moment, I swore I knew her. She looked lost. She turned in a circle and cried and no one helped her. They walked by her and ignored her. Just like we did. When we drove by my eyes met hers. She waved her arms and for a small moment, I swore she screamed my name. Her lips formed it perfectly. Her eyes stopped feeling self-pity and became impassioned. She chased the jeep. But we drove by anyway.

It was us and them.

We got stuck behind a huge crash. A trucker had jackknifed, and between the huge eighteen wheeler and the trucks and cars, we couldn't get through. We turned around and went back.

Dad and Brian fought. I ignored them and pretended to sleep.

I could hear the others outside the vehicle. I could hear their screams and the crying as we slowed down.

"They're taking the women. Look at that," Dad whispered, trying to hide his voice from me, but I could hear him.

"No doubt looking for healthy females. It's just like Doctor Fitzgerald said it would be," Dad sounded smug and scared at the same time. His whispers scared me. I held my breath.

Then I heard a bang followed by another. Then nothing.

"Holy shit. He shot him, Bri. He shot him in the head. We need to get out of here now."

"Turn around, man. Go that way. Up the hill." Brian sounded scared, which made me scared.

"It's the wrong way."

"Who fucking cares. DRIVE!"

The jeep sped up and I felt a huge bump. Then my stomach felt like it was rolling around inside of me. I lost my grip on the seat and was flung up. The thick book hit me in the face. My seatbelt caught me and I saw colors behind my eyes, as I was thrown back onto the seat. It didn't feel comfortable anymore. It felt hard and scraped my skin.

We turned over and over and loud bangs filled up all the air there was.

I heard them screaming and then it stopped. Then it was just me screaming. We stopped moving, but my lips stayed open and my cries were everywhere.

I heaved slightly and looked around. I was upside-down and hanging by my seatbelt. I clicked it, but I didn't fall. The top of the jeep was closer than it was before. I could see blood. Some of it was mine and some of it came from the front seat. Brian was gone. The windows were gone. I heard a groan.

"Em," Dad groaned.

I reached frantically, "Dad. Dad. I can't see you." His headrest was up and the jeep was bent and crumpled around him. I slithered out the back of it and dragged myself onto the dry, brown grass. There were other cars surrounding us and in no better shape than the jeep. In the distance, I could see other people, but not many. I could see them noticing the accident and pointing.

"Em, the others will want our stuff. Run," he whispered harshly and coughed.

I dragged myself to his window, which was gone. His body was stuck, pinned by the jeep. I pulled on the door handle, but it didn't budge. I cried and scratched and slapped at the jeep. I kicked at the door, but it wouldn't move. I was too small and too skinny, and I couldn't even dent the metal. All my anger, pain, and fear wouldn't even scratch at the cold, hard door.

He looked bad. His body was upside down, but not hanging. The jeep was all around him, snug.

He moaned again, "Em. Run. You can run fast and far, don't let yourself give up. Take this and run. "

He held nothing out for me to take, but his hand was bent funny. I sat on the grass beside him and cried. I could feel the defeat.

He licked his lips and looked at me with the most frightening eyes I'd ever seen. "Run, Em. Run and get to the cabin. Go up that mountain to the right of us. Climb up until you come to a dirt road. Follow it until you come to an old farmhouse. From there, it's across their hayfield and up the mountain behind their house—to the right." He slipped his bent hand out and grabbed mine. I could feel his fingers click when he bent them. "It's us and them, Em. I'm still with you. You can feel it, you'll always feel it. But right now, I need you to be a brave girl—the brave girl I trained for exactly this moment. Run and don't help anyone. Don't ask for help. It's everyone for themselves now. They're all sick, Em. In some way, they're all sick."

Blood dripped into his hair from a cut above his eye. I shook my head and cried. I heard a truck behind me.

He screamed at me, "RUN, EM! THEY'RE COMING! NEVER GET CAUGHT, EM! NEVER!"

I backed away on the grass and stood on my bruised and battered legs. They almost buckled in fear, but I did as he said. I swallowed my sobs and turned and ran. I ran across the freeway and up the hill into the grass. Feet made noises behind me, but I had always been fast, even as a little girl.

I heard the vehicle and the gunshot. I heard the others. I knew they'd shot him, if he lived that long.

I ran and ran until I threw up in the grass, and even then, I ran. I ran until my eyes saw things that could not be and heard people I knew to be dead. People like my father. I felt him pulling me up the hill and yelling at me to hurry up. I felt his breath on my face, as he shouted and squeezed my hand.

I ran until I saw the farmhouse. Then I crept and snuck and hid in the shadows of the dark. Then I sat alone in those shadows, too terrified to cry—too terrified to move. But I knew food and water would be waiting at the cabin. All the food and water, I could manage to get inside me. Hunger gnawed at my spine. I stumbled across the field in the dark. I got to the other side and climbed one of the trees there. Its rough bark reminded me, I was alive. Just as he always said it would, pain reminded me I was still alive.

The flashes stop, and the memory fades, and I am alone in the dark room with the smiling statue of Jesus. And again the pain reminds me I am still alive, just like it did then in the big tree at the edge of the field.

Chapter Three

When I wake, the pain is gone, but I've peed myself. The pee is everywhere. My pants are sticky and wet. It smells rusty like blood, but I recall peeing. I recall the pain and the pressure and how good it felt to let go of the pee. I am becoming one of the infected. It's what he put into my arm. I know it. I've peed and cramped. Soon I will wander about and crave flesh...or just die and be eaten by the other infected.

Where is Anna? Has she come for me? Is she captured? I need to be stronger to save her, unless she was truly a hallucination.

The room is so dark that I can't see Jesus, but I assume he is still here. I wonder if he is grossed out that I've peed on the floor and am so weak I cannot move out of my own filth. I wish he wasn't a stone statue, but rather a mannequin. I need new clothes. The image of being infected and wondering the world in robes that I stole from a Jesus mannequin, makes me smile.

I grab one of the bags of glucose and pull the plug from the bottom of it. I drink the sweet water until I feel sick, and even then, I force a little more down. I drain the bag and drop it to the floor, where I then lower my face and arms. The cold of the floor is comforting somehow.

My eyes flicker like the lights in the hall and I know I'm passing out again.

I don't dream this time. I don't remember anything else about before. I just sleep and then wake up.

When I wake again, I lick my lips. They feel chapped and cracked. The pee is dried and when I move my legs, they feel stuck in the pants. I am weak. Very weak. My breath feels like effort. My heart doesn't feel like it's beating at all.

"Find the door and find Anna," I whisper to myself, and maybe Jesus. He's like Leo. He makes me less crazy, because with him there, I'm not talking to myself.

I push myself to my knees and crawl to where I think the door is. I feel along the wall for the gap where the handle will be. The edge of the door evades me. Did the room seal while I slept? I look around in the darkness for Jesus. From what Granny said, he is supposed to be my light in the dark, but even my animal eyes don't work in this place. There is no light in this room.

The wall feels like it is never-ending. I feel like I will travel this wall in a circle, until I go mad and claw my way through it. I wonder if I am in hell. I am being punished for the sins I have committed. I'm not really sorry for any of them. That might be a problem.

I turn and feel for the statue of Jesus. Nothing feels like it will happen fast enough. The air in the room feels like its oxygen supply has been sucked dry. All that's left is the pollution I have made with every panicked exhale. My heartbeat feels like it's been started with a shock, and it's now making an attempt to rip itself from my chest.

It's a panic attack. I recognize it as my fingers touch the cold statue. My fingers meet the cold of his robes and I fall at his feet in a heap. I am like his followers. The ones I've seen who save the children crying alone on the road. The ones who seem kind and gentle, but somehow their eyes make you feel not good enough.

"Help me," I whisper, gripping to his cold robes.

I hear something and lift my head.

At first I think it's Jesus whispering, making me shiver. I am about to become devout for the remaining seconds of my life, when I realize the wind is coming from the door. I crawl away from Jesus, feeling along the floor for the bottom of the door where the air is coming in. It's clean and fresh. Something has changed in the hallway outside. Anna?

I feel the slight cool whisper of air, as my hands reach the base of the door.

I run my hands up it to the handle and hang on for dear life. I turn the lock on the door, just as the handle turns. It gets stuck on the lock.

A voice follows the movement of the handle, "Clear here too." The vibration of the movement jolts through me. "She went up the stairs. Everything else is locked."

I almost leap back screaming. But I force myself to be calm. I hold my fingers on the door and wait. They are checking the hall and looking for me. They know I am gone. I am not alone. The doctor wasn't alone. Where were they when I was killing him? Are they looking for Anna?

Another voice fills the silent air of the hallway, "God dammed, do you know how important she was? For Christ's sake. It's one little girl."

Little girl? Are they talking about me? Am I still a little girl or is it Anna they've lost? My heart is already panicked from the arrival of the men, this doesn't help it calm down.

I try to think, but my stomach is hurting too much. I don't know what to do. If I go looking for them, I might lead the men to where they are. I'm sick, and most likely dying, so it isn't like I'll be much help.

I pause my thoughts when I hear footsteps again, "Get her back or it's your lives."

"What about the wolf?" a man asks.

Leo. I almost say his name aloud.

He's alive. He's near. Fire burns in my belly, but I refuse it. I need to find him. I need him.

The voices walk away from me, growing quieter, "She's sick. She doesn't know where he is. Don't worry about him...find her."

I lose them after that. The hallway is silent again and the wind is gone from under the door.

I pull another bag from my pocket and pull the plug. I drink it down. It tastes sweet and stale and funny but I know I'm dehydrated and sick. The poison he shot into me made me sick but didn't kill me. I need to replace my fluids.

I close my eyes and press my face against the door. I listen for the sounds of boots and guns. I listen for breath that gets ragged, when you're searching for someone. There is nothing. The men's voices are gone. The men who rattled the door and tried the lock, are gone. It's almost like they were a figment of my imagination, like Anna.

I want to turn the handle and just take a peek, but my rules are slowly reinstating themselves and waiting is my biggest one.

I turn with my back to the door, my face to Jesus, and slide down the door. I sit and wait. Patience has kept me alive this long and I won't betray her, or my instincts that tell me to wait. The urge to find Leo is almost driving me through the door. But I know, he won't live if I burst through and they kill me.

I just want my wolf and the smell of the forest. I just want to go home. Oddly enough, I don't think about the cabin in the woods, when I think of home. That disturbs me a little.

I think about Leo, Anna, Meg, Sarah, Jake, and Will, only not in that order. I force them into that order. I think about Will and Jake constantly, but I know Meg and Sarah are my responsibility. Anna is the closest thing, I will ever have to a best friend. I feel warmth in my heart thinking about them. I want to go home and they are the home that my heart recognizes. I don't need a cabin to hide in. I need my friends. My family.

I need Leo the most. I feel the anger and hatred rising in me. If they have hurt one strand of his fur...

The thought creates rage inside of me. I will skin everyone alive, until I have murdered them all. Even then, I know I will not feel satisfied.

I remember who is looking down on me in the dark and feel my face heating with embarrassment.

"Sorry," I whisper to the frozen God.

I imagine he knows the revenge I want. I imagine, at one point or another, he has felt that want. The want to end the misery of others by ending the lives of their tormentors. Tormentors who hold everyone hostage. I want to ask him how his father has left us to this, but I remember what Meg told me. The evil is us.

In this room his arms are stretched out and his face is smiling. He is offering love, and for that we have stuck him in this dark room where no one looks anymore. Yet, even in the dark, his arms are stretched out. Even in the dark, he offers me something—companionship.

My eyes grow heavy and I let myself relax into the darkness, I don't think I will ever escape from.

I don't know how much time has passed. I wake and open my eyes, leaning over. I'm hungrier than I've ever been, but I feel sick. Bile heaves from my lips. I cough as quietly as I can.

I turn and stand using the door again. I click the lock slowly and listen. There is nothing.

I wait an extra second and open the door silently. There is nothing in the hall. The papers are there but the lights don't flicker. The lights aren't on. There is a light at the end of the hall, making the rest of it dimly lit.

I squint, but I see nothing.

I take my first steps out into the dim light of the hallway. My feet shuffle along the papers and cold cement. I can't be quiet. As much as I want to move silently, I am too tired.

I lean against the wall and walk clumsily. I need to find Leo. I need water and food. I need so many things. It feels hopeless. I will never find them all. Not all the things I need.

My pockets are still full of fluid bags and the other pocket has my knife I stole. I reach in carefully and take the knife out.

At the end of the hall, I find an open door. The fresh air seems to be coming from there. Inside is a huge set of cement stairs. I cry when I see it. I push myself to the huge stairs and start crawling up them. I force my mind to shut off and climb. I won't let my brain try to let me lie down or tell me I can't climb them all. Like my father said, I am a strong girl. I can run fast and far. I can't let my mind tell me I can't do it.

I just climb.

It's hard and it hurts, but in my mind I am in the forest with Leo. He is standing next to me. My bow is in my fingers. I can feel a slight breeze on my face. I can feel things in the air. Freedom and peace.

The wind starts to smell.

I can smell food and people. I can smell the towns.

My body knows the food is there and it pushes harder. I climb the stairs with ferocity and strength I didn't know I had left. I can feel the water running down into my parched throat. I can feel the meat between my teeth. I don't even care what kind of meat...just roasted meat that leaves a flame-cooked taste in my mouth.

The light gets brighter and brighter, the higher I climb. When I get to the top of the stairs, I cry harder but my eyes are dry.

There is a huge door. I stumble into it and take the silver handle in my hands. I don't check what's behind it. I burst through it. I stumble out into an alley. There is a garbage bin beside me. It looks like the ones at the breeder farm.

The building in front of me is huge and broken, like in the cities. The wind is full of smells. People, food, sewage, dust, and city. I remember the smell from before. I remember before. I turn in a circle and realize, I am surrounded.

Broken buildings are everywhere. I am in a real city. A destroyed city.

"No," I whisper and look around, horrified.

I see garbage to my right and cringe. I look down at myself to see the pants I stole are covered in blood and a stain from the pee. I am covered in old, dry blood. I shake my head in a twitch and drop to my knees. I was bleeding from somewhere. The blood on my pants is old and dry. It's brown and gross. My hands are also covered. It's cracked and flaking.

I push myself up and walk along the alley. I don't see people, but I know the infected live in the cities. I'm like live bait. I wreak of old blood and urine. I am too tired to fight them or run. I grip the knife in my hand and stumble.

I feel a hand on my arm. I swing weakly at the owner. I see a man with an old shopping cart full of paper and blankets. He smiles an old smile.

"Get in," he says.

I start to fall but he puts my arm over his shoulder and pushes me to the cart. I grab the metal with my hands and let him help me in. I don't understand what he's doing, but I'm tired of walking. I see a red thing flying in the air over me and then I see nothing. There is a red glow all around me.

"Jesus saved me," I say. I don't know why.

"Relax kid. Just stay down. We're almost home."

Home.

This word means so many different things to me.

The cart rumbles along the ground and I try to imagine what home looks like to him.

Chapter Four

Home is a little room surrounded by cement. It's a quiet little corner where I don't hear the infected or the looters or the others. He doesn't smile.

"You made an awful mess kid. The doctor was a pretty important man. They're looking for you." His voice is quiet. He freaks me out.

I blink and stare. I'm lost until I hear it.

"Emma."

My head snaps around. I would get up and run to her too, but I can't move. I'm still hurting in so many ways, but the major ways start to heal the second I see her face.

She rushes me and wraps her skinny arms around me. She buries her face in my hair.

I grip her shaking body, "You're real," I whisper.

She pulls back, her tear-stained face and sparkling blue eyes heal some of the cracks inside of me, "Of course, I never would have left you there. I've been looking for you for weeks."

I flinch, "Sarah, Meg...?"

She cuts me off and smiles weakly, "Only you went missing. You and Leo. Sarah and Meg are at the place we left them, safe." She doesn't say the retreat. She's being careful around him. She sighs and continues, "I panicked when we couldn't find you. We assumed you'd been taken. We didn't know by who, but we saw the trucks leaving."

I nod and try to ignore the shock that's still paralyzing me. "Marshall." I say softly, eyeballing the man in the corner.

She nods, "Will figured he betrayed you and Leo. Sold you out to the military. We got back to the camp, but Marshall wasn't there. His friends said that Marshall did it to free the women; you were the one they wanted. You were a danger to the camp and he traded you for healthy normal women." She rolls her eyes, "He's insane."

I nod slowly, it burns and hurts. He traded me for all those other women and their babies.

She smiles, "You okay?"

I want to nod and tell her I am, but I'm not. I can feel it. I let myself be true to my feelings. She is my 'us'. I shake my head and look down.

She wraps her arms around me, "You will be."

My common sense is slowing creeping around in my mind, checking on the facts I have, "Who is he?" I mutter.

She shrugs, "He found me, needed me to help him find a girl. We figured out pretty fast we were looking for the same girl. I had gotten separated from everyone else and had hid. Then he found me, and showed me where to find you. He needed me to pretend to be a nurse, but then the doctor made me leave before we could rescue you." She chuckles softly, "Then of course, you got away on your own. So we assumed you were hiding and waiting for the military to leave. When they did, we were coming to get you. I went one way and he went the other. He found you."

It's not something I would have done. I don't accept help from strangers. It's the difference between her and I.

He looks around and speaks softly, "We have to stay here a few more days. You're just lucky I got to you first. I looked everywhere for you."

I shake my head in the dim light of the small space. "Who are you?"

"A friend." He picks up a tin and takes a bite.

I glance at Anna but she shakes her head, "You gotta get out of the city."

"Where are we?" I can't tell anything from the small concrete room. It's like a shanty in the towns with board and concrete walls.

"Spokane."

I rub my eyes and try to focus them, "Where?"

Anna laughs, "I said the same thing. We're in Washington, by the West Coast."

I sniffle and wrap my arms around myself, "How did I get here? Why are you helping us? How did all of this happen? Why would Marshall betray me like that? 'Cause I defied them?"

Anna looks confused, but the man's eyes dart suspiciously. He asks nervously, "What do you remember?"

I shake my head, "Nothing. Marshall betrayed me and then I woke up on the cold, metal table."

He nods and eats from the tin. Anna holds me like she may never let me go. I'm okay with that. Exhaustion is attacking me again.

He doesn't look at me when he talks, "You look beat, kid. Sleep. You have to leave the city in a couple days. Rest up now."

I shake my head and fight my yawn, "No. I'm not tired."

Anna laughs and my eyes close on their own.

When I wake again, the man is standing and looking around a boarded-up concrete corner. Anna is sleeping next to me.

I look at the man, but before I can ask him anything, he puts a finger to his mouth and shakes his head. I blink and feel wetness between my legs again.

I hear the noises from whatever he's clearly watching. I hold my breath and look for weapons and possibilities.

His eyes don't leave the corner. He watches and I wait. The noises don't come closer.

After a long time, he turns and smiles. He whispers, "I think we're okay." He looks down at the pile of blankets we're sleeping on. "Did you pee?"

I'm embarrassed and scared. I look down and nod, "I'm sorry. I don't know what's wrong with me."

He shakes his head, "Catheter and a miscarriage. Not uncommon to have bladder issues after that. It'll just take a couple days to clear up."

I look up. I know him. I swear I do.

He passes me a clean change of clothes and a bottle of water, "Get cleaned up. I'll wait over there."

I take the small bundle and frown, "Why are you helping me?"

He laughs, it's sad and weak. "I know your father, very well."

"You knew him? How? From the health food store?"

His dark eyes glisten. He shakes his head, "Lenny wasn't your father, Emma. He was your uncle in a way, I suppose." He turns and walks away leaving me with that massive statement.

My mouth is slack. I don't know what to say or do. I stink of urine and old, rusty blood, and Lenny wasn't my father. Wait did he say miscarriage?

I've had bad days, lots of them. Sometimes it's weeks of them. This is the worst day. I look down at Anna and am happy she is sleeping at least. She missed all those words and the possibilities that lie within them.

I can't stop the tears that well in my eyes. They try to block out the world for me. They try to protect me from seeing the truth. Lenny wasn't my dad? I shake my head; he was my dad. He was.

I stand on my weakened legs in jerky twitches and pull my clothes off. They stick to me and stink.

I use the water and rinse myself, as best as I can.

Worst day ever. At least I have her and soon we'll have Leo.

I dribble the last of the water into my parched chapped lips and walk through the boarded-up entrance of the small shanty. He's sitting on a curb around a corner. He really did give me space to change and clean.

I stretch my legs and feel my body coming back around.

"Where are we?" I whisper.

"Parkade. It's how we parked our cars back in the good old days. These buildings were made up to store cars while people were in the cities. This is the top level. I found this little shanty a while back." He looks at me and grins. His dark eyes look tired, "So which part do you want to hear first?"

I shake my head, "Miscarriage?" The father thing is irrelevant. My father is dead. What does it matter who he was? I was never lied to about who my mother was.

He hands me a small pack and points, "We need to get moving. Talk and walk, okay?"

I nod, "Let me get her then." I slip back inside and speak in a hushed tone, "Anna, come out."

She moans, "Do I have to?"

"Yes, hurry." I hear her stir. I leave her and walk back to where he is. The concrete all around us is broken from the bombs and decay. It's like an old building that's come down on itself. I don't feel comfortable at all. The light that filters in is muted from the bushes and vines. I glance up at him and try to remember where I know him from, "Who are you?"

"Vincent Fitzgerald. I am a friend of your father's. Your real father. I knew Lenny too. I warned him to get out. I found out about the breeder farms, so I told him to make sure he had you as far away as possible." He speaks as we saunter through the broken and crumbling parkade, "Your miscarriage was actually an abortion. It was intentional. They've never impregnated something like you before. The breeder farm you were at didn't even know what they had."

I frown, "What do you mean?" Anna's eyes light up. She looks back and forth between us, obvious of the fact she's arrived mid conversation.

He smiles, "You. You're different. Your mother was married to your uncle. Your father drugged your mother and impregnated her with the first of the Gen babies for the Seed Program. You are like the breeder babies. He used his own sperm to make you. She had no idea it was happening."

I don't understand. I look around uncertain. The cement is crumbling and the old stains of blood and debris are freaking me out. This isn't exactly the kind of place to stroll and chat. But we do, we round corners and walk over debris. Every corner seems to look the same, broken concrete and crumbled walls with huge windows without glass.

I shake my head, "So my dad, Lenny, was my uncle. My uncle, who I never knew, was my dad, but really I'm a baby from a test tube like the babies at the farms?"

He nods, "That's it."

I glance at Anna, who grins like Jake and nudges me, "That explains some things, huh?"

I scowl and ignore her, "Why did they let me believe Lenny was my dad?"

He shakes his head, "You know how you were never allowed to see your uncle?"

I nod, "He had an affair with my mom. My dad hated him. So did my grandparents."

He shakes his head, "I don't know the whole story, just that they ran with you. Lenny and you and his parents. Lenny raised you. You guys all lived, sort of off the grid; Michael couldn't find you anywhere. Lenny was good at that."

Closing my eyes in frustration and confusion, I wave my hands, "Okay, but the miscarriage? Why did they make me lose the baby, if the breeder farms got me pregnant?" I'm lost. Completely. My nerves are on edge and my body isn't strong enough for the fighting we definitely have in store, if we're in a city.

He stops and gives me a sad look, "Experiments. The doctors wanted to see what a breeder baby would be like in a Gen baby. The doctor at the camp you were at with Marshall, did a pregnancy test when you got back there. I guess it's a routine thing for girls who leave the breeder camps, not that many do. Marshall told us that the doctor discovered you were with child. Marshall knew you were special, I don't know how. Anyway, he said he couldn't risk you being pregnant around all those people. He didn't know what kind of a child you would have, or pregnancy. Marshall gave you up to our unit when he found out. We had worked with him before he ran. He had stayed in touch with some of us doctors. I would have saved you before, but the other doctors were quite excited to see what you could produce. You are a special girl, Emma."

I sigh, sickened by it all. "So I hear. You should hear the nonsense about me being some bloody bird." Stupid phoenix bullshit. Stupid parent bullshit. Stupid miscarriage.

He points to the dark ramp going down another level, "We go this way."

Anna grabs my hand and holds it tight.

I ignore her warmth and stop walking too, "I need my wolf, before we leave the city."

His face crumples, "We can't save him. They're experimenting on the animals to see why some of them are immune."

My hand flies at his throat and holds tight. I steel my eyes, "I need him."

His eyes bulge. He nods and licks his lips, "This is why Marshall called us. You have the tendencies of the Gen babies— uncontrollable rage, impulsive behavior, and unrealistic strength. He was scared to let you stay with the camp people, especially pregnant."

That stings—the name Marshall, and the fact I'm some freak who is a danger to the rebels.

I glare at him and lower my hand, "Then don't piss me off. Or your fate will be the same as his."

"Em, calm. We'll get Leo." Anna grips my other hand.

He walks across the wide space to the edge of the building and peers through the grass vine hanging over the crumbling concrete. He points to the far side of the city, "It's that way. He was at a separate building than you. Just outside of the city, other side of the infected areas." The view is disturbing. Crumbling buildings, loads of bushy greenery and debris.

I am lost. I am lost in it all. I need the calm of the forest and the fur of my wolf. I sigh and look at him confusedly, "Why are you helping us?"

He looks hurt. The question hurts him, I think. "We had no right to mess with DNA to that extent. The Gen babies overrun the new cities. They're horrid. They can't help themselves. We screwed with something that was already perfect. Darwin and God were both right. Natural selection was a necessity and man was already made the way he should have been."

He looks lost suddenly, "Science and technology was the end of everything. We made it so we all lived unnaturally long but ate chemically-altered foods and got cancer. We lived unnaturally-altered lives and ate up natural resources and polluted everything." He glances at me and sighs, "The year they decided to put the plan into effect to save the planet, they literally had to chose between Man and Earth. A huge group of officials sat in a room for twenty-eight days and argued. Man or Earth. I can't even imagine, having to make a choice like that. But they did. They made the choice and reset everything. I was on board until recently. Now I'm against it all. Yes, we had to reset the earth, there is no doubt. But the Gen babies, the military, the breeder and work farms are wrong. It's not the vision they shared with us originally. They said the six cities would be based on creating people who cared about the planet. We would build from the rubble and create harmony." He looks impassioned and then destroyed all in the same moment, "There is no harmony. They round up the Blacks, Asians, and South Americans and send them home. Home? They're Americans for Christ's sake. God help anyone with dark skin, or even a slight slant to their eyes, or any kind of accent." He sighs, "Maybe it's better there though. Maybe the places they go is better than here." He slumps and I feel sick.

Not for him. For me. He's a bitter, old man with a guilty conscience. I'm screwed.

I sigh and look at Anna. She looks lost too. I lean against the wall and think about it all, "So I was pregnant for like a minute? My wolf is being held because he's immune? I'm a mutant breeder-farm baby? My dad is my uncle and my uncle is my dad?" I glance at him, "And you're mad because the world is filled with crappy racist people who lie and hurt others?"

He shakes his head chuckling, "That's about it."

Anna leans next to me and crosses her arms, "So her dad made the breeder babies?" She glances at me.

I feel a new sickness. My own flesh and blood is the reason it's all happening.

I frown at Vincent, "How do we stop him?"

He licks his lips, "Impossible. But I'm glad he won't have you. God knows what he'd try."

I look at him and study his face. He's weak. He won't be of any real use.

"You know what you should do? Give up on the other people and just eke a life out somewhere quiet," I say and look down at my aching feet. I miss my boots. I wonder how long it's going to take me to find nice new ones.

Anna laughs, "We know a nice place you could go to. But seriously, you should probably not tell anyone that boring seed-baby story."

He laughs, but it sounds exhausted.

"You married?" I ask.

He shakes his head, "No. She left. She ran to live in the hills." He grins at us bitterly, "To eke out a life."

Anna grins back at him, "Smart woman. Can't say I blame her. You seem long winded and fairly down about a lot of shit."

He laughs again and it makes me think of Jake. I give Anna a sideways glance, "You said you got separated from the others? Where did they go? Who was there?"

She maintains her grin, "Jake and Will. I made Meg stay behind, she was all mad. She said she was almost sixteen so she should be allowed to say. I told her no. Jake and Will went to find food and some infected came, so I ran. I couldn't get back to them, so I kept looking for you. Then I met him."

Will and Jake are in the same city as I am. They're nearby. That makes my heart skip a couple beats.

I freeze when I hear a noise that's not coming from us. Vincent looks at me with panic in his eyes.

I press my back into a wall and wait. They do the same.

Voices echo off the broken walls. I don't know which direction they're coming from.

I don't breathe. I listen. Men talking, laughing. Not infected obviously.

"How many weapons you got?" I whisper.

He shakes his head, "Not enough."

I sigh, "Great. Do I have any magical powers like the superheroes?" I mutter and glance past the wall. Three men are leaning on the cement wall in the area we were walking to.

Vincent shakes his head, "No. Your kind heals faster. You have incredible strength and speed. That, combined with your lack of control over your temper, is obviously dangerous. You learn faster and remember things better. You process things quicker and feel things stronger. Nothing that's going to get us out of this mess."

I glare at him, "How are you scientist types this stupid? I thought the scientists were the geniuses, but you aren't. You're crazy. This is why Lenny hated you all. Why would you make something like that? Just stupid." I glance around the corner at the men. One of them is suddenly missing from the three. My heartbeat picks up slightly. Where did he go?

"Gun, knife, anything?" I whisper.

He pulls a long blade from behind him. I still feel like death, but taking the blade makes me feel a tiny bit better.

I grip it and look back at Anna, "You stay here with him."

She scowls, "I can help you."

I roll my eyes, "Not this time, okay?"

She looks angry, but I flicker my eyes on him. She nods. She knows she has to stay with him and make sure he's legit. Really, I just don't want her near anything. She could get infected. I'd rather it be me.

I look back at the men and see the third man is back and zipping his thick pants back up. The warmth of summer is upon us. I wish I could close my eyes and be back at the swimming hole at the retreat. Instead, I'm in the middle of the broken city, surrounded by bad possibilities. I wish I had those handguns. I watch the men for a second and give up on the mini plan I had. I abandon it and point the opposite way, "Let's go the other way. They have guns."

"We can get out on the other side of the parkade, but there are more infected that way. I saw them earlier." He gives me a sideways glance.

I feel the annoyance and fear coming off me. At least it will fuel the fire inside of me.

He puts his hands up, "Hey, I'm just telling you. It's not going to be easy that way. When I brought you here, I came this way." He points towards the men.

I shake my head, "We won't stand a chance with them." I wish we could happen upon Jake and Will. I don't like not knowing where they are. It feels like they're on my to-do list.

We walk around another corner and down another level, into more darkness. The broken concrete and thick vines make it hard to see. The levels above us collapsed, at some point, and made a huge mess in the dark where we are walking. I climb over a large, broken pillar and try to make my animal eyes work. The dark moves, even when nothing is there. I hate this place. I miss the forest. I miss the birds. Here in the dark, nothing warns you. It waits for you to die so it can eat you too.

My feet crunch and kick things I can't see. Anna walks beside me, silently. She is still the best hunting partner a girl could ask for. His feet behind us are loud. He reminds me of Jake—maybe not the best at survival.

I push away my thoughts of them and listen. If the infected, the others, or the military catches me, I'm dead. My best chance is staying quiet.

We walk along a wall in the dark where cars are parked, looking like rotted-out skeletons. Some of them are crushed by debris. I can see from the bits of light filtering in through the vines on the far side of the parkade.

I give Anna a look. She nods and slowly walks across the broken-up concrete to the edge, where the vines are the thickest. She pulls them aside and peeks through, as I watch Vincent. They almost eat her up; they're so dense, like a real forest.

She looks back at me and points. I walk ahead, looking through the creepy vines and bushes, and see we are almost at ground level. We are only one story up. The alley below us is crawling with the infected. She pulls back and looks at me.

I look around us. We can't drive out. The cars are rotted, and besides, the roads are almost virtually impassable. I take a second look, noticing the far-left side of the alley is empty. The infected move slowly, in comparison to us. They will smell us, unless we can get some kind of bait.

My brain flashes back to the men. They are already close to the left side of the parkade.

I swallow and look at Anna, "I'll be right back. Don't move unless you have to. I'm going to make bait."

She grimaces and nods, "Okay. I'll stay with him." Thank God, I don't want to have a fight with her. I don't want to tell her I value my life less than hers and refuse to chance her getting the fever.

Vincent looks confused. I turn and run, as silently as I can, back across the parkade and up the ramp to where I hear them. I slide against a gutted car and wait.

"A U2 concert. I went with my girlfriend. I was eighteen and she was seventeen. We smoked a ton of pot and went. Everything started about two weeks later. Best memory." A man to the right with a rifle is talking.

The other man nods, "Nice, man. Yeah, mine is a barbecue. We figured it was the last one of the season. My whole unit came over and we got trashed and talked about sports and shit. My wife, her name was Trish. She made the best burger patties on earth. I ate like four. I thought I was going to die."

I bite my lip and wait. I can feel my stomach tighten when I think about it. Regular people sharing regular memories and I'm about to kill them both. Unless they kill me first. I should have died yesterday and didn't. I'm on borrowed time and the bad feeling hasn't left me yet.

Their feet make scuff sounds; they aren't even careful. They must not be on high alert. They must not be looking for me.

I slide along the car and sit at the back of it, waiting for them to pass. The third guy must be off doing something again. He's the one I'm going for.

They walk farther away, strolling and sharing. I watch them, waiting for the moment. Both are in good shape, but they slump and hold their guns wrong. They aren't taking it seriously.

They turn their backs and lean casually. I crawl to the next car. It's the last car before the corner. I look back at them. They're still talking and laughing. I frown. The infected are one level away from them, and they're talking about shit they miss. I break into a silent sprint. It's nowhere as fast as it needs to be, but it's got to do.

I get around the corner and feel it. The cold mean is settling in. The cold calculations start figuring in my brain. The third man has to die. I need bait.

I look back around the corner, but the men are still talking.

I swallow and walk to the edge where the man was. He's still there. He too, looks like he's not taking the job very seriously. He's leaning on his gun and picking his nails. Who trains these people? Maybe my real dad is over-confident. He doesn't feel threatened.

I feel sick thinking about it. My own family participated somehow. My dad must have been a scientist too. My mom must have been a complete idiot.

I slide against the wall and creep, pushing away all the thoughts I'm having. My stomach is a ball of nerves and butterflies, but I want that gun. This side of the parkade has been destroyed completely making a path to the ground of gravel and broken concrete. It looks like an avalanche. It really would be the easy way to come. I sigh and walk down the sloped debris, onto the ground where he is.

I feign a limp and hold my stomach. The knife is in the back of my pants, waiting.

I moan slightly. There is no way I can sneak up on him from here.

His eyes lift. Disgust and confusion settle in. He frowns at me, "Stop."

I shake my head, "Sir, please help me. I ate some food I found and I think it was bad."

His lip curls up, "Stop, where you are." He lifts the gun and points it at me. My stomach tightens more. I could throw up, I'm so nervous.

I shake my head, "My dad is one of the military heads. I got lost and hid from the infected. Please help me."

He tightens his grip on the gun and jerks it at me, "Stop walking, bitch."

I stop and crouch down. I don't like being called bitch. I hold my stomach and fake heave. I don't have to try very hard. I've used this one before.

He comes closer, just close enough. "What's your dad's name?"

"General...General..." I gag and burp.

He comes closer to hear my soft words. I shoot up and grab the gun, slamming it back into him and lifting the barrel. The hit in the chest dislodges his fingers from the trigger. I pull the gun and swing it. It clips him in the side of the head.

I pull the blade from my back pocket, and in one fell sweep, I slice it across his jugular. I wipe it on his pants as he falls. I shoulder the gun and drag him through the alley as fast I can. My guts are killing me.

I round the corner where the infected are. I watch them milling about as I drag him. He's sputtering and gurgling still. I stop and rifle through his pockets. He has a small blade, a water bottle, a picture that I don't let my eyes see, and a bunch of shells for the gun. I pocket them and the knife as I stand up.

I look around. The infected are milling farther down. I bend down and pick up a chunk of broken concrete and toss it down the alley. It lands in between several of them. They look at it and bend down. I sigh and pick up another one. I toss it to the same spot and hit one of the ones bent over.

He stands and looks with his bloody, dirty face. He makes a high moan. I shudder but toss another piece. The ones next to him start making the high moans. I turn and run back to the side of the building. I am gasping for air, my nerves are on fire, and I'm trembling, but I try to stay perfectly still.

The high moans become the ragged screams as they draw nearer to the dead man. It's the third time I've done it. It rots me inside, but it's us and them and I don't know where all my us are. I don't know if they're all safe.

My hands find their way to my ears when the ripping starts. My breath is ragged like their throats. I don't have time to wait and hide. I turn and run back the way I came. I slide my body against the wall where I crawled down and hide. The men should be here by now but I don't hear them. They really are so stupid, as to sit in a parkade surrounded by the infected and chat?

I'm about to crawl up the debris but my stomach does its thing it does where it makes me stop and wait—like it knows something I don't. I freeze and wait.

"George!" one of the men shouts from above me, inside of the parkade.

"God dammed, George. Where you at?" the other man shouts.

My skin tingles. I try not to think about the barbecues and whatever U2 was. I try not to imagine their memories as I finger the rifle in my hands. I hold my breath and my back, tight to the wall.

"Shit!" one man yells and the debris starts moving. He blows by me running down the hill. The second man does the same. As they make it to the bottom of the hill and around the corner to where their friend is being eaten, I scramble up it. I run, not looking back. My fingers dig into the broken wall of the parkade, as I get back onto the level they were on.

I hear popping gunshots as I make it past the cars. I'm shaking and tired but my adrenaline is fired. My feet slap against the concrete as I round the corner. I stop and peek back. No one is following me. I'm sucking air in a wheeze like the infected. I'm probably infected. My throat is probably becoming ruined.

The gunshots are still popping in the air. I jump over the debris and crawl under the broken bits, as I run to where Vincent and Anna are standing very still in the darkness. I almost miss them, but she has the vines parted.

He looks back at me and shakes his head, "What are you? You're not like the other Gen kids."

I scowl, "I don't know. I'm a girl. A pissed-off girl." I don't have an answer.

He nods, "Some girl."

Anna rolls her eyes, "You haven't seen her with her wolf and a pistol in each hand, or better yet, her bow."

I swallow, my stomach is burning still, and I have to pee again. I pull the vines back and look down on the dead infected. The men are doubling back and shooting them in the head where they lay, just in case. It's the first smart thing I've seen them do.

"I need my wolf and we need to get the hell out of here," I whisper.

"We won't leave Leo, Em," Anna rubs my arm.

I nod, "I know. We gotta find Jake and Will."

She swallows and shakes her head, "We have a meeting place outside of the city." She doesn't say anymore. I know she won't, not in front of him.

The other infected have started to come around the corners to where the dead are. The left is now full, but the right side of the parkade is empty. He points to the small, thin alley. I nod. We run to the right side and climb down the debris and broken pillars.

When my feet touch the ground again, I almost collapse. I'm sweating and my body won't stop trembling. We round the corner. One of the infected is wandering about the alley. I finger the gun but know it will draw the others. I swallow hard and pull my shirt up over my face. I panic and try to come up with another option but there isn't one.

I look back at Vincent and Anna, "Stay here." Looking at her makes me sick. I can't have her around the infected. I look back at the big infected man and try to form something of a plan. If I get it, so will she.

The walls of the city close in on me as I search for another way out.

I take a deep breath and try to strategize. If I don't breathe and we wash me off right away, I might be okay. I know I'm lying to myself as I pull the blade and sneak up on the infected. He's large, round and tall. His skin hangs now, though. His body is eating itself. They wander until there is nothing left of them.

I hold my shirt tight to my face with my left hand and creep up to him.

He turns and I swing wildly. He grabs at me but I jump back. His brown, decayed teeth are broken. His mouth is filled with a yellow, foamy paste. It's like his spit has almost gone dry. I gag and slice his throat. His hands grip my arms. I drop the shirt and grab the other blade from my pocket. I click the switch to make the blade pop out. His teeth bear down on me. I stab the blade in my left hand into his temple. His yellow eyes are wide and then he's down. I look at the thick, dark-brown blood on me. The greenish tint and the smell make me gag. I look at it and panic. I start wiping it off on his back frantically.

"Water, do we have water? I need something to clean it off." My heart is in my throat. My breath is short and rough. My throat scratches. I've got it. I'm sick now too. My eyes fuzz out.

Vincent walks up to me and tilts his head, "The breeder babies are immune. You were born immune. It's not the cure. You were given the vaccine."

Anna ignores him and grabs the drinking water. She keeps her body back as she starts pouring it over me. I've ripped my shirt off and am scrubbing my skin. I know it's too late. I'm infected. My head is twitching, "No. No. I'm infected. Look at it. It probably got into my mouth. Anna stay back."

Vincent shoulders past her and grabs my shoulders, shaking me, "You can't get it. You were made immune to it. You can't get sick. You can't even carry it."

I look at him, "No. I was born a decade before the shit hit the fans. The germs mutated."

He nods his head, "Yes! Your body is incredibly strong. You were made to live healthy. No cost to the government. The plan to reduce the population and make people sick was in place long before you were born."

"Maybe, but I can get her sick." I'm trying to take it all in. Immune. Leo would eat the infected. I would keep my distance and not share, but there had to have been times that he had some of them left on him.

The sewers I've crawled in. The dead I've laid with.

I've never been truly sick. Only hurt. I always heal—except when I left the breeder farms. I was badly hurt then. I think about it and still feel the pain. Dragging Anna and Sarah up the mountains, with the injuries I had, I should have died. So many times I should have died. There are a thousand times I should have died or been infected.

Not to mention, I was a little kid living in the woods—I should have died from that. I guess he could be right. If he's right about everything else. Either way, I'm infected or I'm immune, only time will tell.

I look at the slime on my hands and finish wiping it on the dead man's dirty clothes. Vincent passes me a clean shirt. I tug it on, feeling the tears in my throat. All this time spent avoiding the infected, for what?

Vincent grabs my arm and drags me down the alley. Anna takes the gun and walks ahead of us. We stagger and stumble through the alleys until we reach a tall building.

"This is the end of the clean zone," he whispers.

Anna gives me a look; she's concerned. I would be too, if I were her. There is a very real chance, I will give her the infection, even though I'm keeping my distance.

I look at Vincent and scowl. I'm still trying to digest the varieties of things he's handed down to me in knowledge and confusion.

He scowls back at me, "From here on out, it's going to get much worse. The patrols stop here. The infected are bad inside of here."

I feel the horror covering my face, "Worse?"

He nods, "Us doctors and scientists don't go into this part of the city. We stay on the side where the guards are. We use this as a place to keep the infected for experiments. They live in the barricaded areas. Those ones behind us got through. It happens every now and then. That's what those guards were for." He points to a small wall built up of boards and debris. It blocks the alley. I peek my head out of the alley to the right and then the left. There is no one. The streets are empty.

He continues, "Your wolf is about eight blocks down. It's on the border of the city, almost the outskirts. You cross the bridge and get to an area that looks nice still. It used to be a medical research building. The name on the front of it is Luminarc. But the sign is old and decrepit. It says umina. U-M-I-N-A. Do you understand what I'm saying?"

I watch his face and nod, "You're leaving us."

He laughs, "Yeah. I'm not going in there. You'll be safe from the military in there. It's the infected, and possibly the others, that you'll need to worry about."

I don't know him, but I don't want him to go back there. I grab his hand, in an act that is completely awkward for me, "I know where a retreat is. You can go there and just rest. The people will help you."

He shakes his head, "I have to go back and help as much as I can. I'm one of the few on the inside, who are trying to stop it."

I frown, "Why?"

His leathery smile doesn't reach his eyes, "I'm your dad's right-hand man. He doesn't know I'm not on his side."

My eyebrows knit together, "You will go back there and live like this?" The words are awkward.

He nods, "I have to. I'm the only hope for a lot of the women. The facility is quite nice."

"I was there—it was a shit show."

He shakes his head, "The building where you were being kept isn't the facility. It's down the way, closer to the nice part of the city that's still standing. My life there is nice. I'm supposed to be on a convoy this week. The rebels are making sure it's destroyed. I'll be the only survivor. I'm heading there now, opposite direction of where you're going."

His eyes are so familiar and suddenly I see it, "You were the first doctor in the room with the cold table. The one who was nice to me?"

He nods, "I was. I planned on getting you out, but I needed the abortion to be completed. I couldn't release you into the world pregnant. I'm sorry."

I swallow, "Why?" Anna draws nearer to me but I scowl at her, "Keep your distance. I have it on me. I need soap."

She steps back as he ignores us and continues, "You already live with the possibility of being unstable. Your emotions are so heightened, compared to normal girls. It's a problem with the DNA. You don't have normal emotions. You don't feel things normally. Everything is bigger and faster in your world. We don't know what someone like you would make. You have to try not to ever have a baby, Emma." He hangs his head, like he's ashamed.

I didn't have that as an option for myself, not in the world I lived in, but his words hurt me. I'm ashamed Anna has heard them. I'm a freak. How many times could he say the words not normal?

I feel my anger rising, but I force myself to remain calm. A thousand flashes pass behind my eyes as I see it all. I nod,

"Okay."

He grabs my arms and squeezes, "You deserve to be free. Your father is a monster. Run and don't ever come back. Stay hidden away. Stay away from other people. You don't know when your brain will switch and you'll become one of the Gen kids in every way. The rage and irrational behavior is a side effect. Your father doesn't see it. He is constantly trying to perfect them, but he sees only the positives, he misses the negatives. I know you've proven you don't have the irrational behavior, but you never know. Better to be safe."

I almost twitch, thinking about the times I've done things he would call irrational. Would I though? I can justify every action in my mind. I am instantly wondering what Anna is thinking. I can't look at her.

I need Leo.

"How will you get back?" Anna asks him, changing the subject.

He shakes his head, "Don't worry about me. Get to the wolf and get out. You're one of a kind, Emma. You should know that, at least. What you did back there with the infected and the gunmen—you're one of a kind. The other Gen kids are a disaster. I think you are what we had planned all along."

I could spit on him. "I don't care. I just wanna go home." That's not the truth. I want to stop my father who was my uncle. What a mess.

I look both ways, because it's how I still cross streets, and walk across the broken filthy road. I can hear Anna following with the gun. The destroyed concrete crunches under the crappy boots he gave me. I'm exhausted and I haven't even started yet. I climb the wall of crap on the side of the road and look into the street. The infected are not there. I expected hordes, but I don't see any.

I look back at him. He waves. He looks desperate and beat down.

I hate him. Him and everything he represents. "Stupid bastard," I mutter and pull my knives out. I glance at Anna who grins and tightens her grip on the gun.

"I don't care what he says; you're amazing, Em." She nudges me and starts down the hill of debris into the infected zone.

"Thanks." I don't feel amazing. I feel not normal. I guess I always have and now I have a reason to feel that way.

Chapter Five

The infected move fast. Not as fast as we can—thank God. The gun helps a lot. It, and the fact, Anna is a deadly shot. The ones that get close, as we race through the alley, get cut. I already have their blood on me.

We entered the alley and didn't see any at first, but when we got in deeper, we could see them moving about. They never move when you're looking for them. Damned infected.

Their infected blood scares me still, but I assume I'm already sick if I can get it. We get to the end of the next alley. My thighs hurt from the running. Everything hurts. My body is weak from the little food I've eaten and the way I've laid around.

I look behind at the horde of them running after us, the high moans are grating on my skin. Anna fires a shot, dropping one in front of us.

I heave for breath and look around. I see a building with a smashed-in window.

"Anna, here," I shout and run to it. I smash out the glass more and leap into the window. She is in and falling on me, before I can get out of the way.

Before I can scream for her to get off of me and get away from the possible infection on my clothes, the stink hits my nose, filling my eyes with water.

"Sweet God," Anna gags and covers her face.

I can't ignore the stench of rotting flesh and possible sewage. The room is, no doubt, filled with germs. I don't know how they work but the room is bad. There isn't anything in here but office equipment, but the smell must be coming from somewhere.

I grab the bookcase at the side of the wall and tip it over. It slides across the window. My head is jerking and twitching as I gag and heave. Anna moves another shelf against the one I put there. I can taste the dead in the air.

"Leo and then the forest," I whisper, trying to calm myself down.

"I can't wait for the forest. I can't wait to go swimming," she mutters.

I move a leather couch in front of the bookcase and run to the door of the office.

She follows me. The hallway is dark. Instantly, I want to turn around but I can hear the infected at the window. Their high moans and screams make my skin crawl. The stench in the hallway is worse. I step out into the darkness. The only light is coming from the door I am leaving behind. I walk quickly into the abyss with my hands extended, running my blood-soaked knives along the wall. My left hand drops into a doorway. I lower my hand, searching for the knob. It's locked. I continue walking. My feet meet soft things and crunchy things, but I keep walking. I'm grateful for the dark and for her.

"Thanks for coming for me," I whisper.

"You did it for me. No one leaves their family behind."

Her words bring tears to my eyes. Even after everything she's heard, she still calls me family. Even though I'm not a normal kid/woman/girl.

The high moans are the only sounds, beyond my breathing and the scratch of my knives on the wall.

I ignore when my right hand slips into a doorway. I need to get out the other side, opposite the infected horde behind me. The feeling of their hands grabbing for me, lingers on my arms. I shiver as my left hand drops into a doorway again. I grab the handle. It's unlocked. I open it slowly. The air is stale but less like rotting flesh.

Dim light filters in the room.

The high moans sound like they're in the building, as I slip inside and close the door. I lock it and drag a desk from the inside over to the door. It's a small office with rotting furniture and dust. Layers of dust. The smell in the stale air is the dust and mildew getting into the furniture. The small windows are closed. They don't open but there is a door.

"That looks like what we're looking for," she mutters.

It still has a sign over it that says 'Open in Case of Emergency'.

"Feels like an emergency," I mutter back. She laughs.

I grip the lock and take a deep breath. The windows show no signs of life, just broken-down shit and bushes. The city is slowly becoming the jungle again.

"See anything?" I ask. She shakes her head and scouts the street.

A scratch at the door startles us both. I turn, holding my breath and waiting. Not only have they made it inside, but they can smell us. I'm not sure how they can smell us over the rotting things in the dark hallway. Then I look down at my crotch and wince. The miscarriage. It's disturbing on so many levels.

I look out the windows again, as I turn the lock and open the door. I should have waited. I'm panicking as I peek my head out, but the scratches have become thumps on the doors.

The fresh air of the city is welcomed. My nostrils are burning from the other smells. I look both ways and step out into it. God only knows, what waits for us.

Anna closes the door and we turn and run. I don't even care if more of them chase us, we just need to run. I need Leo. I'm close, I think.

Something moves to the right of me, but I ignore it. I run. It chases us, but the gun goes off.

In its place, I can hear footsteps behind us. I get to a wall of debris, like the one I climbed over to get into the infected section. I jump at it. I'm clawing and climbing. Anna is doing the same. We scramble up fast and furiously. I can hear them behind us, the ones who saw us running in the alley.

My hands slip on the boards, as pieces of things under my feet break. I don't look back. I look for Anna; she's at the top. I pull and climb. Something grabs at my boot as I get a hold of a metal bar and pull myself up. I curl up into a ball on the top of the junk wall and look back. I lean against the top of the debris wall of junk and take deep breaths. Anna nudges me, "That was scary," she heaves for air.

I nod.

The infected are making their way to the bottom of the wall and crowding around us. They breathe hard, making whistled sounds that will haunt my dreams forever. I am eighty-percent certain, I will be wandering aimlessly with them in a week—once the fever is done burning my brain. I don't believe everything he said to me. I don't want to. I'd rather be dead than manufactured. I look down at the green goo and filth covering me. There is no way I have escaped getting the infection, if I can get it.

I turn my back on them and look at the road ahead. There is a small bridge that lies in ruin and a road that looks like a highway. I'm at the edge of the city. I would sigh relief but I'm more terrified of the things outside of the city.

The infected we can outrun or kill, but the things outside of the city are strong and armed. I glance back at the city and swallow.

"That looks like the place, the doctor was talking about," she points to the side with the bridge.

I nod, "Yeah, I think it is."

The infected try to climb the wall. Their shrieks and screams are distracting and frightening. I see them differently now, though. Up close I can see it, the faces of what used to be human.

Anna looks at them and shrugs the gun up higher on her shoulder, as she starts the climb down into the open roads. I follow.

I still feel the bad feelings from the days before. I still feel my impending doom. I nudge her and mutter, "I had this bad dream a few times when I was in the room. It was about Leo and he was in a cage. He looked hungry and scared. His ears were twitching like a cat's. They do that when he gets nervous. He looked at me from the cage and smiled his sloppy-wolf smile. His tail wagged. But I could see a man behind the cage. Leo couldn't see him. I tried screaming to him. I was jumping up and down and pointing but Leo just smiled at me. The man was wearing one of the space suits and holding a red-hot poker. He stuck it in the cage and Leo's fur singed. I could hear his howl. It's still haunting me."

She shudders, "Creepy. You know he'll be fine. It's Leo."

I chuckle, "He's survived far worse, I suppose."

"Yeah, God... he was so nice when that horrid kid of Mary's was always mauling him. Little brat."

I laugh harder and we continue in silence. We know how to move quietly and not be seen.

The wind whistles and replaces the sounds of the infected. The clean wind is exactly the way I remember it being, fresh and warm. The smell of rot, sewage and stale cooking is gone. I'm grateful for it, but at the same time, I miss the closed-in feeling of the city. Now my eyes dart nervously. Every speck of gravel that is dragged across the ground, sounds like footsteps. It sounds worse than the simple knock at my door. The memories flash in my mind when I let my mind wander. My doubts still think I made the wrong choice. Looking at her, I know I made the right one. I hold my knives and walk, pushing the memories away. She came for me. She is my 'us'.

Loving them all, and missing the ones not with us, hurts me in a way I cannot understand. It hurt when my mom died. It hurt when my dad dragged me away from my Granny's house. It hurt the most, when my dad died. But none of it hurts the way, being away from him does.

His eyes and the way he watches me—he's always got my back. I feel tears threaten my eyes. I've never needed anything the way I need him. He is the one who was there when I was small and scared. He's my first family member after the world ended and I was alone.

The closer we get to the small cluster of buildings in front of us, particularly the one that says U.M.I.N.A., the worse the fears get in my belly. I'm terrified of what we will find.

I pocket one of the knives and jog up to the first building, Anna slides along the wall with me and looks the other way. I slip along the side of it, away from her and glance around the side. It seems cleaner here. I hear something I haven't heard in a while. A truck. I freeze and wait for a better idea of where it is. I look back at Anna; she's listening too. It's coming towards us. I turn and run for the far side of the building, following Anna. She heard the truck's direction too. She moves like I do. She is getting better and better at this life. That would make me sad, but we don't have time for that. I look back the way we came. I don't see anything.

We stand there breathing softly and wait. The truck's engine has a slight squeal. We crouch in a bush and wait. The truck drives by slowly, patrolling. It's a pickup with two men in the back with huge guns. Guns like I've never seen before. They turn to the right and disappear into the tidy area.

"The others?" she whispers.

I shake my head subtly, "Worse, military."

I hear her swallow, "What does that even mean?"

I shake my head again, "I don't know. Wait here. Cover me and shoot only when you have to."

She gives me a look.

Sweat is pouring down my face. My nerves and exhaustion, combined with the midday summer sun, are brutal. I creep back to where I was, trying to forget the dry feeling in my mouth, and the ache of starvation in my stomach.

I glance up to the top of the buildings. I notice movement. I realize it's just like the camps. I lean against the wall and watch them. I'm never going to get him back. I turn and wave for her to follow me. We run around the building, going in the opposite direction of the guards. I round the corner and fight the feelings of rage and hopelessness that are brewing inside of me. I'm feeling psychotic enough to make my hands shake.

I take deep breaths and glance up. No movements. Looking down the road, I can't see anything, just buildings with huge lettering and parking lots like the breeder farms. Things are clean here like the farms too, like nature is kept at bay by something. It isn't overrun with bushes and trees and vines like in the city.

I hear voices. Women's voices. I freeze; Anna stands right next to me. I hear her fingers slide against the gun as her grip tightens. We lean against the building and look out into the road. Two women walk with matching guns and bandanas on their heads.

"You think they're part of the army?" I whisper.

"I don't know. What should we do? Want me to shoot?" she asks softly, crouching down.

I shake my head and whisper, "Get in the bush and play possum. They have guns and those matching bandanas; they're guards. This must be their patrol."

I curl into a ball next to the bush I am beside and she follows, doing the same.

"Don't move till I say it's okay. No matter what," I whisper into the warm silence.

The bushes hide her and the gun. I tuck my hands behind my back, holding my knives. I let my face go slack.

I lie there and wait. If they're any good at their job, they'll find me. If they're really good they'll just shoot me dead. It's what I would do. But after seeing the training on the other guards, I have hope I'll be alive and well, within minutes of them both being dead.

The voices get louder, "Oh, I know. I heard she was at the farms. It's sad but we all have to do our part." She sounds cold and detached.

The other lady doesn't sound the same. She sounds upset, "She was seventeen. It isn't right. I don't give a shit what anyone says, she was too young."

The other lady's voice grows tense, "Well, when you are in earshot of the others you better sing a different tune, Linda."

"I will."

They're almost on top of me. I relax my breath and play possum.

"Oh my God—look. It's a girl." One of them rushes at me. It's the distant-sounding one. Her hands are warm when they touch my arms.

"She might be infected, Luce. Masks."

"She isn't infected, no fever. She's sick; look at her. She's pale."

I take a breath and open my eyes.

The cold lady has dark hair and soft brown eyes. She smiles, "You okay?"

I nod and swallow.

"You been bit?"

I shake my head but I'm covered in brownish-green blood. I look like I'm carrying the infection.

"Can you get up?" she asks. The other lady watches me with sharp, steel-blue eyes and holds her gun on me.

As I get up, I move my hands fast. I slice the first lady across the throat and grab and spin her. The other woman fires but she shoots her friend in the back. I toss her friend aside and kick her legs out from under her. When she goes down, I stab into her heart hard. I pull the gun away and her bandana. I tie it around my throat the way they have it. I take the one with blue eyes and drag her into the bush. Looking around, I pull her shirt off. I rip mine off and pull on hers. We take their boots and pants too. It's against my rules, but I need clean clothes and we both need better boots.

They aren't amazing but they're better than the crap Vincent gave me.

"Get up," I whisper.

We rifle through the pockets and find the card that is the door key.

"Put the bandana on the way she has it."

We drag them both into the bushes and grab their guns. A truck comes along with men and women in it.

"HALT!" a man shouts, just as we leave the two dead, naked women.

We stop.

He narrows his eyes, "You fire a shot?"

I shake my head.

"You hear a shot?"

I turn and point back the way I came, "No. We just came from there and a truck was driving by. It had a fan belt that was making a squeal. We didn't hear anything but that."

He looks that way and nods.

I'm trembling inside. Anna is completely silent.

"Eyes and ears open, both of you," he points forward. The people in the truck drive on. I'm sucking air, like I've held it for a year. I think I've peed my pants a little. I look down at the small wet spot and shake my head, "Damn, new pants too."

Anna looks and smirks a little, "You having an issue?"

I fight a grin, "Yeah. Whatever they did to me is like my monthly situation combined with no bladder control."

She shakes her head, "We gotta get home."

"Okay, next part we act casual like this is our patrol," I nod up ahead.

We walk along the side of the building and I see it. It's across the wide road.

UMINA

There is no one. I take a breath and try to control my heartbeat. I feel like running in the other direction, when I take the first step to cross the street. The pavement here looks like before. The windows aren't stained with blood and dirty hands of the infected, like everywhere else is. It looks like the infected have never been here before, like the farms. I cross the road, trying not to look wide-eyed and psychotic. We walk past the building as casually as we can.

My skin prickles with fear and excitement.

I can feel him, he's close.

We walk around the back of the building, like we are doing our job. When we get to the backside, I see something that makes me sickly uncomfortable.

"Oh God," she says.

I swallow and glance at her. I shake my head, "It's okay."

She turns pale, looking at the bins—huge bins, like at the breeder farm.

I shudder and we walk up behind them. I can smell rot and trash as I climb the stairs. I don't look around. I just try to act like this is the way we're supposed to go.

I open the door with the keycard in my hand and hold it open for her. Inside is a hallway, not a room like the farms. It isn't like the breeder farms at all. It's more like an office building. I don't know where to go or what to do.

I close the door, taking a deep breath, and glance back at her. She has the same lost look, I imagine is on my face.

We walk through the hallway until we come to a room with an open door. There is a sink in the room. I leap at it and turn it on as Anna comes inside and closes the door. Cold water comes splashing out.

"Oh my God! The water runs and there's soap," she whispers.

I gasp and shove my hands under it. I scrub until I am raw and my knives are clean. Then I plunge my clean face in the water. I let it pour into my mouth, swallowing as fast as I can. I want to drink more, but I don't. I know how water sickness feels and I'm more than likely leaving here with guns firing at me. I back off and let her get at it. She scrubs herself completely and then gulps the way I did. I pull her back, "You have to stop. Too much after so little, makes us sick."

She burps and closes her eyes "I miss the farms sometimes."

I let a small laugh escape, "I know. I miss the food. Remember Sarah got Cook to put that sauce on everything?"

Anna smiles brightly. Her blue eyes sparkle in the dim light of the room. We're so close, I can feel it.

The feeling like I'm going to die hasn't left me, since I was strapped to the metal table. I still feel like it's going to be any second, but when I look at her, I know I have to get her to safety. I have an obligation to protect her. She came for me. She called me family.

I wash my face, hands, and knives. I want to take the clothes off, but until I get some replacements, I can't. At least my hands and knives are clean. Anna does the same. The soap smells exactly like the stuff in all the washrooms at the farm.

I turn and open the door to the hallway. It's long and looks like the breeder farms. I see stairs and hurry to the exit. Anna is behind me the whole way, moving like I do.

We don't look in the doors, we just walk. I open the door that has a sign and says it's to the stairs and run down them. I want to curl into a ball and hide but he needs us. He wouldn't hide like that, if it were us missing. He took the dart for me.

I open the thick, heavy door at the bottom of the stairs. It's filled with plants and mist. I'm confused.

"What the hell?" she whispers.

I shake my head, "I don't know."

The heavy air feels like it has just rained in the forest. I walk through, looking for other people. Plants grow, like in the greenhouse Granny had, on counters and the floor. Water sprays from pipes above. I slip through, terrified.

"Where is everyone else?" she whispers.

Again, I shake my head, "I don't know. It feels like a trap."

Our hands tighten simultaneously on the guns we're holding.

I walk to the door on the far side, gripping my gun and looking all around me. It's too easy, something isn't right.

I unlock the door with the card and crack it open a tiny bit. I listen. I almost close my eyes and try to listen like I used to do. I don't hear anything, but my ears don't work as well here. I don't like it here. I just want to go home.

God-damned Marshall. I clench my jaw and open the door wider. I freeze as a woman in a white coat walks past the door away from me. I hear Anna suck air against my back.

The lady doesn't notice us or turn around. Her long, dark hair is shiny and pulled back in a ponytail. She walks away through another door and closes it. I take a deep breath and open the door, enough to peek my head in and look about the hallway. The light is on full power here. It's weird that it's so clean and there's no infected here. There aren't a lot of them left, but there are enough that they should at least come near here. We didn't see anything after we left the city. Why haven't the military firebombed the cities to kill the infected? It doesn't even make sense, except the creepy thing Vincent said about experiments.

I just want to get back to the borderlands. I want the feel of a bow in my hands and the wind on my face.

We slip out into the empty hall. Every step feels like I'm wading through mud. My body is exhausted and weak, but my need for him drives me forward. I'm running on sheer hatred and stubbornness. I got it from Lenny. I don't care what Vincent said,

Lenny was my dad. I don't care what any of them say.

I grip the gun tighter and try to control my breathing and heartbeat. I round a corner to find a door with a glass window. I look through to see cages and desks. A man mills in front of one of the cages and writes something down. He looks only a little older than I am. They're more than likely, expecting us. I know they are. I open the door and point my gun at his face.

He glances up with a smile that drops as quickly as the thing he's writing on.

"What are you doing in here?" he asks nervously.

I walk through the door. Anna closes it but maintains her gun on him.

"Don't move," I say quietly. I'm actually listening to the rest of the room behind him that I can't see.

He shakes his head, "The food and medicine are on the other floor. There's loads of it."

As amazing as that sounds, I shake my head, "We just want the place where the animals are held."

He swallows hard, "What animals?" His eyes dart nervously.

I growl, "I will not hesitate to kill you."

He looks defiantly at me and shakes his head, "The gunshot will bring down a whole lot of military people."

I sling it over my shoulder and pull my sparkly-clean knife out, "I know."

He flinches and steps back, "Please, don't kill me."

Anna moves forward, "She said not to move."

I don't need to look back to see the hardened look on her face. I know that look well enough. His eyes show the loss of strength and courage. He slumps and shakes his head, "Which animal?"

I pause and look at Anna. She shrugs and says, "All of them."

He raises his head and his eyebrows, "What? All?"

I nod and realize what she's doing, "Yes, all."

"Behind me, around a corner and through a steel door. The cages are back there." His voice is soft and defeated, but I see something in his eyes.

"Do you have any rope or anything?" I ask.

He shakes his head.

I see clear plastic tape on the counter and nod my head at it, "Pass me the tape."

He frowns, pauses and does it. He passes it to me but still doesn't make eye contact. Something is wrong. He's planning.

I grab his arms and tie them behind his back. He doesn't fight me. I walk him around the corner to the steel door. I open it but his feet stop the door. He is backpedaling and fighting me.

"N-n-not this d-d-door."

I glance back at Anna. Her eyes narrow. She shoves the gun in his back, "What's in this room?"

He looks back, his face is flushed from scrambling, but I have his arms up his back. "The wild cats. They caught them eating the infected. They're immune. Most animals are."

I see movement behind the door and drag him out. I close the door, just as an angry mountain lion stalks up.

Her eyes are savage and vicious.

He nods his head, "The dogs, wolves and bears are that way."

Anna shoves the gun in his back again, "You were going to let us go in there?"

I drag him the way he nodded us, towards the door with a glass window and the animals are in small cages.

I rip open the door and open the first cage I see. A large, golden dog wags his tail. I can see a shaved side where sores mark his skin. I feel hatred burning inside of me. I shove the man inside of the cage. I close it and shake my head, "How could you? He's a sweet dog."

He closes his eyes, "We need to understand how their immunity works with the mutations."

I kick the cage making him jump, "Then you shouldn't have made the disease. Assholes."

Anna is opening cages. I turn and see his eyes instantly. He's in a cage so small that when she opens it he has to drag his body through, like he's crawling out of a hole. He shakes his fur and leaps at Anna. She drops the gun and wraps her skinny arms around his thick neck. I skid on my knees crossing the floor.

When I bury my face in his fur, it doesn't smell right. He makes noises like I've never heard before. He's mad at me. He nips my arms and claws at me with his paws.

"Leo," I sob into his fur.

Anna is bawling too. I pull back; he closes his yellow eyes and pants. He looks content. I wipe my face and hug him again. He continues his noises but then the purring sound he makes hits, and I know he's happy.

"I'm sorry, Leo," I whisper and rub his huge ears.

I look around at the room—cats, dogs and wolves. I can't risk letting the wolves out; they aren't Leo. They're real wolves. I jump up and let out the cats and dogs. The room starts to fill with panicked animals. I notice a back door. I run to it and open it. It's a long set of stairs going up.

"Anna, let the dogs and cats out the door we came in."

She hugs him once more and then jumps up and frees them all. She makes kissy noises and the cats and dogs follow her. All but the golden dog. He wags his tail and stays with me. I roll my eyes and sigh.

I look at Leo, "Take your new friend here and go to that door." I give him my look and then the door. He's up and at the door before I have to repeat. He still speaks to me in our way. It makes me smile. He speaks me and I speak him.

I point, "Anna, stand inside of that doorway with Leo. Don't let him come back into this room, okay? Don't close the door completely. Just open it a slit."

She looks confused but does it. The golden dog follows her to the stairs. He pants and wags and doesn't seem to notice where we are.

The three of them slip into the stairwell. I see her blue eyes in the crack of the door. I take a deep breath and hold my gun firmly in my hands. I click the first lock on the cage to one of the three wolves. I walk backwards and click the second lock. My heart is pounding in my chest. I try to control it and walk backwards. The first wolf nudges his door. He starts to slip his huge body through the opening. I click the final one and leap for the door as the first wolf jumps at me.

Anna opens the door and slams it as I land in the stairwell.

She pants and looks up at me, "That's some trap you just set."

I nod and take a huge breath, "I know. Whoever opens that—is dead."

I look at Leo and notice the shaved spot on his side. He has sores that match the golden dog's. I wince but his eyes catch mine and refuse to let me be sad. He nudges me and whines.

Anna starts up the stairs. She gets to the top, turns the lock, and then the handle. I've never been more grateful to see sunshine in all my life.

"It's the side of the building; the one we came in from," she whispers.

The golden smells the air and tries to get through the crack that she has the door open. She shoves him back, "Back, Buddy. Let me see if it's safe."

Leo whines again. I nod, "Just go. It's gonna be bad here in like two minutes."

She scowls, "I can't see anything."

I point at the dog, "Let him out."

Her look doesn't improve.

I shrug and finish climbing the stairs. I look out the crack and open the door. I look at Leo. He crouches and crawls from the door. The golden follows, not crouching.

I follow them, holding my gun and looking around. I see the movement on the roof, but he's looking the wrong way. He doesn't see us yet. I wish I had my bow.

"Where is the meeting place?" I look back at her.

Her face turns red, "The camp. There is no meeting place. That was a lie for the doctor." Her words make me sick. Jake and Will are in the city somewhere.

We creep along the wall. I hear a truck.

"We gotta run for the forest," I say and whistle, making Leo dash. He runs as fast as he can for the woods. The golden follows him, thank God.

Anna smirks, "That dog is as bad as Jake."

I laugh, regardless of the fact we are more than likely about to die.

"Walk casually," I mutter and fight my smile. The truck comes around the corner. They wave at us and continue along.

I'm pouring sweat and aching ridiculously.

I glance back at Anna, "Turn for the woods." We cross the immaculate street and head for the road that leads into this area. It's a small road, single lane. It's opposite the city. I don't need to see Leo to know he's in there waiting for me.

We walk casually, but the sound of my heart tells me that we are anything but casual. Not to mention, Anna's increased breathing.

The road is so close, but it and the forest, feel so far away.

I glance back at Anna; her blue eyes are huge.

"We got so lucky," she says.

I nod, "Too lucky," and keep looking around. I feel like her words jinxed us. The golden comes out of the woods, wagging his tail. I'm sure Leo is in the bush watching this, shaking his head.

Anna nods, "Yup, Jake."

We drop down into a ditch. I lie on my belly instantly and peek up over the side of the ditch. The rooftops have movement, but it's still casual and relaxed. No one has noticed us.

"You think it's an act?" she whispers holding the gun tight to her.

I swallow and watch them milling about up on the rooftops, "Not sure. I want to say no, but I have a terrible feeling." I look at her and fight the memory of opening the door to the cabin. I don't regret it, but I hate that I could be there. I could be safe. I miss that feeling.

She furrows her dark eyebrows, "Stop giving me that look. Just say what you're gonna say. I know I messed up."

I frown, "Huh?"

She sighs, "Jake and Will... I know I screwed that up."

I bite my lip and look back at the rooftops. The men are gone.

"Shit." I jump up and run for the woods. Her feet behind me are faster than mine. She beats me across the street and into the woods.

Our feet move fast. The golden runs around us, he thinks we're playing. I could throw up, I'm so nervous.

We run hard and far until I gag into the bush, just like I did the first time I ran for my life. I grip the branch next to me and shake. My body isn't strong anymore. I spent everything I had, freeing Leo and running from the infected. Or I'm infected.

I wipe my mouth and try to catch my breath.

Anna and Leo look the same. Same worried eyes.

I shake my head, "I'm fine. Just exhausted or infected."

She shakes her head, "He wasn't lying. You can't get it. He told me he spent the first few days you were there, trying to infect you. You're immune and can't even carry it."

I shrug, "We'll see in a couple days." I put the back of my hand to my forehead, "I think I have the fever."

She rolls her eyes, "You're sick, dummy. But only from being weak." She turns and continues up the huge hill. I have no idea where we are.

"So you really have no idea where Jake and Will are?" I'm so angry with her for that, I could spit fire.

She shoots me a glare, "I told you, we got separated. I think they'll go back to the camp."

I run my hands through my hair, scratching my scalp, "I need a swim or something. I'm funky and gross. We gotta find some water. Look for fir trees."

She gives me a look and rolls her eyes, "Is that even true?"

I ignore her and walk behind Leo. I've been watching his ears and tail. He always knows when there's trouble. I keep looking back, but no one is there. They weren't chasing us. They were no doubt busy, saving whoever opened the wolf trap.

Leo's pace picks up. I try to keep up, but I'm nearly wheezing at this pace. The golden runs around us, sniffing and peeing. He is so Jake, that it would make me laugh, if I wasn't near death.

"Can you find the camp from here?" I ask and gag again.

She shakes her head, "You asked that ten minutes ago and I said yes to it then. You're driving me insane."

I'm about to snap on her, but the forest gets dark and blurry. I stumble and fall into the bush next to me. The smell of the bush is the last thing I register.

I wake with a start, seeing the forest.

Lifting my fingers to the back of my head, I feel the bark of the tree I'm against. I move my other fingers and smile when they dig into his thick, downy fur. He nuzzles into me and makes one of his noises. I glance down and everything feels alright with my world. I don't know how long it'll feel this way, but I'm grateful I feel this way now. I feel like right now is pretty important, because my body is shutting itself down. I'm dying. But the wind is on my face and his fur is in my fingers, so it's okay if I die. I've been waiting days for it to come and I think it has.

I swallow and look around. My eyes adjust to the bright forest, the morning forest. Where is Anna?

I look back at Leo and wonder if she's left me and Leo stayed to guard me. I snap my lips together and try licking. My throat is thick. She's left me because the infection is hitting me. My spit is thickening and my skin is aching.

I slide my fingers into his fur and grip on almost. I knew I could feel it. I knew I could sense, I was going to die. I've feared it my whole life, ever since I read that pigs have a heightened sense of their own demise. I read it and had a bad feeling that I was like the pigs, somehow.

I hold him and wish I could tell him to eat me when I turn. I don't want to wander and kill. I've done enough of that.

The light from the sun filters through the huge canopy high above us. I close my eyes and see the light of it through my eyelids. I can almost feel the warmth of the morning sun.

Vincent's words start to creep around in my mind. All those women, children, babies, people... all hurt by my father. Sickening sadness rolls in like a thick fog. My baby. It's not something I ever thought about, not really. But now that it's gone, it hurts a bit. More than a bit.

Leo senses it. He shoves me and nips at my arm. I don't know how to make it hurt less.

My evil brain flashes images of the little, white-haired brat at the retreat. I laugh, but it comes out as a cough. I glance down at the yellow eyes that are watching me, "I think I might have dodged a bullet there."

He cocks his head and pants. He probably doesn't remember the evil little brat.

"We don't want to have something like that to be responsible for. You and I both know, Meg is enough trouble."

He nods and I swear he remembers the name.

I laugh at him and cough again.

A voice breaks my self-pity, "Talking to yourself is the first sign of madness."

I snap my head around; I would know that voice anywhere.

"Jake!" I try to cry out but my words are stuck in the instant pain in my chest.

He rushes me and wraps his arms around me.

"Am I dreaming?" I mutter into his thick shoulder.

He lifts me off the ground and cradles me in his arms, "Oh my God. You're alive," he whispers into my shoulder, squishing me into him. "Of course you're not dreaming, you're all bones. You're so skinny, Em. You wouldn't be this skinny in a dream. Or bleeding."

I look down at my legs and see it, blood stains on my thigh. My face is warm instantly. I ignore it and enjoy the fact he's holding me.

"How did you find me?" I ask, but the answer is there in the shape of a golden dog. He bounces around the forest joyfully.

Anna walks up smiling, but behind her I see something that hurts me more than anything. Seeing him makes me want to cry. I don't know why. Jake lifts me up and makes me feel happy, but seeing

Will walking up behind his sister, breaks the hold I have over my emotions. I clutch to Jake as Leo circles our legs, rubbing around me and letting me know he's there.

Will's face hardens as he walks towards us, but I see it in his eyes... I think. I think he's relieved to see me. Or he's very angry. I can't ever really tell with him. When he gets to us, he pulls me into his arms and I feel it. I feel the safety of my cabin, the reassuring words of my father, and the touch of Leo's fur all wrapped up in one thing...this embrace. He smells the way I remember, but holds me tighter than I can breathe through.

His body trembles and wraps around mine completely. This is the safest place in the whole world.

"I'm sorry, Em," he whispers into my hair, "I've got you now."

Chapter Six

The sniper in the tree is probably the greatest thing I've ever seen. I would sigh and smile, but I'm surviving on the high of my friends being with me.

Will scoops me in his arms and starts walking faster, "I'm taking her to the med tent."

I struggle, "Will, I can walk." They've been taking turns carrying me for days.

He shakes his head and clenches his jaw, "No." He actually speaks through his teeth.

I roll my eyes and look at where we're going. The tents come into view as we crest the hill. The bustle of the camp and the smoke of the fires are the first things I notice. Leo's hackles are the second. He looks angry, like he knows we were betrayed.

Will takes his huge steps until we are on the far side of the camp. People see him and raise their eyebrows. They almost smile and then don't. They must see the look in his eyes. It's the same one that's keeping my mouth shut. There isn't any point in arguing with him; he's an ass.

His fingers are almost clawing at my skin as he rounds the tents, and I see the doctor who fixed me last time. Will walks right up to him and snarls, "I need her seen immediately."

The doctor looks up, like he might say something but then changes his mind. He looks at me and smiles, "Hey, it's you."

I nod.

He looks me over and points to the same tent as last time, "This way."

Will carries me in. He places me on a cot and stands back. Leo follows and sits at my bedside. I look at the two of them and shake my head. Poor doctor has no idea how bad it'll be if I don't live through this.

He smiles softly, "Want to tell me what's wrong?"

I swallow and look at Will. The doctor reads my eyes and turns to him, "You can wait outside."

Will shakes his head, "Nope."

I feel anger curling around my insides and tightening everything up. I look at the doctor and scowl, "As you know, there was a baby in me, it's not there anymore, and I'm bleeding still. I've been peeing my pants; I had something in there…a tube. I pulled it out and peed everywhere."

I can't look at Will. I want him to have that stupid smug look on his face, but I'm scared it's going to be something else. Something I can't deal with.

"How did you know that I knew about the baby?" the doctor asks.

"Vincent Fitzgerald told me." I lift my face and accidentally catch the disturbed look on Will's face. It's a frozen angry look, but then sadness, or something like that, crawls across, like the weather changing in the sky. His eyes meet mine, "You were pregnant?"

My mouth drops. I lick my lips and close them. I nod and look down again. I'm ashamed. I don't know why, but I know the feeling is shame.

He crosses the tent, shoving the doctor out of the way, "Who? How?" He grips my arms.

I push him off of me, "The farms," I whisper.

He doesn't move. He looks forward. His blue eyes are cold and mean. He stands and leaves.

He's disgusted.

My lip trembles. I want to believe, that because he was at the farms, he has no right to judge me. But it doesn't feel like that. I feel disgusting.

The doctor takes my hand, "It's okay. How did the miscarriage happen, then?"

I feel the story sitting on the tip of my tongue and I don't know if I should say it or not. Will he kick me out of town, if I tell him what I am?

I blink, holding my breath and then just say, "I'm not normal, I don't think."

His eyes grow in size as I retell the story Vincent gave me, and the events that occurred, as far as I was aware of them. I wasn't aware of what he knew and didn't.

His hands creep to his lips. He sits on the wooden makeshift stool and holds himself.

"I knew you were pregnant, and about the breeder babies, and the way things were—because of you rescuing the women, they told me all about it. I never knew the mutations were being implemented before the breakouts. I knew the mutant children were bad, but this... This is horrid. Adult Gen babies." He is gray. I'm a mutation. I think that's bad.

I nod, "It was the man who fathered me. He did it to my mom. He's one of the scientists. I think."

He nods, "That's the most horrible thing I've ever heard. I never would have told Marshall you were pregnant, if I had known what he would do with the information. I just wasn't sure about you going back out there fighting, if you were with child." His thoughts are interrupted by a scream. It's blood curdling.

I jump up but he holds me down, "I think you should stay here." I want to fight him but I can't. I lie back on the cot and feel the water I've drank swish around in my belly.

The screams get much worse. I cringe, "It's the infected. They've made it into the camp. Or the others. They followed me." We've been followed. I never even thought about it all, I was so sick. I

75

expected I was safe with Will. He has a bad way of making me feel like that.

Now they're here. They've made their way in, and everyone is going to run or die, and I am to blame. Marshall was right, I should have been kept away from other people.

The doctor stands and runs from the tent.

He is white as the sheet I'm lying on, when he comes back in after a few minutes.

"It's not the infected." He washes my arm and puts a needle in, "You're going to need to rest."

I blank out then, with things still to tell him, like I might be infected, I might be immune, and that I'm not mad he told Marshall.

I wake on a soft bed and snuggle into the sheets. It's almost as good as being home. I reach around the bed for Leo. I don't find his fur. Opening my eyes, I see I'm in a small tent, not the medical one. Anna is sitting in a chair beside my bed, eating a leg of meat.

She smiles with crap all through her teeth, "Hey!"

I wince, "Hey." My voice is a croak. I lift the sheets and see nothing but a pair of cotton underwear and a baggy t-shirt. No blood, thank God.

"How are you feeling?" She takes another huge bite, making my tummy rumble.

"Hungry." I watch her eat. She reaches down next to her and lifts a plate. She passes it to me. I take a leg of meat and bite down. It has sauce; nothing ever has sauce anymore. I moan; it almost tastes like Granny's chicken legs.

She nods, "Good, huh?"

I chew and sit up. I smelled the food and forgot about the fact my throat is completely dry. She sees the face I make and passes me a jug. I push the chicken to the side of my mouth and chug the fluid. I shudder from the sweetness.

I pull it back, making a face, "Is that juice?"

She smiles and nods, "Awesome, huh? Trina—over with all those ladies that stand in the circle and scare the men—she makes it. I love it. Loaded with vitamins. Made from some berries she grows. You need it, trust me. You almost died."

I scowl, "What?" I sip the juice again. Being prepared for the sweetness of juice and not water, like we've all had for a long time, makes me enjoy it.

She bites the chicken and talks with her mouth full, like Meg does, "Yeah, they almost didn't get you back. You lost a ton of blood. Doc has kept you asleep for a week. He figured you 'hem-something' and that it was bad."

I look past her, "Hemorrhaged." I read about it. It's bad in a time where you can't get blood from other people. I know my blood type, but not everyone will. Not that I probably have normal blood. I have mutant blood. I need to find out what mutant means.

I look at her and wonder how much she's told her brothers. They'll be done with me for sure.

She wipes the sauce from her face and takes the juice from my hand, "Leo is with Jake; you know how those two are. He still hates Will though."

I laugh.

She smiles and drinks again, "You okay?"

I swallow the lump of chicken in my mouth and nod, "I will be. I need to stop my real dad, whatever he is to me. When I stop him, I'll be okay."

She smirks, "You better be careful, you'll become that flashy crow everyone keeps saying you are."

I look down and shake my head, "It's not that."

She kicks my foot, "I know. I was kidding. Good to see all that time in isolation never mellowed you out."

I wrinkle my nose, "I don't think I mellow out."

She grins, "Jake mellows you out."

A smile crosses my lips. I bite my bottom one to try to stop the spread.

"Man, your pasty face even got a bit of color there for a second," she laughs but seems uneasy still.

I look at her, "Are you okay?"

She shakes her head, "No, but I will be. Some of that shit scared me, bad. Being lost in the city was too much to take. But we got Will, me, Jake, you, and Leo. We just need Sarah and Megs and I'll be okay. I need some downtime maybe."

We think the same. I like that.

Her eyes dart around. I kick her this time. It takes more effort than I'm prepared for. "What?" I ask and drag my leg back into the bed.

She sighs and picks her teeth with her tongue, "Will put Marshall in something the doc called a coma."

I close my eyes instantly and absorb it, "He what?"

"He beat him to near death. The only reason he's alive at all, is Jake. Jake ripped Will off and stopped him from killing him," she sounds annoyed.

I open my eyes, climb off the bed, and stalk from the tent in my baggy t-shirt and underwear.

"Emma, you're awake." I see a lady I barely recall. I walk past her, scanning the grounds for the tall lug.

The wrong one comes bounding over, "Em, what's wrong? You should be in bed."

I walk past him, "Where is he?"

He chuckles, "You gotta calm down. The doc says you're pretty sick." He grabs my arm.

I tug it away, "Jake, where is he?"

He sighs, but doesn't have to say anything.

"You should be in bed," a voice says from behind me.

I spin and almost lose my balance. I would sit but I'm too damned angry.

His eyes steel when he looks at me, "Bed."

I cross my arms, "You can't tell me what to do. I'm fine. What the hell did you do to Marshall?"

He crosses his thick arms back at me, "I did what I had to."

I don't know what to say to that. "I needed answers from him."

He shrugs, "He needed to pay for what he did to you."

I scowl, "He betrayed me 'cause he thought... stuff. I needed to know how he knew... stuff." I can feel heat creeping up my face.

He shakes his head, "You need to get back to bed." He takes a step but Leo is there instantly. He stands in between us.

I grab his fur and use him to keep myself steady, "You can't tell me what to do. You don't need to defend my honor. I coulda taken Marshall. I wanted answers."

He takes another step but Leo growls. Will stops, giving me a look.

I grin hard, "What are you going to do? Leo will eat you before you get another step in."

He snarls at me, just as Leo snarls at him. I point, "This is an impasse." I read about it in one of Granny's books. There was a princess with a dragon and she fought with two swords. She was badass.

He shakes his head, "We aren't done talking, but you need bed. Go."

I feel like I'm about to lose the chicken and the juice, so I turn to Jake, "Help me back to bed?" I say quietly. The crowd has gathered.

He beams and winks at Will. Leo growls and fakes at Will who jumps back a bit.

Jake laughs, "C'mon Leo."

Leo watches Will for a second longer and then walks to us. He rubs against Jake, making me laugh.

Jake helps me back, but doesn't let me off the hook, "You acted like an idiot. You need to stay in bed."

I feel my brow pinch together. I don't like it when he's mad at me. Leo and him give me the same look and usually it involves some degree of doubt or sarcasm.

Anna is still in the chair, chewing and drinking.

I lie back down and curl into the blanket, "We need to go check on Meg and Sarah."

"Maybe in a week or so," Jake says and crosses his arms. The twinkle in his eyes is still there. I sigh in relief. It's the thing I wanted the most in the world, to see that twinkle. I swear it's food for my heart. He makes me believe that things could be okay again, maybe. It's saved me, when I was sure I had no heart. I never had a reason to hope before, not even before we ruined the whole world.

Leo whines and nudges me with his cold nose, "You okay, boy?" I ask, watching his eyes. They still seem like they're full of fire and life. He pants, making me smile as I run my fingers through his fur. The thickness seems lessened than before we got taken. I can't imagine how it was for him.

"Did you check him for any wounds?"

Anna swallows chicken and nods, "Yeah. We had doc look at him. He got feisty about it, but Jake did the whole stand up really tall and crossed his arms like Will. Then Doc just looked him over, said he seemed fine."

I shake my head at her, "You're eating like Meg. What's the matter with you?"

She laughs, "I was starved for weeks."

I roll my eyes and look at Jake, "How did you guys lose her?"

His cheeks blush and I realize, it was him. He runs a hand through his hair and smiles, "It was a misunderstanding. I thought Will was going back to see if she was okay, but I guess it was supposed to be me."

I shake my head and hold my hand out for the juice. She passes it to me, "Did they check me for infection? Did they check you?" I ask Anna and keep my eyes off Jake.

She nods slowly, "You've asked this too many times. You really are immune. Stop asking me about the friggin' infection. I'm fine. No infection in this body."

I swallow and shake my head, "Yeah... well... you don't know when it could happen to any of us."

She picks her teeth, making me frown, "Stop it."

She kicks at me, "Shush. I've been living amongst the undead and pretending to be a nurse and killing shit. I'm allowed to have a few moments of acting like a savage."

Jake shoves her, "Yeah, moments. Keep telling yourself that."

She snarls at him.

"Where is the golden Jake-dog?" I ask looking around.

Jake looks confused and Anna's almost choking, she's laughing so hard. She hits her own chest a couple times and moans, "He found that circle of old ladies and befriended them. He's ditched us."

I roll my eyes, "Sounds about right."

I look at the huge beast next to me and grin, "You stayed, right boy? No ditching us for old ladies, like the Jake-dog."

Jake frowns, "What Jake-dog? What does that even mean?"

Anna snickers, "It's so true. He was clumsy and happy like you.

Dang dog."

Leo is making the purring sound as I run my fingers through his fur. It's making me sleepy doing it. I move over on the single cot. He assesses the situation and climbs up gingerly, not trusting a bed off the ground. He tries to spin and get comfortable, but instead ends up giving me a sideways look. We all laugh. He lies at my feet, covering them and the entire lower half of the bed, but keeps his butt to me.

The smile almost hurts my sore, exhausted face.

Jake is laughing still, "Guess you know how he feels about you lately."

I shake my head, "I don't blame him. I would have been so angry if he got me shot and caged."

Anna smiles, "I think he's mad 'cause he wants the hunt. He's been coming with me but he seems weird. You know what he's like with you; he doesn't do the same things with me and Jake."

"Jakey, we need to have some help over here to lift a few barrels," Will lifts back the tent flap. I cringe when I hear the name Jakey. I hate that damned name.

He doesn't make eye contact with me, but Leo lifting his head might have something to do with it.

Jake leaves with him, "Be back in a bit."

I look at Anna, "What is the deal with the Jakey?"

She rolls her eyes, "It was what our mom called him. Every morning it was 'wakey, wakey, Jakey the snakey' and Will used to get so excited when it was his turn to say it. Jake was always a sleeper. Even when he was a baby, he was lazy as hell." She shrugs, "Will always just called him that. He was pretty little when Jake was born. They were old and trouble by the time I was born. I was princess Anna."

A snort escapes from me, before I can stop laughing at her.

She glares, "I used to like nice stuff. I was so little and all those

Disney princesses and shows were my favorite."

I nod, "I see." I don't. I can't see her like that.

She passes Leo the bone of the leg, that she has eaten to nearly clean, and takes the jug of juice from me. Leo nibbles at the meat carefully. I reach for the bone but he growls.

"LEO!" I snap. He cowers. I stroke his head and turn his face. He sees my angry eyes and lowers his head in shame. I look at Anna, "Cooked bones are bad for him. He could get hurt."

She shakes her head, "I have never heard him growl at you."

I stroke him and slip the bone from his ashamed face. I pass it back to her, "Leave with it quickly." I say calmly, "Bring him a raw one." She gets up slowly and leaves the tent. I stroke him softly, "What did they do to you, baby?"

He turns and faces me. His soft Leo face is back, but he still seems funny, 'off' maybe. She's back and tosses it on the ground of the tent. He gives me a look. I nod once. He humbly picks it up and crawls under my bed. I can feel him under me, like the Princess and the Pea, but with a wolf.

"He seems weird." She sits and tucks her feet up.

"He might be worried about me, he might be upset about Marshall being here, or he might be slightly traumatized from the captivity. Could be anything," I mutter and try to ignore the lump under my back.

"Want me to stay again?" she asks.

I nod.

She gets comfy in the chair and closes her eyes.

I close mine and feel safe with her there. "I need a new bow," I say when my body starts to relax.

"I got your old one. I found it in the basement when the building never blew."

I open one eye. She smiles at me, "I knew I would be seeing you again, so I saved it."

I smile back, "Thanks."

She shrugs, "You're my sister, Em—even if you never pick which brother you like better. Although I will say, it seems to me Leo has chosen for you."

I snicker, "Yeah, he sure likes Jake."

She grins, "Not as much as he likes me."

"Nope. Besides me, Leo loves you the most," I close my eyes again and drift away into a clean sleep. No bad dreams, dirt, or infection—just Leo, the woods and Anna.

Chapter Seven

The walk down the hill makes my stomach grumble with nerves. I can't help but think nonstop about the goodbye I gave Marshall. I snuck into his tent before we were leaving and watched him sleep. I wanted to shove a pillow over his face, but I didn't. Doc was watching me and it felt wrong to do it, without him being able to fight. I leaned down low to his face and returned the whispers that he had given me so long ago.

"I should have killed you when I had the chance." I looked back at Doc and smiled, "You keep him safe for me."

He smiled nervously and I left the tent.

Jake nudges me out of my daydream of smothering Marshall, "You excited to get to the retreat?" Seeing the farmhouse scares me. I don't know why.

I ignore it and nod anyway, "I need to figure out how I'm going to stop my... uhm... them." He isn't my dad. Lenny was my dad. Lenny has been with me every minute of this life; he has kept me alive. His wisdom has made me who I am. The terrible things they did to the baby I was, has been kept at bay by Lenny and Granny and Gramps. I was loved. Lenny might have been a weird dad, but he loved me. The man who fathered me doesn't know me, never has.

I take quiet steps, clutching my bow. My quiver is on my back. I miss the guns I had, Mary's guns. I feel bad for losing them.

We get to the place where the others were and I smile when I see me, Will and Anna are all looking at Leo. He looks normal, but he's sniffing the air. He recognizes home. Jake is scratching his head and looking at a bird in the tree next to him.

I shake my head, "Let me go ahead with him." I walk up to where Leo's standing. Will grabs my arm, "You're still weak."

I shake my head, "I'm not." I am a little, but it's not enough to tell Will about. Honestly, even the doctor was amazed at how quickly I healed.

I pull from his hand and creep to Leo. My animal eyes return with my nerves and instinct. I see a hare in the far right and some leaves rustling behind it. Something is hunting it. I pull an arrow and relax into the pull. My breath whispers along the bow as I watch the bushes. The hare hops away, while whatever it is stalking it stays still—it smells us.

Leo watches it and then looks at me. I shake my head, lowering the bow. Whatever is behind the bushes is scared of us; it's clearly not the infected. We slip down the hill slowly, watching out for movement and listening for changes in the patterns.

I hear Will behind me; he's closing in on us. I scowl at him, making him stop. Everything he does annoys me.

Leo and I crouch, stalking through the woods silently. When I see the light of the field and the break in the forest, I stop and nod at Leo. He crouches low and stops moving. I jump into the tree nearest to me and climb fast. My skin aches, my calluses are gone. I'm getting soft.

I pull and lift until I'm high enough that my guts ache. The farmhouse looks empty. I miss it. I miss that life. The simplicity and peace. I want for that to be my way again. I want Jake, Megs, Sarah, Anna, and Will to live with me and Leo. I close my eyes and listen, as the wind sways the branch I am in. The wheat tickles and touches, the dust in the driveway rolls across the gravel, the breeze brushes against the house like it's painting it or stroking lightly, and nothing else moves.

There is nothing. No ragged breathing or high moans or campfires burning in the wind. There is no sign of life. The house looks the way it always does. I don't like that. That is unsettling. Why would they have left a good house with a working well?

My heart tugs me in the direction of the house, and the supplies I know I have stashed, but my fears tell me that we need to give the house a wide birth. Leo pants nervously.

I look back and nod. Will speaks softly and they all move down the hill slowly. Anna still has her rifle, my old one with the silencer. They stashed it and all our things at the camp when they came looking for me. They traveled light.

I watch the field as they walk down the hill to me. Nothing moves around the house or field in a way it shouldn't.

When they're close, I climb down, "I'll go first and climb a tree at the far side. When I'm across and up the tree, you all make it across one at a time."

Will nods, "Be fast."

I ignore him and crouch next to Leo. We slip out of the forest and into the wheat. I glance at him and whisper, "Ready?"

He pants at me, but I can see the yellow in his eyes is darkening. He's ready. We bolt at the exact same moment, running hard and fast across the field. I only have my bow and quiver. Normally, I would run the field with a huge pack and supplies. I am much faster without them. It's almost freeing to run this fast.

We break the forest at the same spot as last time. I leap into the huge tree and haul myself up the branches. I pull an arrow and scan the field.

There is nothing but the line in the wheat where we ran. I see Anna come first and then Jake. Will brings up the back end of them. Anna breaks the forest and spins, pointing the gun back at Jake. He flinches when he sees it and scowls. She ignores him and watches the field. Will comes last. I watch for an extra second.

"Nothing," I say. I'm almost disappointed.

We start the hike to the retreat and I can feel the excitement building inside of me.

Anna leads with Leo. Jake naturally falls into pace with me, leaving Will to bring up the back end.

"What are you, Em?" he whispers.

I feel a look flash across my face but I fight it, "Nothing. Why?" I hate that he knows something. Did I act differently?

He grabs a stick and snaps it, "I heard what Marshall said to Will. He said he knew almost right away, you were a seed. I just don't know what that means. Will started to kill him and that sort of ended the conversation." He grins and my heart skips a beat. His cheeks flush when we make eye contact and I want to get lost in him, like the girls in the romance books.

But I can't. I'm not like those girls.

I feel a burning pain in my eyes as they fill with tears. I look down when I realize I'm crying. I shake my head, "Marshall was right."

The back of his hand rubs against mine slowly. I let it. I let his touch mean something. I need it to, for some unknown reason. He always makes me feel something I like. I don't know what it is, but it's good and maybe pure.

"Are you like the breeder babies?" he asks after a minute.

I nod once, "Yeah, like that. It's a long story, but basically I'm like that."

I can hear the grin in his voice when he speaks, "I knew you were more than just a regular girl."

I glance up at him and shake my head.

His grin stays on his lips, but I see it leave his eyes when he notices the tears. We don't talk about it again but his hand encompasses mine. I notice suddenly he gives me a different sort of safety than Will. He makes my heart feel safe, like it's protected in his hands when he holds mine.

I notice Leo's ears go back and I drop the hand, pulling an arrow instantly. Anna has the gun pointed out, scanning. Will catches up, looking around savagely.

"There should be scouts by here," he says.

I notice it; we are at the big trees again. There should be armed guards in the trees.

I break into a run. Leo follows me. Fear for Meg and Sarah pulls me along. I run hard, oblivious to the sounds behind me, oblivious of whether they followed or not.

I smell the camp, before I see anything. I hear them, and then finally, I see it.

Laundry is hanging in the trees, people are laughing and talking, and everything looks like it was, only more relaxed. I come to a stop when I see her. Leo doesn't stop he races to her and knocks her to the ground.

"Gosh darned, stupid crazy wolf!" she cries out, as he lies on top of her licking her face.

I grimace and laugh through my gasping breaths. Meg swats at him. He does his frisky-dog thing and hops about playfully. People seeing him have stopped talking and moving.

"WOLFIE!"

I turn my head to see the blond demon running for Leo. I whistle once. Leo is up and running for me. He stands behind me, panting and looking sloppy. Meg runs for my arms. She knocks me back a bit when she hits me. I wrap around her skinny body and hold her tighter, than I think I've ever held anything. I feel a million things I can't put my fingers on, but relief is the biggest.

"Sarah?" I whisper.

"Swimming lessons with Mary," she mutters into my hair. I can hear the sobs in her words. She trembles in my arms. Anna and Jake catch up to us. Meg pulls back and grins at him. I shake my head and sigh, but a sound overtakes all of us.

"WHAT THE FUCK ARE YOU THINKING? GET THEM BACK IN THE TREES AND ON ROTATION NOW!" Will is screaming at a group of men. His words are savage growling at the end of the shouts.

The men lower their heads.

"They all listen to him?" Anna asks, almost laughing.

Meg snorts, "Well, I done told them, taking them guards outta the trees was a stupid idea. They told me to shut the hell up and play with the kids." She rolls her eyes and picks something from her teeth. "Soon as Will left, they all started slacking off. Been making wine and beer and been drinking." Her eyes flash something, "Been a bit scary round here lately. I was giving y'all two more weeks and I was taking Sarah and going to a town."

I frown at her, "No one hurt you, right?"

She shakes her head, "Not me. Hell no. Mary runs a tight ship with the kids now. They raised the age of all the something-something, too. No minors doing any dating till eighteen." She sounds bitter but I smile. She sneers at me, "You wipe that smile off, Em. You are to blame for the lack of fun, we been having."

I cross my arms, "I have been having enough for everyone."

That makes her grin at Jake and nod, "I can imagine."

Anna laughs, "I'm going swimming."

I nod, "Me too." Meg looks nervously at the camp, "Well, you can't leave me here now." Seeing her face, I glance around the retreat and notice the people are watching me. The blond demon is even gone. He was there a second ago. I had rushed to Meg so fast, I didn't notice where he went.

I search the angry faces for the one that I know will die protecting me. He's there, scowling away at me. I grin at him and walk away from it all, towards the swimming hole. I have dreamt about swimming again for so long. The shower at the first camp was nothing compared to what the swimming hole is going to feel like.

I walk to the edge of the forest, to the path, but I can feel their eyes on me. The laughing and joking has quit.

We enter the path and I stop, looking at Meg, "What happened?"

She swallows and shakes her head, "They said you was bad. You was one of them bad ones and you was being sent to the city to live with the others like you. They said Marshall was protecting us all from you. But I swear, I never believed it. I even protected your name but they didn't care. They believed you was evil."

It hurts. I left my mountain home, saved their loved ones, risked my life to protect them all, and I am the evil one. I don't even have a defense. Marshall somehow knew what I was, what I am. It hurts. I push it down and walk down the path to the swimming hole. I strip my pants and shirt off and toss them aside. I kick my boots off and dive into the water. I see her. Her blonde head of hair is shiny and wet. I push my hands in and swim as hard as I can for her. Her face lights up when she sees mine.

"EMMA!" she screams and swims for me. She can swim. I fight the tears in my face, the hate in my heart and the betrayal that's rotting my guts.

When her little hand is in mine, I pull her into my arms and close my eyes. I tread the water and squeeze the life out of her.

"Oh, Sarah," I sigh, "You're safe." The attachment feels stronger, like I am linked to her even more than before. I didn't even know how much I worried about her until this moment. The water ripples around us. I look up to see the kind eyes of Mary. I smile, "Thank you."

She shakes her head, "She was amazing."

I shake my head, "I saddled you with it all and I think it's been more than you'll tell me."

Her eyes speak the words she can't, because the little ears with us don't need to know about how bad things got around her. Sarah is a sharp girl; she no doubt noticed it all anyway. She'll tell me later.

Mary clears her throat, "It was my honor."

I wrap my arm around Mary and hug her too. I notice the way I fold myself around them; I'm not so wooden anymore. Things are different about me now.

Sarah sees Anna and swims to her. I glance at her and Jake diving in and smile. But Mary's hand on my arm and the tension of her grip, swings my head back around. Her eyes have changed, "You gotta go. Take her and Meg and get them the hell outta here."

I knew it. I knew I had sensed a change. "Why?"

She shakes her head, "Marshall has them all convinced that you are some kind of evil."

I sigh and look back at Jake, Anna, Meg, and Sarah. I feel a ticking start in my body.

"Is that baby of yours a breeder baby?"

Her eyes tell me the truth of the matter. I nod, "You love him and treat him with kindness, but you aren't giving him enough rules. The only reason I'm not like those freaks in the city is my Granny and Gramps. They loved me, and my dad Lenny would tan my hide if I got out of line. You need to give him rules or he'll become like those things in the city. We aren't right in the head." I swim away before she can ask questions. There's a fire burning in my belly that is making me feel sick.

I climb out of the water and pull my dirty clothes on. I notice the way they stink as I pull them on. I miss doing laundry and being clean and being alone. I miss everything but I'm in too deep.

Leo is waiting for me on the trail. He knows what I'm about to do. I can see it in his eyes. He nudges me . I shake my head, "No." I scratch his ears and walk past him. He nudges me again, but I continue up the hill.

When I get back to the camp I see them crowding and talking to Will, who looks angry in a whole new way. I climb onto a stump and whistle. Leo jumps onto the wide stump with me, almost knocking me off of it.

A man glances at me and points, "You need to leave."

I cross my arms and wait for them to gather. My belly is churning like something is tearing it out. I almost want to run away, but I need to fix it for my family.

The voices rise and the anger approaches. Another man shoves in front of the other people and points, "You're a danger to us all."

I watch his face. His confidence is based upon the other people; he glances nervously at the crowd for support. I lean in to Leo whose hackles are up. He growls at the group. Will is stalking towards me. He scares me way more than the other people.

A woman makes her way to the front, "She saved us, you idiots. She isn't a danger—she's a savior. She stopped the farms."

A voice from the back shouts up, "They burned my town looking for her. She is trouble. We should give her back to them men."

That brings my attention around, "What men?" My tone is harsh and cold.

The woman in the front gives me a frightened stare, "Men came for you. They were looking for you. They said Marshall sent them here. Told everyone you were unstable and dangerous, not human."

It stings for a minute, but I swallow it. "Did they take anyone with them?"

She swallows and looks down, "They took a couple of the younger girls. Told us that we needed to replace what you stole from them."

My stomach burns more. My heart is picking up in pace. It makes Leo snarl at the closest man. He backs up.

"YOU LET THEM TAKE YOUNG GIRLS?" I shout at the crowd.

Will gets to the stump and drags me off. I pull my arm from his.

He turns and shouts, "This camp is going to lose its democracy and become a dictatorship, like the other camps in about two minutes. One more person speaks or makes a move, I end that."

The looks on the faces of the other people are intense. Some follow him, I can see that, but others are scared of me.

Me.

That almost makes me laugh. I glance at Leo and know it's probably him and not me.

"Will, she needs to leave. She brings danger."

I feel like screaming, "I am a person like you. Only I'm not a coward. If some men strolled into camp, I would never have let them take girls. I am not an idiot like you. You are pathetic. The minute Will leaves the guards are taken down, so men can stroll into camp? The kids are forced to hide while you pigs make wine and beer and drink too much? The women aren't safe? What the hell was the point in having a safe haven, if you can't keep it safe? You should be ashamed of yourselves. I have never harmed you, any of you." I turn away and walk to the path. I'm shaking and angry. I don't try to control the rage I'm feeling, but I know I have to. I crawl into the bushes and sit on a log. My body aches from the pain in my heart.

Warmth wraps around me. His fur covers me. I dig my hands in and hold on.

"I wanna go home," I sob. Before I feel any sorrier, I hear twigs snapping next to me. I brace for Leo to attack, but he doesn't. Another person joins our embrace. I smell him instantly.

"You ever want to tell people all the bad things you been through, so they'll feel sorry for you and be nice to you?" I ask.

Jake chuckles, "They aren't worth the time it would take, but yeah. I want them to know everything you've been through. They believe Marshall is so great and he's an asshole. He's hurt you. I wish I had let Will kill him."

I blink tears down my cheeks and look up at him, "I don't have any answers or courage or strength. I'm just me. I don't know what to do next. I am sad—sadder than I've ever been. I think I was so excited to get here, and now that I am, it's disappointing. Like we got nowhere else to go in the world."

I see Will standing behind him looking down on us. His face is pained, "It's called postpartum. It's from being pregnant and your body making all the hormones. The baby dying hurts you, emotionally. You don't even know it. It's common in women who have miscarriages and abortions. The doc was telling me some of the things we could expect."

I swallow and nod, "I have felt like a giant baby since then."

Jake looks sick, "You were pregnant?"

I nod, "They put a baby in there at the breeder farm, when I thought I was going for routine checks. I didn't even know. They didn't even tell me they did it. We were there for a couple weeks and we went for routine checks constantly." I don't know why but the sentence makes me ashamed, like I did it somehow.

He winces and holds me tighter to him, forcing my head down and kissing the top of it. He's like Leo, he doesn't need to talk about it, just hug it out.

"We need to leave here, Em."

I close my eyes when I hear Will's voice. I take a deep lungful of Jake, "I know, but we take everyone, Sarah and Meg."

"That's dangerous." His tone is that one where he doesn't want me to argue.

I glance up and shake my head, "Something bad is happening here, Will. The women are scared. I'm not leaving Meg and Sarah here. We gotta stop leaving people behind. If we aren't coming back here, then I'm not hiking that damned hill again."

He sees my face and nods, "Fine. Where are we going?"

I swallow and look at Jake, "The new city. You remember the way?"

Jake's eyes widen. He looks at Will who is stoic and giving Jake no obvious hints on what to say, so he stammers, "Uhm... uh... y-y-yeah."

I sniffle and wipe my face, "None of us is sick. We should pass through the gates easily."

Will frowns after a second, "They will try to take you and Anna and Megs for sure."

I stop and think, "We dress Megs and Sarah like boys. It's blood work; they aren't checking gender are they?"

He sighs, "I don't know. We need a solid plan though."

I grin, "It's a long walk, we can plan along the way."

He looks like he might strangle me, "When have we heard that before?"

I sneer, "Well, it's what's happening. We sleep tonight and leave tomorrow morning."

He nods, "I'll tell the savages that I am taking you out of here. We leave at sunrise."

It hits me, "You acted like you weren't on my side!"

He licks his lips, "I needed answers. Better for them to think I was with them." He turns and walks away. I don't like that.

Jake hugs me tighter, "We need to get outta here, Em. We should leave tonight."

I pull away, looking up into his beautiful blue eyes, "You don't trust him, do you?"

He swallows hard and twitches his head back and forth, "He isn't the same guy he used to be. They did something to him; they broke him somewhere along the line. He went crazy on Marshall and he's been weird about you. He built these places with Marshall."

I don't like that either. "Shit," I mutter, "I don't know what to do."

He looks down at Leo, "Will, will be fine if we leave him here. We need to get the heck out of dodge. You and the girls need to leave now. I can come back for Will when we get settled and safe somewhere."

He's right. I hate it but he is. My nerves are back as I stand out of his grip and look at Leo, "Stay here and guard the path. Don't let them come down to the water and surprise us."

Jake nods, not realizing I'm talking to the wolf. Leo stands and walks to the path where I'm pointing. Jake follows him, making me smile past the millions of things flying through my mind.

I can't help but see the similarities in the romance novels Granny had. The bad hot guy was always really bad, and the girl always missed it, somehow. I hate that I kissed him and that he made my heart pitter-patter. I want to hate him. I realize I'm muttering to myself when I meet Mary on the trail. She snickers, "You okay?"

I frown, "No. You need to tell me how bad we're talking."

She looks back and shakes her head, "I was leaving in a couple days with Megs and Sarah and my boy. I wasn't staying here, no way. We'd be safer in a town."

I scowl, "Come with us." I don't trust her enough to give details.

She nods, "When?"

I shake my head, "Talk to Will. He's working out the details."

I am testing her and I see the team she's on when her eyes flash, "You can't trust him. He's still in charge of this camp and those people who hate you. This isn't that kind of world; you can't trust people. I know you think he's going to save you, but you're one girl, and this is an easy life here. He isn't going to trade the easy life for traveling and being on the run with you. He's not that one-woman kind of guy."

"Be ready then and I will signal you to make a run for it."

She smiles, "Okay. Who is coming?"

I shake my head, still watching her face, "I don't know. Us girls."

She seems satisfied. I'm terrified she isn't real either. My stomach is screaming to run from her too. I nod toward the pool of water, "I'll get them and put them to bed in a tent. We can see about leaving tomorrow in the morning, before daylight."

She scowls, "That's early in the summer."

I nod once, "Okay. That's the plan then." I turn and hurry to the water. We're leaving now. I don't know what's up, but the magic in my belly is telling me we gotta leave now.

Meg sees me first, "Get them out." I say. She hears the panic and waves at Anna and Sarah. They swim over. Anna sees my face and grabs Sarah's hand. She drags her to the edge of the water and pulls her up onto the flat rock.

"We are leaving now."

They look at me. I don't need to explain.

Anna hauls her clothes on, as I hold up Sarah's shirt for her. Meg is dressed and on the path. We run up the hill to see Leo and Jake there. Jake is petting him and acting nonchalant.

I don't hear anything else. No birds, no noises, no people. I sneak up on Jake and whisper, "What's going on?"

He jumps, looking shocked, "Dude."

I frown. He shakes his head, "No one came."

I look past him; it's quiet in the camp. I point to the left, "We go that way, run for the opposite side of the hill."

He looks stunned, "We're leaving now?"

I nod.

"What about Mary? She said she was coming tomorrow."

I want to slap him in the head, "No. We leave now. We have enough people to be responsible for." I look back, "Anna, get Sarah down the left side of the mountain. Meg, go steal some food, knives, and water. We have the rifle and the bow. I'll get Jake down the side over here; he's too big to go that way with you.

Meet at the bottom of the second big hill." I remember getting arrows down that way.

Anna grabs Sarah's hand and they're gone before I even turn to face Meg. She grins and vanishes amongst the tents and trees. I grab Jake's hand and pull him. He crunches and plods along. I grip my bow and hold my breath, so I don't snap at him. Leo scouts ahead. The guys in the trees aren't back up yet. If we hurry they won't even notice us leaving. We're still hungry and cold and wet; even in the hot summer sun, the forest is cool and damp.

"I don't understand why he came all that way to get me back with you and Anna, if he was just going to betray me here," I mutter and continue dragging his huge ass down the hill.

"I don't know if he will betray you, but I don't trust him," he huffs and puffs behind me.

I look back, "You seemed pretty sure a few minutes ago."

He shrugs and climbs over a fallen log, "He's acting weird, Em. What do you want me to say? He isn't the same person he used to be. His moods are weird. He was insane when we were looking for you—insane. Then we found you and he seemed like a psycho, all angry and pissed. He beat Marshall to near death. He screamed at Anna when she found us and had you in the woods. He shook her so hard. I don't trust him. He was desperate to get here, now they don't want us. He loves this camp. He's lost his damned mind. We can come back for him. We know where he is."

I break into a sprint when we hit a flat area. Jake is close to me; he's huffing but keeping up. We make it to the bottom of the huge hill. I point to a bush, "In there."

We run for the bush and jump into it. Leo lays next to me, in the ready crouch. Jake is bent, trying to catch his breath. There is no movement I can see in the woods. The slope makes it impossible to not be seen; there are no trees that are big enough for them to hide behind. I point to the right, "I'm going to find Anna and Sarah."

I hear a twig and look over to see them creeping up to us, "You don't have to," Anna smiles.

I laugh. I know she heard Jake coming down the hill.

We hide in the bush and wait. My guts hurt. They always hurt. Our little band of us feels huge and weak compared to the rest of the world.

"Where's Will?" Anna whispers.

I look at her and shake my head, "He's staying, I think."

Jake nods, "He's losing it, dude."

She opens her mouth to get angry, but we hear Meg. We both look up to the hill to see her trudging down with a small sack and a boy. I sigh, "What is that?"

"That's her boyfriend," Sarah says in her little voice. I feel my face tighten, "Shit." Sarah smiles, "His name is Ron. He's pretty nice. He's sixteen."

I roll my eyes and look at Leo, "At least he's not thirty." I put a hand out, "You stay." Leo sits but his eyes never leave Ron. I watch the hillside behind them and pull an arrow. "Anna, if I have to fire, you know to run. This is the same valley you would have come up through to stalk Leo and me before. Go to the house and hide in the trees—I'll find you. We're close to the cabin, so make sure Jake doesn't fall in the hole." I give her a look. She nods and smiles at Jake. He rolls his eyes and sighs, "It was one time."

I sneak from the bush with the arrow tight. There is nothing coming down the hill but Meg who grins when she sees me. "This is Ron, he's sixteen so if you're gonna beat his ass, just know he's some loony religion that doesn't believe in sex before marriage." Coming from the only one of us who believes completely in God, it's weird she says the religion is loony.

I scoff, "Get behind the bush and shut up." Ron, a boy with shaggy dark-blond hair and a cute face, grins some crooked teeth at me. He gives a slight wave. I scowl and watch the hill. Nothing moves, but that means nothing. We are dealing with Will. He's sneaky and mean. Holding the arrow tight, I know I can't shoot him. He makes my heart rate go nuts and my insides hurt, but I can't shoot him."

I see something; my animal eyes pick it up. I look back, "Run! The cabin is up the hill on the far side. Anna you know the way...." They're already running, before I have a chance to finish the sentence. We are close to the side of the hill where the hole is. I've hunted the mountain on the other side of the valley we are in. It's actually a miracle I never stumbled upon the camp. It's one mountain away from my cabin.

Leo creeps up next to me and crouches.

I focus my eyes again. I see the blond head of the little boy and the shiny brown hair of Mary after a second. I groan and look at Leo. He makes a face and I nod, "I know." Will is walking with them. The three of them are all I see. I relax the bow and feel like I'm about to have a hissy fit. I rub my eyes and wait for it.

"WOLFIE!" he shrieks across the valley when they're close enough to see us. Leo lowers to the ground.

"WHERE WOLFIE GO?" he shrieks again. I crouch down with Leo and rock back and forth on my heels. They cross the woods to where I am panting and processing how to get rid of the little brat. Leo licks his lips and I shake my head, "No, let's not go extreme just yet." Leo yawns and gives me a sideways glance.

"WOLFIE!" he screams and claps his hands. I stand up suddenly. Her hand clamps around his lips when she sees my face. My lip twitches, fighting the sneer and venom that so badly want out.

He starts to cry when he sees my face. I reach up and grab his chubby cheeks, "STOP!" I shout. I pull my hand away, "You want wolfie to bite you? You want the infected to kill us all? Stop talking."

Mary looks horrified, "What is your problem?"

I point around me, "I have killed tons of infected in these very hills, not to mention the military guys. My problem is that if that draws the attention of either, I will run as fast as I can. I will save my own ass. It's who I am."

Her face goes white. She looks around, "Shhhh. Andy, Mommy needs you to be a quiet boy. The bad people are in the woods."

He makes a face but he sees mine and stops. Will doesn't talk. His arms are crossed across his wide chest. The shitty look on his face tells me we may be having a conversation later, one where his fingers leave bruise marks. I narrow my eyes when I look at him, "Whatever you're thinking, don't. I'll kill you."

His lip lifts into a crooked grin, "I wasn't thinking anything."

I feel the hatred burning off me in his direction, "Whenever you get that look, I get bruises. I'll kill you first."

He clenches his jaw, "You ran off and left me." He takes a breath, calming himself.

Mary puts a hand on his arm, "Let's just go on. If these woods are dangerous, we need to get going."

Will takes the blond demon and stalks past me. I look at Mary and feel it all over again. I am at the door of my cabin, about to turn the lock and help Anna but my stomach is telling me I will regret it.

I glance up the hill again but nothing moves, "I thought you didn't trust him?"

"I don't," she answers flatly.

"They didn't follow you?"

She shakes her head, "They just wanted you all gone. Will let them in on the fact, Marshall isn't running the show anymore. Why didn't you tell me he was in a coma—thanks to Will? That improves how I feel about him."

I back up holding my bow ready, "Not me."

I turn and walk across the valley behind Will. The blond demon doesn't make a sound the whole way up the hill.

Chapter Eight

The sight of the cabin makes me feel sick. Not ill, but scared and horrified. "Wait here," I whisper and sneak out of the bush. I creep across the yard to the front door. I glance in the window but the curtains cover them perfectly. I turn the knob but it doesn't budge. I knock lightly.

Jake opens the door after a second and smiles at me. I could smack him, but I don't. I turn and wave Will and Mary over. Leo is already through the front door. He seems anxious and excited.

Anna has the wood in and supplies on the counter. She's cleaned out the storage hiding space we had.

Jake points at the fire, "I lit it."

I laugh and close the door.

Will looks confused, "What is this place?"

I sigh, "Home."

Jake eyes his brother up, "Em grew up here. She lived here with Leo."

Will takes it all in, "I can see you here; you suit this level of control."

My jaw drops but Mary is too excited for me to fight back. She plops down on the sofa and moans, "Oh, sweet Jesus." Her son climbs up on her and curls into a ball. Anna and Sarah hand them bowls of soup.

"Tomato," Sarah says like she is very proud. They must have run the entire way and set up the cabin for us all. We were slowed from Mary and constantly checking for followers. I made us take a small detour too, just to be sure we weren't being followed. Leo scouted back, just like he used to. He stretches out by the fire and relaxes. I sit against him and take my bowl of tomato soup from Megs.

Will sits on the smaller couch, watching me. He wants to talk. I want to shoot him with an arrow. Maybe we'll do both.

The soup is good. It's salty and tasty. I canned it in the summer, when I managed to get the canner from the farmhouse up the hill. It was heavy and made the trip three days instead of one, but I managed to get tons of veggies and soups canned. I even made spaghetti sauce from Granny's recipe book. I nearly died when I found a huge container of salt at a house. It made my life better in too many ways to count; soaking blisters is at the top of that list.

I sigh when I take a bite. The smell and feel are the same. The heat of the fire, the smell of the dusty cabin, and the taste of Granny's famous tomato soup with salt, real sea salt.

"Damn, this is good." I look at Mary and smile.

She sips the bowl and moans into it.

I laugh and look at the rest of us. I realize then and there, I've done it. I let it feel good for a minute.

Anna knows what I mean. She smiles back at me, "We made it."

I nod, "Yup."

Sarah comes and sits beside me. She sips from the bowl and grins, "Almost as good as Cook's food at the farm."

I grin, but the comment silences the room. She's eleven; she doesn't get the pain that word has for the rest of us. I know that feeling. I never seem to know what pain other people have and always say the wrong thing. I don't know it's wrong until I see the pain in their eyes. I glance up at Mary, "Sorry for snapping at you."

She shrugs, "I assume he's a regular boy. I forget he's one of them."

I wince. She puts a hand out, "I mean..."

I shake it off, "It's fine."

Sarah snuggles into me. I wrap an arm around her and kiss the top of her head, "We need to clean up for bed."

I drink back the rest of the soup and put my bowl down. "There are three beds and the couches turn into beds. Meg, you will bunk with Anna, me and Sarah in the first bedroom. The beds are bigger in there. The little room—we'll let Mary have. Boys, you can sleep on the couches. The toilet works in the bathroom, but not with a lot of toilet paper. I haul it up the mountain, so please don't use a ton. There is an outhouse in the yard—it works great. I put lye in it whenever I can find some. The well is drinkable water. I would boil it just because."

Mary scoops her son up and walks to the smaller room, "Thanks, Em."

I nod and stand, pulling Sarah with me. She yawns and wipes her eyes. I point to the room, "I'll get some wash buckets outside. Go in there and wait for me to bring them. Do not get into the beds without checking them for bugs. I haven't been here in months."

I walk to the buckets and head out the front door.

Will scoops them from my hand and passes me the bow, "You guard my back and I'll fill them."

I nod and pull an arrow. I listen to the darkness surrounding us. Leo pads along behind me.

I lead him to the well. In the dim light of the moon, I see him waste the first few pours and smile. He knows.

"Why did you leave me behind?" he asks.

I hate myself for it and sigh, "We thought you felt like you had to choose between the retreat and me, and you chose them. We thought you might let them take me."

I hear his tone change to the defensive, "Emma, what do I have to do, besides carry you for miles, to show you I care about you? How about when I came for you when Marshall sold you out? Or when I defended you to Marshall?"

I step back from him and hold my arrow tight, "I have seen you go from fine to psycho in a short span of time. You've been fairly mean to me, Will."

"You still really don't trust me?"

I shake my head into the dark night, "No. You have to earn trust and you scare me."

The water stops and I see him shifting in front of me. He takes a step forward and I lift the arrow. He walks right into it. I gulp when I see his face and he presses his chest into my arrow, "Do it. I'd rather die, than have you think I'd hurt you on purpose."

I release the tension and step back. He takes a huge breath of air and lifts his hand. I flinch, but he passes me the bucket of water he poured. In the dark, I make out the face he's wearing and it breaks my heart, "You really think I'd beat you, don't you?"

I shake my head, "Not on purpose, but maybe because you can't control your anger or see your rage. I know I make you mad, and you make me mad, and we are crazy together."

He closes his eyes, "That makes me sick."

"Me too," I whisper. It does. I want him, I don't know how I know or why I know, but I do. I want him to hold me and kiss me, take our clothes off, and make me feel things I don't know if I can or not.

"I want to make you happy, make you smile, and be with you— protect you," he whispers back.

I shake my head, "I know but the hurt in you and the hurt in me makes us a bad combination. Two hurt and broken things can't ever make a whole thing." I read that in a romance novel and I never knew what it meant before.

He steps into my space, looming down over me, "But Jake makes you complete?"

I swallow, looking up at him, "He does. All those things you want for me, the smiling, the happy, and the peaceful—he makes me those things."

The look on his face is breaking my heart in the dark. I want to close my eyes and stop seeing it, but I don't trust him enough. I step backwards, "I can't be with either of you, Will. No matter what I want in the world, I have a separate goal. It's gotta get met. If I don't stop him, no one will and shit will never change. I gotta be the hero of my story and my story doesn't have anything to do with a boy and girl—just a man and the monster he made." I never read that in a story. I made it up, but I imagine it's exactly what Mary Shelly was thinking when she wrote Frankenstein. I grip the handle of the bucket and back away again.

"You aren't a monster, I am. I'm a monster, Emma. I made you scared of me and it's too late to fix it. I'll never get the chance to repair the damage I did. Nothing is gonna take away from the fact, that I hurt the only thing in the world I ever loved." He steps away and grabs another bucket.

I don't know which to respond to, the fact he called me a thing or that he loved me. My chest feels like it's going to explode. I almost gag on my way back to the cabin. Jake opens the door when I touch the handle. I jump and slosh the water on myself. He takes the bucket; his eyes search mine for things, I don't know if I can hide. Leo goes in the house with Jake.

I turn and leave again for more buckets of water. Will passes me the next one in silence. I don't know if that's worse than his talking, both rip my heart from my chest.

I pause and watch him fill the next bucket. The dark hides just enough things from me.

"I can't love right," I blurt out.

He looks back at me, "What?"

"My love isn't normal. I love too fast and too much and hate too fast and too much. Nothing about me is normal. I loved Jake the first time I saw him and same for you. The thing they made me, makes me not feel things like other people. My emotions don't work properly. I feel some things too much and others not at all. The doctor told me never to love and never to reproduce, 'cause they don't know what I'll make. He told me I couldn't ever be normal." I turn and leave quickly. I'm ashamed the words are out there in the dark, floating around. I don't want him to know how I feel about him or the flaws in my system. The door opens, but instead of handing Jake the bucket, I walk past him and drag it to Mary's room. I knock and pass it to her, "For washing." I carry it in and sit on the bed. The blond monster is sleeping. I look at him and feel it, the sickening connection to him. His instability is mine.

"You okay?"

I spin and shake my head, "I'm not. They made me pregnant and then killed the baby. I bled all the way to my knees for days. I peed my pants from the tube they stuck up there, that I pulled out. The doctor told me I'm not normal; my real dad is the one who's behind all of this breeder-baby nonsense. My mom was patient number one for it." I plunk down on the edge of the bed and stare at the wall, "I don't know what to do to feel safe again. I used to feel that here. Now I feel sick. Something could happen to any one of us and that scares me."

She drops to her knees in front of me, "Em, that's normal. Before I had Andy, I was so selfish and free. Then I got taken and they made me get pregnant at the farms. I had a seizure and ended up in the medical ward. When the doctor wasn't looking, I got away. I gave birth alone in the forest and then Marshall and Will found me. They too had escaped from the farm but years earlier. Marshall was a doctor—he saved me. They brought me to the retreat; it was new then. I was a mess, I cried for months. I lied about Andy being a real baby. I had nightmares about them taking him and making me go back and have more babies. The panic and stress were overwhelming. Then one day, Will dragged me off and gave me a firm talking to. Andy was showing signs of me being a bad mom; he cried all the time and was nervous. I couldn't breastfeed him. My milk dried up from the nerves. Will made me see the things, I was imagining weren't real."

I feel a bit bad for judging her and the brat, sort of.

She squeezes my hands and I notice the tears making her brown eyes shiny, "You are scared because you have people to care about. If it was just you and your wolf, you'd be calm—he can take care of himself. But you're not. You have Sarah, Meg, Anna and Jake. They all need you, even if it's just for friendship. You're a young woman growing up in a world where love and bright spots are few and far between. Take those moments and cherish them. If you fall in love a hundred times between now and the minute you die, be grateful you had so much love. If you only love once and it's deep and passionate, be grateful for the constant love and companionship of that. We don't live in the world of guarantees anymore, but that doesn't mean it isn't a world of possibilities. You're young, love everyone and anyone who will love you back and treat you with respect."

I nod, "Thanks, Mary. I needed that."

Her warm brown eyes make me relax. She lifts up onto her knees and brushes her lips against mine softly. The soft sweetness of the kiss pulls the air from my chest.

She sits back on her heels and smiles sweetly, "Good night."

I stand off the bed and walk from the room muttering, "Night." I close the door and press my back against it. I like it when she kisses me.

I walk back out the door to the well, where Will is carrying back the last couple buckets. He stops and looks at me. I put a hand on his chest, "I don't want anything from you but respect. I think if you can respect me as a person and treat me with kindness, we can be friends."

He looks confused but doesn't move, "Is that what you're offering me?"

I nod.

He smiles lightly, "I don't want to be your friend, but if that's important to you, then it's important to me."

The heat where my hand is rested on his chest is burning, "It's important to me. I want to be a normal girl—after I kill my dad and destroy everything he has built." I feel the slow grin crossing my lips.

"Yeah, that'll make you normal," he laughs.

My grin matches his. I take a bucket from his hands and turn to walk away. I expect his hands on my arms, spinning me around, but he doesn't do it. He respects the friend request.

"You know before the world ended, people got to know each other before they met in real life," he says.

I look at him, "I remember that. My friend Rachel's mom left one day to be with a man in Canada. She never met him before that day; they played video games together. Rachel and her dad were devastated." I had forgotten about that.

"Might have been the better way to get to know people. No infected and worldwide disasters to contend with. It was just plain talking and being the person you wanted them to see. Not like now, where I spend most of my time wishing I could show you the person I was once."

I glance up at him and try to see the man I want him to be, "Maybe." I don't have fancy words to make him feel okay, I wish he was a better man. Not just for me but for everyone. The fact he wishes it too, makes me hopeful.

I nudge him gently, "Maybe one day, the world will come back and we can get to know each other again."

His eyes burn, ignoring the smile on his lips, "I can wish for that, I guess. Or I can just start being the person I want to be, when I'm with you."

I laugh, "I won't hold you to anything." I open the cabin door and feel the twinkle in my eyes, "I also won't hesitate to shoot you, if you get mean again."

His eyes don't change, "Fair enough." He waits for me to walk inside. I catch a glance from Leo. He doesn't like it when I'm alone with Will. He doesn't like Will. I don't really blame him.

Chapter Nine

The hike down the mountain feels like something I have never felt before. I glance at Anna and smile, "Feels like we have family to come home to, huh?"

She nods, "It's the first time I've ever felt this. There is someone waiting for us, at a place that's home. We have people, Em."

I sigh, "I almost don't want to jinx it and be too excited."

"Can we get a truck or a car?" Jake asks.

Anna flings a stick at him, "Stop being a baby."

He looks exasperatedly at her, "Dude, it's far. You don't remember how far it was; it was a long ways."

She sticks her tongue out at him. Will is quiet, hopefully not moody. He hasn't said much since we talked the other night.

"Where would we find a truck? With gas?" Will asks and walks faster, "We need the time to plan."

Jake nudges against me, "She don't need a plan, Will. She'll just bust the doors down and kick the shit out of everyone—*Terminator* style."

I shake my head and ignore the flames crossing my cheeks. Anna looks as confused as I am, but Will laughs. I like it when he laughs.

I glance at him, "I was thinking maybe we could go to the breeder farms, get nurse and doctor outfits, and then drive into the city, like we just finished shift. That's what she called it right, Anna?"

She winces, "Yeah, shift."

Will nods once, "That's a smart idea."

Jake hovers; he's starting to make me uncomfortable with his clinging to me. I don't know what to say to him. He slips his hand over mine, cradling mine and swinging it. I look up at him and shake my head, "Eyes on the wolf."

Anna snorts, "He expects you to save him."

I frown mockingly, "He should know me better than that—I always run."

He wraps an arm around me and squeezes me. I trip him on purpose. He goes down like a falling tree. He grabs me and drags me down with him. Leo growls. I laugh putting a hand in the air, "It's okay, buddy."

Leo doesn't like it. He shoves Will and growls. Anna drops to her knees fast and calls him. She's shaking she's laughing so hard.

Will looks pissed, "Jake attacks you and he tries to bite me?"

I laugh. Anna puts her hands out, "Come here, boy." He walks to her, still eyeballing Will and lowers his face. Jake grabs my foot and tries to drag me back.

I look back at him and am instantly pulled up roughly. I'm about to pull an arrow and shoot Will in the ass for manhandling me, but his face stops me. He puts a finger to his lips. I crouch and crawl to Leo. I put my fingers in his fur and watch them. It's a group of military. They have the bandanas around their throats like the people in the city.

Jake crawls to us. I push him down into the grass and put a finger to my lips. Will looks at me, "We could take their truck."

I nod. Three of them are out of the small pickup, walking around. One is in the driver's seat. They are looking and wandering about; they're looking for something.

We creep down the hill closer to them. I lick a finger and put it into the air. The wind is slight. I pull an arrow and pull it back. I glance at Anna and wink. She sights her rifle in.

I take a breath and wait for her first shot. I see the red mist and release. The arrow takes down the man next to the one she shot. The last person pulls their gun and slaps the truck, "ATTACK!"

She downs him as I take the driver down. Will and Jake are already dragging the first guys into the grass when we get down there. Jake grabs guns and tosses them into the back of the pickup and Will jumps in the driver's seat.

"The bandanas." I say and pull them off a person next to me. Jake makes a face when I toss him one.

We tie them on and climb in fast. Jake sits up front with Will. Anna and I ride in the back with the weapons and Leo.

I don't pay attention to where Will's going. I watch the countryside go by quickly.

Anna smirks, "You and the boys are in a real pickle."

I shake my head and shout back at her, "No. I am friends with them. I can't be more. You heard the doc."

She shrugs and looks at me. I see how much she's aged, "If I loved someone, Em, I would just love them. The world is so friggin' screwed up; if you find something good and you don't grab onto it, it's like you're laughing in the faces of the people who have all died. My dad loved my mom. He would want all three of us to try to be the kind of people other people would love and cherish. He would be pissed, if even one of us were unhappy in this life. It's so short and the guarantees are gone. There is nothing left but what we make."

I raise my eyebrows and stroke Leo's fur, "Who got old and philosophical?"

She laughs, "I don't know what that means."

"It means you're looking at the meaning of life and contemplating the essence of happiness and the things we need to find that happiness. At least that's what I think it is. I don't really know either. I just know whenever my Gramps got like that, my Granny would call him that."

She grins, "It's a good way to be, I think," and points back where we came from, "We just shot four people—people who had loved ones and family probably. I don't feel bad. They chose the wrong side. They would have killed us in a heartbeat."

I look where her hand is pointing, "I don't feel bad either. We probably should though."

She nods, "We should, but that world is gone. The world we live in sucks. It sucks ass, like Marshall would say. There is nothing but bitter sadness. If I find a boy who makes me happy and makes me forget about the other shit, I'm latching on with both hands. I'm going to make him love me and I'm never leaving wherever we end up. Shit, I'll build a cabin next to yours."

I laugh, "We'll need a few of them. Mary seemed pretty attached to that one and so did Meg."

Her eyes burn the way Will's do, "Yeah well, I told you the first day I was there, I would do anything I could to stay there. I still mean that."

I frown, "You'd still sacrifice me?"

She nods and plays with Leo's huge paw, "You suck. Of course not. But I would sacrifice Mary and her kid. I feel nothing for them. Meg, me, you, Sarah and my brothers, that's my family. Mary is not my problem."

I leave it at that. I don't want to admit, I still sort of feel the same way. I hate that. Or, maybe, I hate that it bothers me.

She hands me a piece of jerky. I chew it and wish we were back at the cabin. I tear some off and give it Leo. He licks my fingers gently. He seems to be settling again.

Will drives until the truck runs out of gas. It's dark again when it sputters. The warm air has cooled off and I'm frozen.

He parks, "It's not far from here."

I look at Anna, "You remember the way?"

She looks around, "Yup. This isn't it."

I give Will a shitty look. He laughs and offers me his hand, "Trust me." I pass him a gun, instead of my hand and slide off the truck.

Leo jumps down and looks around. Will grabs another gun and starts walking. I look at Jake but he shrugs. We don't speak; the dark isn't safe to talk in.

We walk until we reach gravel. I stop and look down at the gravel road, "Is this a driveway?" I've only ever felt this in driveways or crappy, old roads.

"Yup." He doesn't look back; he just walks. He pushes something, "Through this small gap; It's a gate."

I don't like it. Leo stays near me, nudging me. I have an arrow pulled and ready. I wish I had those handguns. We crunch along, not quietly at all, following Will's silhouette down the driveway. I see something dark against the sky. It's huge. I stumble at the same time as Anna. The gravel ends and we're on concrete. The massive black thing grows, as we get nearer. My fingers itch to pull the arrow back. Bad thoughts filter in my brain—thoughts like shooting Will in the leg and running, dragging Jake out of there, knowing Anna and Leo would follow.

Lights flick on blinding me. I pull the arrow back farther and squint, trying to see anything.

"What the fuck, man?" Jake asks squinting.

Anna has the gun up and ready. Will puts his hands in the air, "Bernard, it's me!" he shouts.

"Me who?" a voice calls back.

"Will, asshole."

The lights dim. I still have the spots in my eyes, but my vision clears. I see a massive mansion with the door open and a man inside of the doorframe.

Will walks up and greets him with a weird handshake of sorts. They one-arm hug. Will points, "You are going to want to meet her."

My stomach drops. I pull the arrow that I've relaxed when they shook hands, back again and point it at him.

Will shakes his head, "This is Star's brother. He's ex-CIA. He knows your dad for sure." He ignores the fact I have an arrow on them and looks back at the Bernard guy, "Her dad is one of the seed-Gen guys. She's one of the first seed babies."

The Bernard guy grins, "You are not Michael's kid? Oh my God—I have always wondered what became of you. They did studies, early on, with your DNA but then your uncle ran." His voice is deep and calm. He points at the house, "Please come in." Jake steps forward but Leo growls making him stop.

Anna holds the gun to Bernard, "Will, what the friggin' hell is going on?"

Will crosses his arms and tilts his head like we're being annoying, "This guy knows everything there is to know about the new city. All the ways in and out and where her dad is. I'm tired, can we please go inside?"

I am about to lower the weapon, when I hear it. My skin shivers and my stomach drops again. It's Star.

"Will!" she shrieks and leaps into his arms. She kisses him on the cheek and then jumps out of his arms and attacks Jake, "Jakey."

I have had about all I can take. I lower the arrow and wave, "See you in the city, Will. Thanks for being honest from the start." I turn and walk down the pavement. I hear his long strides following me but Leo's growl stops them.

"Em, don't do this, please. Call Leo off. Anna, come on." I walk and listen as Anna follows. Jake isn't far behind us when Star calls out, "He's not kidding, Emma. My brother knows everything. He can help you."

My skin is covered in goose pimples. I don't even know why I hate her. I stop and look at Anna, "What do you think?"

She shakes her head, "I'm with you. I'm beat but I'm with you. If we're sleeping in the woods, then so be it."

Jake grabs my arms, "But sleeping in a bed in a mansion would be nice."

I look back at the huge house and Will's face. I sneer, "He's a jerk."

He sees the exhaustion and comes running over. Anna grabs Leo and strokes him. Will jogs up, "Guys, this is a good idea."

I narrow my eyes, "If it was such a great idea, why didn't we discuss it?"

He points back, "Because you think things about her and would never take help from her brother, even if it's a good idea."

I scratch my head and think about it for a second. I sigh, "One night and he doesn't do experiments on me."

He grabs my hand and pulls me along, "I love it when you compromise. Guys, this is a nice house and has full power. Showers—hot showers."

I look at Anna. She mutters something about her weak spot and we follow him back.

When I walk to the front door, Will grips my hand. I think it's so I won't slap or attack Star. He drags me inside and I am instantly transported back in time. It looks like a hotel lobby. There are lamps lit and fineries we just don't see anymore. Leo strolls in next to me, nudging. I run my fingers into his fur and hold a chunk.

"Will, you never said a huge wolf was part of the group."

Will chuckles, "He's part of it."

I scowl, "How long have you known we were coming?"

He glances at Will, "Well, Star mentioned something."

I give Will my death stare and look around.

Jake whistles when he walks in and Anna grins, "Shower is which way?"

Bernard, who doesn't look a day over twenty, smiles and points,

"Top of the stairs to the right."

I jerk my hand free of Will and turn to the stairs. Leo stays at my side. He does it when he's nervous. Houses make us both nervous. I stomp on the stairs. They're sound. The whole house is. That's rare. I thought I had found the only stairs that were intact, mostly houses not destroyed in the blasts.

I realize I'm excited about a hot shower. I follow Anna up, and when we open the door, we fill the space with gasps. The bedroom is massive. The bed is lush and gorgeous, like in a picture. The dust is minimal and the whole thing looks kept up.

"I think he cleans," I mutter and look around. Leo walks to the bed, sniffing and checking for surprises.

Anna ignores us and rushes to the door to the right. She turns on the light and looks back at me with a grin, "Can I go first?"

I laugh, "Yeah, but save me water."

She squeals, ripping her clothes off and disappears into the lit room. I turn to see Jake in the doorway.

"Hey."

He runs a hand through his dark hair, "You okay?"

I nod.

He leans on the door and points back at the door across from us, "I'm going to take the room across the hall. He said we have to shower one at a time, water pressure or something." I see the smirk I love cross his lips slowly, "Unless you wanna just shower with me?" he tries to be serious.

I bite my lip and shake my head.

He frowns but the grin is still making attempts, "No? Okay. Just thought, maybe, it would be faster if we showered together."

The sound of the water pouring and Anna humming, feels like it's taking over the room, or the space is shrinking with him in it. I step back but he steps forward. My heart rate picks up and he makes me feel the thing that Will always makes me feel. I shake my head again, "No."

His blue eyes search for something. He steps back nodding, "Okay. Wow. I feel like an idiot. I thought you were smarter than this. You want him because he's strong and smart in the forest? Really?" His eyes aren't friendly and sweet. They turn and I can see the hurt on his face. "I would never hurt you, the way he has."

I swallow hard, "It isn't that. I just want to be your friend, Jake... yours and his. I need to focus my energy on killing my other dad and ending the things he does. I don't want to have to choose who I want to be with. I can't be with anyone. I have to stop my dad. I have to free the other girls."

The anger stays in his bright-blue eyes, "For a girl who walked away from everyone and never cared about anything, you sure got some serious causes now, don't you?"

I don't have any real excuse for why I am so determined now. I nod, "I'm related to the monster who started it. I know the truth of it all. I feel like it's a heavy weight on my shoulders, and the only way to get rid of it, is to kill him and end it all."

He turns and walks from the doorway.

I look down at the hardwood floors and try to push away the bad feelings inside of me. I hate the way I feel, like I have to choose one of them. I hear footsteps and close the door quickly. I turn and press my back into it.

Anna comes out with wet hair and a huge towel wrapped around her. She points, "That was amazing."

I push off the door and walk to the bathroom, "Good. I need it." I close the bathroom door and pull my clothes off. They stick to me from getting dressed when I was still wet. I leave them on the floor next to hers. They look like a pile of dirt on the clean, bright floor. The shower is a walk-in kind. I turn the knob and step in. The heat from the shower is instantly relaxing. I take misty breaths of the steamy air in. I shampoo twice, scrubbing my head free of the debris and dirt. It feels like the dirt coming off of me has been there since the breeder farms. I haven't felt clean since. Not real clean, like I used to before I opened the door to the cabin and let them in my life.

I finish and leave the bathroom in a towel. I'm not ready to put my dirty things back on.

Star is standing in the room holding a stack of clothes. She smiles, "I brought y'all some of my things."

"Short shorts and tank tops?" I ask.

She flinches, "No." She places them on the dresser and turns.

"She didn't mean that," Anna says quickly and shoots me a dirty look.

I nod, "I'm sorry. I don't know why I said that." I'm not sorry and I do know why. What I don't know, is why she makes me so angry. Why I hate her. It's unnatural the amount of anger I have inside of me when she's around.

She gives me a look, "He's never picked me, you know. Since he met you, it's been you. Before you, it was no one. He never cares about anyone like that. He helps everyone but he doesn't let anyone in." She opens the door and leaves and I feel awful. I try to make it go away but it won't. It eats at me. It's a horrid feeling.

Anna laughs when she sees my face, "Oh, you feel like shit now, don't you?" She grabs some of the clothes and pulls them on. I sit on the bed and try to just let the bad feelings eat me up, like they're trying to.

"What is this?" I hold my stomach.

"Guilt. You feel guilty for hurting her, for no reason. You acted like a jerk and now you have to suffer through it until she forgives you, or you can go back to not giving a shit." She straightens the t-shirt and looks at me, "I feel amazing. That was incredible."

I look up at her and smile weakly, "Hot showers have to be the thing I miss the most about the real world.

The door flings open. I stand to see Star walking back in. She looks savage. Her hand comes back, I see it too late. The sting of her hand across my face burns instantly. She shouts, "That's for saying I dress like I want to be raped and always being hateful to me! I never did a thing to you!"

She turns and storms out of the room again. When the shock wears off, I smile at Anna, "That feels better in my stomach." I rub my cheek and glance at Leo, sleeping on the bed. His one open, yellow eye closes.

Anna laughs, "Even Leo thought you had that one coming."

I nod, "I did. At least she hits like a girl."

I pull on the clothes and walk out of the room after Anna. Star is leaned against the wall at the top of the stairs. She shakes her sobbing head, "I'm sorry."

I frown, "I deserved that. I had no right to say that about you. I have no right to judge you." Anna gives me a look I don't understand, but she isn't happy. She mouths, "SORRY!"

I stammer, "I-I'm s-s-sorry."

Star sniffles, "I just didn't understand why you hated me from the start."

I frown and look for answers; there are none. I hate that Will kissed me and then kissed her. I shake my head, "I just never was around other people."

Anna points laughing, "This is her—way more social. See how she doesn't really move her lips much, she never cries, and she is always kind of hard-ass? This is nothing. You should have seen how bitchy she was, when I met her. We've slowly been fixing her."

My jaw drops. Anna winks when Star smiles. I don't know what just happened, but I don't like it. I turn back to the room and grab my bow and quiver. Leo gives me a look. I nod. He climbs off the bed and follows me out of the room. Anna eyes me up, "You know it was a joke right?"

I nod, "I'm hungry." I'm starved actually. We haven't eaten much and I need something.

Star laughs, "He has tons of food downstairs."

My gaze narrows, "How?"

She shrugs, "He is a smart guy. He knew this was coming. He was preparing for years beforehand. He stays in the city for work and brings food."

I cross my arms, gripping my weapons, "He's your brother?"

She nods, "Stepbrother. My mom married his rich dad when I was little. They died almost right away, and me and Bernie came here."

I tilt my head, "How did you get caught?"

She shrugs and I see her sparkly eyes turn flat and dead inside, "I was stupid. I didn't want to listen to Bernie. I went out of the yard. He told me to stay here while he was going to the city. He didn't want me to come because I was at breeder age. He didn't think he would be able to protect me."

"How old were you?" I can't stop myself.

"Fifteen, almost sixteen. They made a few of us stay behind when they got to the farm." She shudders, "Then Will came. He was with Marshall. Will just kept hitting and hitting. They were dead but he couldn't stop. I can still hear the sound of it."

We all shudder together. She stares for a minute, I know she's reliving it. She shakes her head, "Then they brought me to the camps. I showed Will the way back to here. He and Bernie became friends. I went back to the camp with him. I couldn't stay here and do nothing. So I help the wounded, give massages and try to be of help."

I feel sick again.

Her eyes sparkle again, but it's the tears in them that makes them shine, "When Marshall betrayed you, I decided I was done. They don't want to fix things. Marshall wants to make it look like he's putting in an effort, but it's so that the camps will still run. He wants people motivated to work and gather and stay together but it's an act. He just doesn't want to do any of that shit alone. He may not have agreed to the breeder farms or the military, but he would be in that city, if it weren't for the fact he's diabetic."

Anna frowns, "He is?"

She nods, "Yup. The only reason he's out in the woods like that, is the diabetes. The city has a no-sickness law. I still think he traded you for a free pass. He knew what you were."

I swallow the bad feelings associated with those words, "How do you know?"

She winks, "He was fond of my massages. He told me when you came back from the breeder farms, that he figured you were one of the early seed-Gen babies from the breeder farms. One of the ones they experimented on early. He said you were dangerous like those kids in the cities—unruly and unpredictable. I could see it."

I flinched.

She shrugged and wiped her face, "He said that he could tell right away. Then you got ambushed and he admitted to being responsible. He said he was protecting the camps, but I think he did it to get a free pass to the city. Rebuilding a city has been his main focus for a few years."

Leo whines and yawns. I look at the bow, "I have to get him something to eat." I walk past them both, with Leo on my heels. We walk down the stairs and out the front door.

I hate that I'm a seed-Gen and that I'm different. I stalk across the concrete to the gravel and sigh, "Stupid gravel." We crunch along to the far side of the yard. It's huge and surrounded by a wall of massive trees. Leo crouches and runs into the woods. He disappears. I follow along and wait for my eyes to adjust. I pull an arrow and lean against a tree.

"I wouldn't go in there, Emma." I sigh again when I hear Will's voice calling me.

I whistle. Leo comes running back to my side. We leave the forest the same way we came in, "Why?" I call back.

"He booby traps everything to keep the infected out."

My hand instantly goes to Leo's fur. I grip it tight and walk back exactly the way we came. I'd seen yards like this.

He put his hands in his pockets. When I get close, I can see he's clean too. "He said to tell you, he has steaks and things for Leo."

I look at Leo and nod, "Ok."

He doesn't move, so I walk past him.

"Wait."

Turning, I see his clean-shaven face in the dim light of the sky, "What?"

"Star and me have never had anything. You know that, right?" His tone is low like he's testing the water. "You get that when I explained it before, it was the truth?"

"Yeah, she told me. I don't really care." I hate lying to him, but I hate him assuming I do care.

"She treats me the same way she treats everyone. She is just flirty and sweet to everyone."

I put my hands up, "It's fine."

"You don't need to be jealous or whatever..."

I cut him off, "STOP!" I storm past him, almost dragging Leo by the fur. I can feel the muttering trying to burst from me.

He grabs my arm and spins me around. My knee comes up fast but he jumps back, narrowly missing a hard hit to the groin.

I step back, "I said not to touch me. I'm not jealous of Star. Asshole." I back up, pulling an arrow and holding it on him.

He puts his hands up, "I'm sorry. I didn't mean like jealous. I meant..."

"I don't care what you meant. I'm done with it. We're friends. Let's be friendly; don't make me shoot you." I nudge Leo. He looks up at me and backs off Will, when he sees my face.

I turn and walk to the house, but my arrow stays taut in the bow. I don't look back at him; I listen to him. He walks behind me softly.

"I can't believe you almost hit me in the nuts," he calls out.

"You're lucky you're fast. I have boney knees," I mutter back.

Leo growls back at him.

"When is he going to quit hating me?"

I turn and shake my head, "When you stop scaring him. You act like all the fuckers he's saved me from. You think you're the first guy Leo has had to pull off of me? You think he hasn't dove in and saved me a thousand times? He hates men, just like I do. He doesn't trust them anymore than I do. You all seem to have one thing on your mind, and you seem to think you should be allowed to have it, even if we don't want to give it. Leo and me have seen things like that tons. Men grabbing arms and spinning girls. Making them kiss them and dragging them into the bushes. You know what that sounds like, when you're ten years old? You know what it sounds like, when people take what isn't theirs to have? It's enough to make you never want anything to do with anyone."

His face is pale in the night, "Em, you know I would never do that."

I shake my head and fight the god-damned tears that just keep coming, "No. No, I don't know that. Your own brother and sister don't know that. You act like... like..."

"You?"

I laugh, "Yeah. You act crazy like me, but you have no excuse. You had family and friends and people. I get you went to the farms Will, you suffered. Big deal. They didn't put a baby in your belly and then kill it just to see what it looks like."

He steps forward and I see the square of his jaw tense, "You think what happens to the women in the farms is more brutal than what happens to the men? You think they don't have it hard? You think

I don't wonder if any of those babies out there are mine too? Babies I won't ever know about or see. They took my rights too. The only difference is, I didn't get to go to sleep, Em. I was awake while they took it, and when they were done I got shoved into the work farms with all the other men." He spits on me with the last of his words. I didn't realize how close we were, until that moment. His breath huffs from him down on my face and I can see the steel in his blue eyes, even in the dark.

I don't know what to say. I don't even know, what I did say. His lip is trembling like he wants to say or do something that I think I want him to do. No matter what I do, I can't stop myself from wanting it. Leo senses it and presses his cold noise against my hand. I jump and step back.

"I'm hungry." I turn and walk away and promise myself that if he grabs my arm, I will shoot him in the damned leg.

When I get inside, I hear laughing; I walk towards it. Smells are like promises in the air of food and drink. I round a corner and walk towards the light. They're in a huge kitchen with lights and food spread across the long counter. I stop and stare. It's like the restaurants I went to with Granny. They had whole counters of food and you could pick what you wanted. Jake grins at me over a heaping plate of food. He motions for me to come. I hear Will and then feel the heat of his body pressed against the back of me.

I sigh and lean back into him, "That's a lot of food," I whisper.

Will speaks softly, "It's a lot of food. Bernie shops in the city. He's allowed in and out of the city."

I nod, "So, he's friends with my real dad then?"

Will's hand runs up my arm, "Put the bow down and come and eat. We can talk about it, okay?"

I look back at him and nod. I let him take the weapons from my hands. "I can still kill you with my bare hands."

He grins and looks like Jake for a second, "You don't have to, you have a pet wolf."

"I hate you," I laugh.

He nods, "I know. I'm okay with it."

I walk to the huge counter. Star passes me a large square plate. I've never seen anything like it. It's heavy and thick. I take some of everything. I don't even know what it all is. I know there's chicken, steak, potatoes and beans, but the rest are casseroles or something. They're all in tinfoil packets and steaming hot like TV dinners. I used to like the fried chicken TV dinner. I grab a fork and carry my plate through the door that Jake went through. Anna and Bernie are sitting next to each other talking. He's young looking, but I can tell he's older. He has dark hair and dark eyes and his skin isn't tanned but it's olive colored.

The eating room is fancy—everywhere in the huge house is fancy.

I sit next to Jake and look down on the plate. I don't know where to start. I dig the fork into the potatoes and take the first bite. It's hot, salty, and perfect. I close my eyes and moan.

I open them to see Bernie staring at me.

"What do you know?" he asks.

I shake my head, "Nothing."

He chews his bite, "Can you start at what you remember?"

I swallow and nod, "I know my dad moved us around a lot. Then he bought a health food store, my grandparents bought an old house, and we all lived together. My mom died when I was pretty little, so it was just us. They hated my uncle for having an affair with my mom. My dad brought it up a lot." It feels weird sharing the tiny details of the world before.

I look at Will as he sits next to Star and starts eating. Taking another bite, I continue, "My dad was always crazy about technology. He didn't like cell phones or computers much. Granny had them all, but she was pretty basic with them, looking up recipes and stuff. She let me have the technology though, but only for gaming, movies, and books. I wasn't allowed to interact with people online. We lived in a small area and my dad made me go to survival camps and made me do training on the weekends. He was obsessed with the end of the world. He called it the meltdown. He said the world was going to have a meltdown. We were supposed to go to the family cabin before the meltdown, but Granny and Gramps didn't believe. They wouldn't come. He would disappear a lot and I would stay with Gran. Then the sicknesses started and the chaos hit, before we could go to the cabin. He made arrangements for us to stay with his friend in a bunker. We left it too late to get to the bunker, and ended up ditching our car in the roadblocks, and running through the hills to the place where his friend lived. We stayed in the bunker for a while. It was supposed to be short term, until the chaos was over. He figured the sick would die off fast and we could just go to the cabin."

My mouth starts to water. I stop and take a drink from the glass in front of me. It's water. It sparkles in my mouth. I clear my throat and finish the story, "The day we left the bunker was the last time I saw my dad. He and Brian were fighting and I could feel the jeep driving over things, bumpy things on the road. People were still out... walking. Some were sick. Some were little kids who were alone. We drove until we couldn't, because of an accident. Something happened. The others or the military came and shot someone on the road and took the women. Dad kept saying it was just like the doctor had said it would be. Now I know it was the doctor who saved me in the city. He had warned my dad a few times about the bad stuff coming. Anyway, he and Brian started fighting again and the jeep crashed. Brian was gone and Dad was trapped and hurt. I crawled to his window but he couldn't move." I hold my empty hand out, "He held his hand out with nothing in it and made me take the nothing from him. Then he screamed at me and told me it was us and them and I was never to stop running. I knew how to get to the cabin, so I ran. I left him there to die in the jeep. I ran and I never looked back. I got to the cabin a few days later." I look at my empty hand and know it's the most I've ever said in my whole life.

I can't look at them all. I don't want to. I don't want their pity; I know it'll be there in their eyes.

I take the next bite and swallow, but the lump in my throat makes it hard.

Bernie speaks after a moment, "Lenny must have been the health food store owner and Michael is your uncle?"

I nod and force myself to keep eating. The salt and taste is gone though.

"I was twenty when the world ended. The CIA had scooped me up when I was nineteen. I saw this coming down the pipes. I started preparing immediately. My dad never used this house so I took it over and converted it; took it off the grid completely and started stockpiling." He talks like he's proud. He sips from his glass, "I helped build the new city and stayed in the good books, so I have access to food and things, but I don't believe the propaganda. The hype that only breeding the healthy will rid the world of the sickly, and forcing the sick to the borderlands, is the way to keep the city clean. The kids like you, they're maniacs. The ones your age aren't as bad, but the ones about thirteen and younger are insane. You dad is obsessed with perfecting them. He's turned into a monster himself. Too much playing God, if you ask me."

I lift my eyes from my plate, "Can you stop him?"

He nods, "Yup. We have to kill him. I'm sorry, there is no other way."

I shake my head, "Why have you waited until now? Why haven't you killed him before this?"

His eyes glisten, "He's a genius and very good at talking. I used to believe."

I frown, "What made you stop?"

He laughs and glances at his sister. I don't need any further explanation. She is oblivious to the fact, he has looked at her. Only Will and I caught it. He clears his throat, "I just stopped. I had heard about the originals—the first generation of babies. It was the early stages of it so very few women were impregnated. They weren't certain what they were doing, what the results would be.

You mom and a handful of women were impregnated under the guise of it being hormone therapy. I know Michael was outraged that his brother took you. He searched high and low for you. Lenny, was apparently a master of living off grid. Michael's parents hated the fact he had betrayed his own brother."

Anna chimes in, "How did Lenny know?"

Words form in my mind. Words I'd heard for years, that only now are making sense. They flash into my mind. "He was sterile," I mutter.

Bernie nods, "He was. He was sterile from a job he had done, when he was a young man in the army."

The words he ranted when he screamed at her, start to make sense, "They went for tests because she wanted a baby. He never told her, he was sterile. She thought it must have been her, but when she found out she was pregnant, he knew she'd had an affair with my uncle." I was under the kitchen table with my ponies and Disney princesses. I was little. I heard him yelling at her. I heard her crying.

He laughs, "She didn't remember the many times she'd come for treatments and whatnot. She would have thought it was hormone injections and regular doctor appointments. They all thought that."

My heart nearly stops. I look up at him, "They?"

He nods, "They. The other moms. They were all his kids."

The gleam in his eye disturbs me. I think it's respect, but I'm not sure. I feel horror and rage building inside of me.

I get up from the table. I wish I had brought the plate, but I don't. I just leave. I need to get away.

I run for the room and then the bathroom. I lock the door and sit on the toilet with the lid down.

"They?" I whisper into the darkness of the bathroom. "They?" I've had brothers and sisters all along. How many? I shake my head and try to block it all out. She had believed she'd had an affair, hadn't she? I remember that. She loved my uncle.

I drop to my knees and lift the lid. My stomach empties. I wipe my mouth and collapse onto the floor. What was happening to me? How had I become so soft and weak? I crawl to the door and open it. He comes in and I close it again. He curls around me. I don't cry. I don't have any tears left. I don't want to be that girl anymore, anyway. I dig my fingers into his fur and wait for the end of the world to come again. If I close my eyes I'm back home and we're in bed. It's soft and warm and the only thing I have to do tomorrow is laundry for one, find food for one and boil water for one. Leo can get his own.

But I open my eyes, and the world where everything I did for one is over. In its place, is a world where I can't see all the faces of the people who need me. They've become a sea of faces, and in the dream that starts to form in my exhausted mind, they all look like me.

Chapter Ten

The hard floor leaves me feeling bruised, when I push myself up. Leo yawns and stretches. I get a whiff of his dog breath and shudder. He doesn't seem offended by it. He continues to pant in my face. I pull back, shaking my head, "Oh that's bad, Leo. Wow. You need some mint leaves."

I always made him eat them, especially after eating the infected.

The bathroom is quiet. I listen beyond the door but nothing moves. I catch a glimpse of my face. It brings back the haunting dream. My greenish-blue eyes and light-brown hair stand out in my mind. I'm not an original—I'm a copy. My mom and uncle never loved each other. He used her, the way he now uses the world around us. She imagined it was love somehow. She was an idiot.

The hate in my eyes is cold and meaner than anything I've ever seen before. Leo scratching at the door, brings me out of the bad thoughts filling my head. My stomach grumbles and I swear I'll finish the meal before getting upset and running off again. God knows what else they have to tell me.

When I open the door, I have to jump back as Will falls inside on the floor. He sits up fast, like he's dizzy.

"What are you doing?" I ask.

He looks back, his eyes are tired and puffy. He shakes his head and rubs them, "Sleeping," he says it like I should have known he would be there.

He takes up the entire doorway, waking up and getting his bearings.

"You slept here all night?"

He nods and yawns, "I was going to crawl into the bed, but Anna was there, passed out with Bernie's cat. I tried waking her but the cat hissed at me." He pushes himself up and looks down on me,

"You alright?"

I shake my head, "I don't know. Where's the cat now?" I look past him, hoping it's gone. Leo loves cats in a bad way. A couple times they've come to me for a pet and a snuggle, which always ended badly.

"He ran off," he laughs and leans on the door, blocking me in, "You okay?"

Looking up into his blue eyes is like getting lost watching the water on a lake. I smile my fake pleasant one that I have used on people, who I was about to either rob or trick.

He doesn't buy what I'm selling, "It's okay if you're upset and want to talk about it."

I laugh, "Okay, you first. Let's share our feelings." It's cheeky and something I might have said a decade ago, when my dad was being a jerk.

Will laughs with me, "Breakfast?"

I nod and shove him through the doorway, "That sounds about right." Leo walks past us and through the door to leave the room. He makes sure he gives me one extra-crappy wolf look, like he's telling me he's watching and I better behave. It's the same look Granny gave me, when I was a kid. Lord knows, Leo is probably Granny reincarnated.

We walk down the hall to the stairs, where I catch a glimpse of Anna walking next to Bernie and leaving through the front door. I glance at Will.

He laughs, "Not every guy is a piece of shit looking to get laid, Em."

Leo is at the bottom of the stairs near the door. I run down them and open the front door, calling out to them as they cross the front grass that now resembles a field, "Take Leo! He wants out!"

She looks back at me and grins, patting her legs, "Come on, boy."

He looks up at me and then Will. I tilt my head and raise my eyebrow. He gives me the same look he did upstairs and saunters out the door after Anna. I watch them for a minute, before Jake comes walking over with Star. She's in long pants and a long-sleeve shirt. I have never seen her so covered before. I want to comment about the fact she even owns them, but I have a feeling it might be rude.

"What's crawled up your ass?" Jake asks as he peers out the door after his sister. Star giggles.

I shake my head, frowning and walking back inside. "Good to see you own pants, Star," I mutter and walk down the hall. If they can be rude to me for no reason, then I guess it doesn't matter, if I am too.

Will chuckles and walks after me, "You know sometimes you are a real bitch."

I look back at him with daggers in my eyes, "No one asked you to come. In fact, I recall not even telling you I was leaving."

The table had food spread across it again. I grab a plate and load up with sandwiches, cheese, meat and apples—real apples. Not applesauce or apple butter or canned fruit. I sit on a very high stool, like the ones that were in the café Granny liked.

Will goes around the counter and piles a plate up extra high, "I know you think you can do everything alone and you don't need help, but you aren't alone. Maybe you don't need us but we're here."

I frown and shove meat into my mouth. I block him out as he rambles. I know if Bernard tries anything on Anna, Leo will eat his ass. I hope that if Star tries anything on Jake, he won't have any issues telling her to take a hike.

"Did you hear me?" he asks.

I shake my head, "I'm hungry and tired and not really in the mood for a lecture. I got plenty when I was a kid."

He takes a bite of a sandwich and shakes his head, "You need to listen to me—we need a plan for the city. If we show up, they're going to grab us and put me in a work camp and you in a breeder farm."

I pick at the meat on my plate and narrow my gaze, "The doctor/nurse angle doesn't work?"

He shakes his head, "I don't know."

"Why are you helping me with this?"

He snorts and finishes the bite, "Because I want you, Emma. I want you and me, and that god-damned wolf, to go and live and be together. If I have to endure getting bit and shoved to the ground every day for the rest of his life, I will. If I have to walk into the lion's den and help you kill your dad so you can go back to being a hermit, I will."

I don't trust him, or his words. "That's a lot of work for some sex. You could probably get yourself a nice girl, who won't make you jump through hoops every time you try to get near her."

He grins wide, like he's about to boast, but he doesn't say anything. He winks at me and opens a can of something. He takes a drink and makes a face. I can't fight the laugh.

He puts it down and shivers like he's gotta pee. "Oh my—wow. Oh God. That's shit. Don't drink that." he shudders again.

I snicker and finish my plate of food. I haven't felt full and relaxed in a long time. It's making me tired.

I get up and leave him in the kitchen. I need a nap in a bed, not on the bathroom floor.

Climbing the stairs, I notice the strangest feeling I have ever felt overwhelming me. I don't care. I'm tired and beaten down and I don't care. Anna is going to have to take care of herself. Leo will protect her, but I'm too tired to run out there and monitor her with a thirty-year-old man. Something is wrong with me, but I'm too tired to figure it out or go over the feelings I have.

I climb into the bed Anna and I were going to share, and pass out, almost instantly.

When I wake, I feel warmth next to me. I reach out for him to run my hands through his fur. There is no fur and he stirs and clears his throat. I open one eye and frown, "Why are you in here?"

Jake smiles, "I was worried. You've been sleeping for like eight hours and you seem weird. Thought you might want to talk about it all."

I shake my head, "Tired, too tired."

I close my eyes and let the bed take me again. I feel his fingers brush through my hair.

"Em, you don't have to be so strong. You can let me in."

I open one eye, "There is nothing to let in. I'm a science experiment. My real father is a bowl of mixed ingredients, my mom was an idiot who was tricked easily, and my dad was the only person who ever tried to keep me safe from this all. Well, Dad and Granny and Gramps. I still have to stop him, I have to. I need to end this." I close my eyes and nestle into the blankets. He wraps his arm around me and pulls me into him. It feels nice, like the sleep on the couch, when he had a fever and kissed me. I don't want him to kiss me now though. I want him to hold me and care about me, but I don't want him to kiss me. It's not like that for me, even if I want it to be.

I drift off again.

My eyes shoot open when I hear a scream. It had blended into my dream at first, but with my eyes open, I know I'm not dreaming. Jake is passed out on the bed. I shake him till he stirs.

"You hear that?"

He shakes his head, "What?" The scream rips through the halls again. It's a high moan.

"Infected," I whisper.

He moves closer to me. I grab my bow and quiver from the floor and pass him Anna's rifle, "Don't shoot me."

He makes a face, "Funny."

We climb off the bed, moving slowly. The sound comes again, only now I think there are two.

The little hairs on my body are standing on end. Peeking around the corner of the doorframe, I see nothing. I slip into the hall. I can feel the heat from Jake behind me. I ignore him and focus.

I hear the ragged breathing coming from the bottom of the stairs.

When I reach the end of the hall, I see the matted dirty head of the sick. It was once a lady with long, dark hair. She had ripped pants and shirt. Her body is emaciated with backbones showing through the holes in the ripped clothing. Old scabs, running sores, and the ragged breath are the things I focus on. I pull back the arrow I've pulled and let it go at her head. It slices like it would have a watermelon. Jake gags. I ignore him and walk down the stairs, past the dead lady. Her stink and rotting flesh bring the fear of the real world into the safe haven we have been enjoying. When I get to the kitchen, I see him. He's shoveling food from the counter into his decayed face. He eats a piece of napkin with cheese on it.

Behind a cupboard to the left, I catch a glimpse of a reflection in the steel fridge. It's Anna. She's holding a knife. I pull the next arrow and hold it steady at him. He looks up from his meal, flashing a milky eye at me. I release the arrow as he screams the high-pitch moan.

"Anna?" I whisper.

She slips from behind the cupboards, "They came up the driveway so fast."

My heart starts to panic, "Where's Leo?"

She swallows, "Outside still."

I hate the look in her eyes. She's scared of me or scared to tell me something.

I turn and run for the front door. The hot air of the summer day hits me, as I run from the shade of the front porch. I see him, fighting four of them. I pull the arrows fast. I take down the first one closest to me and run closer. I have the second arrow pulled and ready. I watch the head of the monster bob and move. I release the arrow and miss.

"Shit," I mutter.

I pull another and take him down.

Leo takes the third to the ground, but the fourth one jumps on his back. I pull an arrow and hit the large infected in the back. He doesn't flinch or stop. I pull another but it hits him in the arm and almost hits Leo. I pull another but run at them. I dive onto the pile. As his slimy face turns to face me, I stab the arrow down on his eye. He stops as Leo rips the head off the one he's got. He looks back at me and growls. I get off him and the dead. Looking around, I see we are not alone. They came in a huge group, the biggest I've ever seen. They are a swarm, like in the city.

My breath is heavy as I assess the situation.

Only Leo and I can fight them. Everyone else risks exposure. I still don't believe I'm immune, I can't help but feel like I should run.

Jake comes out the front with the rifle.

I walk back slowly, watching them shuffle towards me. One scream fills the air. I shudder.

Will comes out the front door, snatching the rifle from Jake's hands. He tosses me a gun like I have never seen before. I shake my head, "You use this one." I pass it back and take my rifle. I site the first one in. They're moving quickly across the gravel to us.

The sound of their crunching feet on the driveway is frightening. I pull the trigger and a body drops. Will does the same.

"You should go inside and lock the doors, take them with you," I say, mostly because there are too many for me to fight them and worry about him.

He shakes his head, "After you."

I grit my teeth and pull it again. I drop the rifle and pull my bow and quiver again. I can shoot faster with arrows. Leo crouches and attacks to the far flank. He knows if we're shooting he needs to stay to a side.

I drop two more and see a shape beside me. I glance over as Anna grabs the gun and starts shooting. The three of us have enough distance to kill them, plus the few Leo kills. The ones who weren't killed properly twitch in the driveway, as the last one falls to the ground.

Bernie comes out of the house with a mask and gloves and an odd-looking contraption. He walks up to the infected dead and shoots flames at them. Some scream or twitch. I gag when the smell of the cooking flesh hits me.

"Leo."

He lifts his head and looks at me. I slap my leg and walk to the side of the house. I pull the garden hose that I gave him water from the other day. He comes and lets me hose him off. Normally, I would find a water source and force him to have a bath, but this works. I spray chunks of skin and bone from him. The dark blood is harder to get off. He lifts his face and lets me clean his muzzle. We've been doing it since we were little; he knows the routine.

I spray myself off and glance over at Will and Anna talking, "I'm going to shower and then I'm leaving."

Anna scowls, "We should stay here for a while."

I shake my head, "You're staying, I'm going."

Her blue eyes light up with her stubborn fire. She and Will make the same face. "I'm coming."

I shake my head, "No. You're not coming. Most likely, I'll end up in a breeder farm. You definitely will. I can lie and say I'm twenty-eight—you can't. Will is older too. They won't breed us if they think we're older. We can look like professionals. Bernie is going to take us in, like he's on a food run." I've come up with the plan while I was sleeping for a whole day.

Will nods, "That works."

I give Jake a look too, "You and Anna will be safe here with Star and Bernie."

Jake crosses his arms and leans against the doorway, "I don't think this is a good idea for one, and for two, I can pass for twenty-eight far better than you can."

I shrug, "Yeah, but you have sucky survival skills and you'll be a liability."

His face tightens, "Whatever." He turns and leaves for the inside of the house.

I walk after him, but grab the feet of the infected lady. I drag her out into the front yard. I walk back in, grabbing the feet of the guy, and do the same thing. I look under the sink for cleaner.

"What are you looking for?" Star asks.

I turn back to her, "Bleach."

She walks past me and into a doorway. She comes back, seconds later with a huge jug. I pour it onto the stone floor and start cleaning the greenish blood from the floor.

She grabs rags and starts helping.

"You should have a mask," I say.

"I'm immune," she mutters.

Instantly I feel sick. I look up, "What?"

She nods, "I can't get it. I'm like you. It's how I knew Marshall was right about you."

The reality of it all starts to hit, "How old are you?"

She swallows hard, "same age as you."

I frown, "What?"

She nods, "We have the same dad, I guess."

I don't want it to, but it changes everything. She is instantly part of my 'us'. "Your mom?"

She nods, "Yeah. She wanted a baby and there was a fertility clinic. My dad was older. He couldn't have kids easily. She went for treatments and got pregnant. The man she was with died and she met Bernie's dad. He became my dad. I thought I was his, but Bernie told me the truth a few years ago. We noticed the differences." She flashes a scar on the underside of her arm, "And I got bit."

I gasp, "You were bit?"

She nods, "Yeah. Bernie figured it out. It changed everything for him. He stopped working in the city so much, moved out here where he had the house off the grid anyway."

I had assumed it was the rape of Star that changed everything.

Her face lightens, "You know it doesn't matter who our dad was. Bernie's dad raised me, he was sweet and kind and he loved me. My dad from before Bernie's dad, was a sweet man too. That's the people that matter. The man in the science lab doesn't matter."

I scowl, "Why did Marshall let you stay but kicked me out?"

She grins, "I hide my mutant blood better than you do. He never knew. But when he turned you out, I left, just in case."

"You heal fast?"

She nods, "And I run fast. And I'm strong."

I snicker, "You hit like a girl."

She sticks her tongue out, "I blend."

I feel a cold shiver and wipe up more of the dirty, bleached goo off the floor.

Bernie walks in, stinking of cooked, rotten flesh. He grins, "You girls having a chat?"

I narrow my gaze.

He grins like a fool, "Small world, huh?"

I don't know what that means. I look back at the floor and clean.

"Emma, I am coming too. You are not leaving me here," Anna

comes storming into the kitchen.

I see something in the corner of my eye and am up fast. I grab her arm and hold it out, "What's this?"

She looks down at the greenish goo and red blood on her arm.

"It's their blood—I fought with one in the yard before we made it inside. I'm going to wash it now."

I close my eyes, "They don't have red blood, Anna."

I hear Will's footsteps, "What's going on?"

"She's got a cut with infected blood all over it," I mutter and pull her to the sink.

Will crosses the floor fast. He grabs her arm and holds it out, "For fuck's sake, Anna. What is this?"

Her lip trembles but her eyes stay hard and focused, "I didn... didn't know."

"Pour the bleach on it," Star nods at the huge jug.

I look at her and Bernie and wish it were one of them. Bernie nods, "We can wash the cut with bleach, but wiping the infected blood might force it into the wound."

My hands tremble when I hold her arm out. Will's tremble equally as he lifts the huge jug. Anna's eyes glisten, "If I get sick, you kill me, okay? I don't want to wander around killing things."

I shake my head, "We'll find a cure."

Will looks like he might just tear the arm off. He barks at me, "Hold it over the sink!"

I drag her arm over the metal sink. He looks at her, "This is gonna sting."

She bites down hard and nods. He pours it and she starts screaming.

I feel my own body reacting, like it's happening to me too. I'm clenched and scared and shaking with her arm. I hold it out as he wipes with a clean rag. The green goo is gone, and in its place, is a whitened, deep gash. The edges of it start to look like cooked chicken. She writhes in agony.

He pours once more and wipes again. I turn on the tap and pour cold water over the wound. Bernie passes me soap. I wash my hands first and then the bleached wound. It feels toughened and hard. We've scarred her arm brutally.

Tears stream down her cheeks, as she sniffles and sucks in her air in jagged breaths. Will washes his hands and wraps his arms around her.

"Emma, come clean her in the shower now!" he barks again.

I follow.

Jake follows too. He looks sick. I imagine we all look the same.

Will leaves her in the bathroom with me and a plastic bag, "All clothes in the bag."

I rip mine off first and then hers. I start the shower and drag her in. She is still crying and holding her arm.

"I'm gonna get sick and die, Em," she whispers through the tears. I haven't seen her like this since the front door of my cabin.

I make lather with the soap and clean my whole body. The lye soap stings against my skin. I rinse and make the lather. I scrub her body like I would Leo. I don't think about the fact, I'm touching another person. I think about saving my family.

I wash her hair and pick the tangles with the conditioner. It's the same stuff as at the breeder farms. It's disturbing how much I like the familiar smell.

We stand under the water in silence. She glances up at me and shakes her head, "You don't let me infect them. You kill me. You swear to me now."

I nod, "I swear." The sick part is, I do. I would kill her if I had to. I would kill anyone, except Leo. I know I couldn't ever kill him.

Chapter Eleven

The dusty road we take isn't like the one we came in on. It's a back road with no broken-down cars or burned-out vehicles that have become giant planters.

"The city is not like anything you've seen before. People live without engaging each other too much. They don't really speak to one another on a deep level, it's fake and functional. They're pleasant, overly pleasant. Everyone is afraid of everyone else, like they will be turned in to the officials. If you break one of the five laws, you are either sent to a work farm or sent to the borderlands.

I frown, "What's wrong with the borderlands?"

He looks at me in the rearview, "I will bet living in the borderlands was hard, even for you, in the beginning?"

I nod, "I was ten. Don't get me wrong, your shower is amazing and having food so easy is too. But wasn't that, all the stuff that brought us down in the first place? Why aren't we trying to rebuild and be simple? They should be grateful to go to the borderlands and discover the true meaning of rebuilding the world."

He shrugs, "Well, imagine it's the beginning for you all over again. These people have lived a cushy life for a while. Most of them never leave the cities, except to work in the breeder farms. They believe that they're trying to make a difference. They believe that the only way to save humanity, is to breed out the sickness and disease, by breeding people of superior quality. They believe they are the best of the best quality people. Most of them see the sickness of greed, disease, and war mongering as the evils that existed."

I cock an eyebrow, "Why don't they breed themselves and just stay in their perfect city then, and leave the rest of us alone?"

He nods, "Oh, they will. They are starting to rebuild society. There is controlled breeding within marriages now."

I shake my head, "I don't understand why they still keep the breeder farms open then?"

His eyes dull, "He's obsessed with perfect people. He wants to build an army of perfect people to protect the future from ever becoming the decayed society, we once were. People like you and Star who don't need a lot to live, who never get sick and need treatments. Me, Jake, Anna, and Will will probably get cancer one day from the fallout. Most people will. The soil, water and air were all polluted. We will get cancer. It's inevitable. We've all made the mistake of eating things people find or grow and drinking water from contaminated wells. The borderlands are worse than anywhere else. There isn't a lot of healthy food. The retreats and camps are better than the towns. The towns are really bad."

I nod, "You sound like my dad."

He raises his eyebrows, "He probably knew a lot about the conspiracies. I guarantee he knew about you and what his brother did. It's all very disturbing. It probably tainted your dad, made him crazy and obsessed. I know I have moments. Some things disturb me. You know why the breeders are killed off? 'Cause they get sick after three breeder babies. They can only ever have three at a max. The babies are designed to take everything from the mother, like a parasite in a host. It makes a very healthy baby but leaves the mom weak. By the third pregnancy, those women are dying, they just don't know it."

I look up at Will. He bites his lip and looks away from me.

"If we stop the breeder farms and destroy the work camps, what are the odds people will just go back to normal?" I ask after a minute.

He shakes his dark head, "I don't know, Emma. There are a lot of believers. They did have a tough time in the very beginning. They did live a rough life in the start."

"What about the people who don't believe?"

Will turns and looks at me, "We lived amongst them at the camps. Those are the non-believers. They don't believe in the breeder farms or the work camps. Most of the scientists I encountered, hated it. They saw the unnatural selection it all was."

I don't get it. I process it and shake my head, "No. The people in the camps didn't even know how the breeder farms worked, until we discovered the girls were dying."

Will sighs, "Yeah, but they knew the breeders existed and disagreed. I'm sure Marshall knew all along; you can't tell me, he didn't."

I make a face, "The cities must know how it all works. They work the farms."

Bernie nods, "Most people know how the work camps and farms function. They probably would disagree if it was their family members, but it's dirty borderlanders. They believe— they believe it's for the greater good."

I cross my arms and lean against Leo. He pants and watches me get further annoyed. I twitch my foot. I still haven't worked out how Leo can come with me. He refused to stay with Anna, even after I shouted at him. He isn't even holding a grudge, which normally he would. He hates being shouted at.

I nuzzle my face into his fur and take in deep breaths. He smells like the forest still, somehow. If I close my eyes, I can feel the trees against me.

Will grabs my arm, "You have to be civilized."

I scowl, "I can do that just fine."

He gives me a look that makes my cheeks blush, "Em."

I chew my lip and then sigh, "I think I can. I remember when I was a girl and Granny would swat me for saying rude things and being mean. She was always swatting after me. When her friends were there, I was to be seen and not heard. I was to cross my legs nicely and not chew with my mouth open." My brain almost hurts trying to remember the many rules she gave me. "Uhm, she said I had to keep my elbows off the table, not bring animals in the house, always flush when I was done, and always wash my hands." I tap my fingers against my legs and point at him as a smile breaks across my lips, "Not to interrupt people when they were talking, with stupid thoughts that could have waited till they were done."

He looks at Bernie and both of them burst into laughter.

I scowl, "What?"

Will shakes his head, "You were just a little savage weren't you, even before the world ended."

I cross my arms and lean back into Leo, "No. I watched Days of Our Lives with Granny and read her books. She liked Dean something and Stephen something and V.C. something. Her favorite was a highlander romance series about a guy named Jamie and a lady named Claire. It was sad." My cheeks heat up as I recall the details of that book. They have stayed with me forever. "Diana Gabaldon. I won't ever forget her name." I can't help but wish Will was more like the Jamie guy. He was perfect.

Bernie gives me a worried look in the rearview mirror, "You read those books when you were ten?"

I nod, "And eleven and twelve and thirteen. She left bags of books at the cabin. She read when she was there. Nothing else to do. They never hooked it up to electricity. Dad insisted it stay off the grid, like you."

He smiles, "You were born for this weren't you?"

I shrug and look out the window. I have a feeling they're laughing at me, even if they aren't laughing out loud.

"She was born to fight. Look at the scowl on that face," Will points back at me.

I laugh and shake my head, "You're a jerk."

"Emma, seriously though, you need to behave. One slip up will ruin the whole thing."

I glare at Bernie, "I know that. I'm not an idiot. I know Anna is at risk. I saw the gash this morning." I think about the sweaty feel to her skin and fight the ache in my heart. Her situation is making our trip to the city a two-part excursion.

My stomach stays a ball of nerves as we approach. I don't see anything different, until we round a corner and I see the white tips of something rising above the trees. It glistens in the sun.

"There it is."

A shiver creeps up my back as I lean forward and point, "Stop here."

He looks confused but pulls over. I open the door and look at Leo, "You know the drill, okay?"

He stretches and jumps from the back of the big truck. Leo stands on his back legs and puts his front paws around my neck. I hug him and whisper into his fur, "Stay away from the people, okay? I'll whistle if I need you." I run my fingers through his fur extra. I need to get the extra touches to stock pile them in my memory.

"I love you, Leo."

He makes his purring sound and hops down. He looks at Will, then me, and runs off into the woods. I see him darting towards the city. My guts burn. I don't want him to be here.

I ignore the feeling and get back inside.

"He'll be fine," Will puts a hand on my leg. I move away from his grip, "He shoulda stayed behind. He's stubborn as shit."

My hands start to sweat as we near the city. The clean pants and t-shirt itch. They were fresh from a package. Never washed or worn. I don't like them. They don't even fit right, but Bernie says everyone wears free-flowing clothes, too tight stores toxins in the body.

The linen pants and shirt feel nice in the summer heat though. Only my hands are sweaty and that's not from the heat. I drag them up and down my pants. I wish I had my bow. Clutching that would make me feel a whole lot better.

I feel the cold, mean look crossing my face. It's like a piece of my self-defense. I can't be around other people without a bitchy look crossing my face.

The city comes into full view. It looks like something from The Wizard of Oz. It's amazing. It glistens in the sun and makes me feel inspired. I don't want to wreck it suddenly.

"You should have stayed back at the house. They're going to know you're not older than twenty-eight." Will adds his own version of a confidence booster, as we arrive close to the gates, of what appears to be, a guard blockade. It's like what Meg told me about. Bernie slows and puts the window down. I can't tear my eyes from the magnificence in front of me.

"Less star-struck," Will whispers. I close my mouth and look at the man approaching us. He has a dark-blue uniform and a huge gun in his hands. He looks a bit older than me and very serious.

Bernie hands him a card like the ones that open the doors to the breeder farms.

"Doctor Sinclair, how are you?" the man asks.

Bernie shrugs, "Getting warm with the windows open."

The man looks past him and nods in my direction, "Who are your friends?"

I watch his dark-blue eyes and wonder if everyone has blue eyes now. His dark hair makes them seem brighter than they are.

Bernie points at Will, "This is Doctor Henderson and that is his nurse. They are guests of mine from a farm a ways out."

He raises an eyebrow, "They have ID cards too?"

Will hands the man his card, "Here's mine."

I pass mine and notice how sweaty my hands are. I wonder if the fake ID card is wet from it.

He looks them over and passes them back, "Okay. Move ahead."

He looks directly at me, "Have a great trip. I hope you enjoy the city."

I nod once. I don't know if I should smile or not.

We drive to the next stop where we are checked quickly for infection and diseases. When we pass through, I'm almost hyperventilating.

Bernie smiles back as we drive into the small city, "You don't have to fret; all those explosions you caused, destroyed any evidence they had on you."

I shake my head in jerks, "They had me in Spokane."

He raises an eyebrow and grimaces, "Oh. I'm sorry."

"Why?"

He brushes it off, "No reason. You made it out—that's the big stuff."

Will looks back at me with a confused look, but I don't take my eyes from Bernie. "What happens in Spokane?"

His eyes dart from mine to Will's and back to the road. "Death experiments. It's where they keep the infected and experiment on them. The old hospital is used to try to find cures, and what the connection is, with the ones who don't die. Most die. It's only like seven percent who live on with the disease."

I shudder, "Seems like a heck of a lot more than seven percent." I look out at the glass and marble city. It's bright and clean like the farms.

"It's like all the color and personality that makes us human is gone," Will mutters and looks out at the people walking in boring colors and not talking.

"They look like robots don't they? It's like a science fiction movie from the early two thousands," Bernie agrees.

I never really watched them, but I can see what they're saying. The people are wooden. Just as I am certain I am seeing the same people walk by, as if the scenery is repeating itself, I see the thing that everyone has spoken of. A small group of four kids about Meg's age walk together down the sidewalk. They have a gleam in their eyes and a swagger to their walk that is menacing. I get a bad feeling in my belly when I see them. One glances at me as we drive past. He smirks at me. I don't like that look. I don't like them.

"They're creepy," I whisper.

We drive past a building that looks familiar. Then I realize it's identical to the breeder farms. My nose wrinkles involuntarily.

The whole city becomes creepy. The kids and the breeder buildings taint it. I nod to myself; I can blow this place up.

"Do they have a back-up explosion button here?"

Bernie looks at me and shakes his head, "No. We'll have to bring in the explosives."

I shrug, "We need to figure out where we'll put it all anyway." I know nothing about blowing things up. I did it when I had to, but the explosives were there.

Bernie pulls into a wide doorway and drives down. My skin prickles as we drive into the darkness. I see other cars but no people. The lights on the front of truck show little dark corners everywhere. I shake my head.

Warmth covers my hands. I turn them over and let Will grip me.

"I don't want to be here. I don't like it down here."

Will squeezes, "It's okay, baby. Stay calm. Remember people will be watching."

I shake, "I don't see people. Just dark corners." The truck turns another corner. I can feel panic starting to become anger. I don't like dark corners in buildings. I don't like new places where I don't know the way out. I close my eyes and stop looking. I take a deep breath, seeing Leo's face. His sloppy-wolf face. I know if I whistle, he will come. If I panic, he will come. He always comes.

I grip Will and know he always comes too. We will get out of the city. Everything is going to be okay. I chant it and pray I'll start believing it.

I open my eyes as the truck stops in a dimly-lit spot. I look at Bernie, "Where are we?"

He points to a door to the left, "My house in the city."

The doctor in Spokane fills my mind. I look around at the vehicles parked and whisper, "Parkade."

Bernie looks at me and laughs, "You remember them?"

I shake my head and touch my fingers to the cold glass, "No."

Will jumps out and opens the door for me. He wraps his hand around mine again. I'm shaking.

"Why can't we ever just fight shit in the woods? I'm good in the woods," I mutter and let him drag me from the truck. We walk around it to the door. It's big and metal. Bernie slides his card and it opens. The doors lock here too? No one trusts anyone. Everything is clean and white and shiny but it's dead here too. They just make the death nicer looking than the dusty shit we deal with out in the borderlands.

I let go of Will's hand as we walk through the door. I see a girl a little older than me. She doesn't look at me. I watch her—the way she avoids our eye contact, only looking at things, and somehow watching me in her peripheral.

She is in the same sort of pants as me, the tan linen but her shirt is baby blue and mine is pale purple. I think Granny would have called it violet.

Her hair is shiny and clean. I know I don't look like that. My skin is tanned and freckled where hers is creamy. She looks like a breeder.

Her green eyes dart at mine momentarily.

Guess not everyone has blue eyes.

Bernie walks down the hall past her. We follow.

She smiles at Will. I see a blush rise in her cheeks and roll my eyes. When we round the corner, I glare up at him, "We can't bring you anywhere can we?"

He looks confused, "Who?"

Bernie looks back confused and opens a door for us. When we walk inside I am awestruck. "People live like this? Freely?" I can feel the dirt coating my skin, compared to the white of the room and the wide-open bright space. The room is bigger than any tent I've seen and brighter than any houses I've hidden in.

Will whistles, "Haven't seen a house like this in a while."

I feel sick, "People die in the woods from no water and no food or eating the wrong thing, and here in the city, you all are living like this? I was in a town a few years ago and the people there were so dirty and skinny, they were eating their dead."

Bernie makes a face and puts his hands up, "I didn't make this war, Emma."

I look at Will for support, but he shakes his head, "We can't focus on the small things. We gotta save Anna."

I swallow it down, the anger and pain. I fight my urge and want to rant or smash things.

Will starts laughing and points out the window, "I can see a group of those little kids beating someone up. I always imagined it was a crazy story to scare people."

We walk to where he is, and sure enough, there is a group of kids beating someone in the alley between the tall buildings. No one stops it. No one even looks at it. They walk past the alley and ignore that it's going on. A van comes tearing around the corner, stopping feet from them. Men in white suits jump out and chase the kids down. It's like watching TV when I was little.

"Why doesn't he stop making them, if they are like this?" I mutter, touching my fingers to the cold glass.

"I don't know. He's convinced he can control them and they'll outgrow their tempers and bad behavior," Bernie stands next to me and sighs, "He doesn't see. None of them do."

I shake my head, "What a waste of time and technology. He built this city and this life, but for what? So those freaks can overrun it and destroy everything he's worked for? Makes no sense."

I turn away from it, looking out at the city. It's small but everything gleams from the glass and metal. It looks new but the people don't. "Everyone looks like they do in the borderlands. They aren't dressed fancy."

Will walks to where I am. The heat of his body so near mine makes me shiver, "There are no factories or cotton fields or anything. They haven't made a new world, they just put up walls and made a bunch of places to live. The work farms get them food and essentials, but really they aren't much different than the rest of us. The furnishings and clothes are scavenged."

Bernie gives us a grim look, "Except they have an army and a population of people. We feel safer in a group. People naturally want to be around other people. We used to say that before, safety in numbers."

I nod, "I feel safe here. I'm not—I'm not comfortable with the walls and the possibilities, but I feel safe. I could close my eyes and sleep and know nothing is going to kill me in the night."

He shrugs, "And yet, this is the most dangerous place for someone like you."

I watch his face when he says it. He doesn't attach emotions to the things he says, unless it's sarcasm. He has plenty of that. I wonder if he ever cries or feels scared.

Will grabs my shoulders, "Let's rest and then we'll head out in the night."

Bernie points to a door to the right of us, "That's the guest room."

Before I realize what's going on, Will takes my hand and pulls me to the door. When he opens it, I frown and look back at Bernie, "Is there another room?"

He points to the door on the other side of the apartment, "Mine." He grins like he's daring me. I look up at Will, "You should go sleep with him."

He laughs and pulls me into the room, closing the door behind us, "I'm not leaving your side. I'll sleep on the chair."

I look at the tiny chair and the not-so-tiny bed and sigh, "No. Just stay on your own side of the bed."

I strip my boots off and climb into the sheets in my pants. I hate bringing the filth of the day into bed with me, but these clothes are cleaner than my body.

I close my eyes and pretend I don't notice the heat or weight of him on the bed next to me.

I drift away fast, mostly because he is there. He is the safest thing in the world. Him and Leo.

I wake feeling heat under and around me and moan. I try to run my fingers through the fur but I find skin, hot skin. I open one eye to find myself splayed across him, like I do to Leo. I feel moisture under my face and wince. I lift my hand slowly to wipe away the spit I've left all over him. I glance up, hoping to find him sleeping still, but I find his grinning face instead.

"Evening, ma'am."

I gulp, "Sorry." I wipe the spit with the sheet.

He laughs, shaking us both and hugs me down onto his chest again. "For a shy prude of a girl you are a naughty sleeper." I pull back but his thick arm traps me to him, "Oh, you aren't going anywhere now. You've been rubbing me and squeezing me all afternoon."

My heartbeat picks up. I feel panic. His words are threats in my brain, but his gentle smile and blazing eyes don't scare me. He doesn't scare me. I realize it now. It's been a game in my mind to keep him at bay, I scare me.

He rolls me on my side, trapping me. It feels tight, constraining but I like it. Like we are in a cocoon.

My hands tremble where they press into his chest.

He smiles devilishly and presses his lips against mine. The heat and intensity of him pressing against me, makes sparks where our skin connects.

His tongue slides into my parted lips. I kiss the way he does, slipping my tongue against his. Our wet lips caress and suck each others. He sucks my tongue and I catch a moan escaping me.

My breathing increases with my hands movements. I knead his thick, muscled back, gripping him and pulling him down on me.

He moves between my thighs, pressing himself against me. I don't know what's happening, but I'm pressing myself against him back. He's gentle and delicate with his kisses and caresses. His hand rubs from my lower leg to my upper thigh. He breaks our kiss and gently kisses my throat. He cups my butt cheek firmly, lifting me almost.

It's not how I imagined it, none of it. He's soft and delicate. He sits back and opens the buttons on my shirt softly, he plants a kiss on my exposed skin as each button comes off. He opens the shirt. My hands naturally lift to cover me. As I cover my breasts, my walls start rebuilding themselves. I shake my head, "No."

He nods and laughs, "Okay." He climbs off the bed and pulls on his shirt. He's panting, we both are.

He looks at me and I see something I've never seen from him—understanding. He isn't mad, he isn't mean, he isn't being sarcastic or rude. He gets it. He sees how scared I am.

I frown and take an inventory of my feelings. I'm not scared. I want him. I want him to climb back into the bed. I want him to rub against me again.

I look at the door and nod, "See if it locks."

He furrows his brow, "What?"

I swallow, still covering myself, "See if it locks."

He starts to get what I'm saying, "It does. I locked it when we came in."

I take a deep breath and remove my hands from my chest. I put them on the bed, gripping the sheets that are still warm from his body being there.

He arches an eyebrow and I nod in tiny twitches. He pulls his shirt off and drops his pants. He takes a step in his underwear and gives me the look once more. I take him in. His body is beautiful. He's muscled and smooth and I want to slowly touch every inch of him. My eyes dart to his underwear and nod, "Yes." I want to touch every inch.

He climbs into the bed and pulls back the covers. His fingers tremble as much as mine do, as he pulls off my pants. We are both just in a pair of underwear. He loops his fingers into the sides of mine.

"Last chance."

I smile, "Yes."

A grin breaks across his face as he pulls them down and I stifle the heart attack, I'm pretty sure I'm having.

Chapter Twelve

I feel different.

I knew I would, but I wasn't expecting it to be as much as it is.

It's a lot.

He keeps giving me a weird look, like he's scared of me or for me. I can just see it in his face, thanks to the last of the sunlight coming in the window.

I frown finally, "What?"

His cheeks are still flushed. He shakes his head and licks his lips, "Nothing. Are you okay?"

I frown, "Why?"

"It's just not what I was expecting."

The comment hurts my feelings—feelings I didn't know could get hurt. I feel myself pulling away.

He sees my look, "In a good way. Not what I was expecting in a good way."

I freeze, "We should get going." I don't want to talk about it and his face is weird. He looks a bit like I imagine Jake would, self-conscience or nervous. He doesn't have the cocky Will face I'm used to.

He pulls me into his chest again and kisses the top of my head, "I love you, Em."

I look up, "Are you okay?"

He laughs, "Yeah, why?"

I shake my head, "You're acting like a girl."

He laughs, "Want me to rough you up a bit?" He cocks an eyebrow.

I roll my eyes, "I'll still shoot you."

He kisses again, "I know you will."

The awkwardness in the air is interrupted by a knock, thankfully.

"You guys ready to go?"

Wili clears his throat, "Yup. Out in two." He looks at me, "You should stay here."

I grimace, "What?"

"Yeah, I was thinking you should stay here, in case we get caught."

I pull back, "No."

His eyes narrow, "It's not safe."

I shake my head, like I'm trying to rattle his words out of my brain. I climb off the bed and fish my underwear and pants out of the sheets. I pull them on fast. I don't like being naked around him, which is weird, considering what we just did.

I pull on my socks and boots and walk from the room, leaving him still getting dressed.

Bernie looks at me with a grin, "Sleep well?"

I blush and look down, "Yeah. I'm hungry."

He points to the kitchen, "I have a bunch of food ready."

I walk past him to the kitchen and grab a bun. I smell it. We never get bread, ever. He always has bread it seems.

"Remember just going in your car and grabbing food?" he mutters and splits a bun open. He stuffs it with meat and cheese.

I do the same and nod, "Yeah. It was so good. My dad never was into the bad food but Granny loved it. She liked those places where the food was spread out and you picked what you wanted."

He grins, "Buffets."

I point, "That's it. Buffets." The word feels weird on my lips, like it isn't real.

Will comes in the kitchen. He stands too close. I step away from him, frowning. Bernie grins and shakes his head. He takes another bun and walks back to the living room.

"What are you doing?" I ask.

Will shrugs, "I don't know—what? Nothing?"

He takes a huge bite and smiles at me.

He never smiles this much.

I finish my bun and pour a glass of juice, "How do you guys have so much juice?" I ask loudly. Bernie looks back at me, "We have orchards. The fruit is trucked in and made into juice."

I scowl, "What a waste of fruit."

He laughs, "We only use the fruit that's going bad for it."

I sigh and look at Will, "People are starving and the city folks have fruit going bad?"

He shrugs and wraps an arm around me. I want to shove him and maybe stab him with something. He's touching me too much and being too soft and weird. I struggle out of his arms and walk to the window. The lights flicker.

Bernie looks up, "They run on solar power energy that's stored throughout the day. Our lights never work until the end of dusk."

I look out the window and watch as the lights of the small city all flicker together and then come on. "They're not very bright."

"They get brighter as they heat up. Everything is run on solar power." He points at the small holes in the ceiling, "Those are windows that bring in the light of the day; we don't need power throughout the day."

I scowl, "I know. I've seen a skylight before."

He chuckles, "Anyway, everything is separate. They run the plug-ins separately from the lights. So the fridge runs all day, but there are no lights on."

I cross my arms, "What's the plan?" I don't want to hear about how genius the city is. I can tell he had something to do with it all—he's too excited about it.

He narrows his eyes and shakes his head, "You seem awfully bitchy tonight." He looks at Will who has stopped eating and points at him, "Leave her alone." He has the warning tone.

"Stop!" I use my own warning tone.

Will frowns, "Babe..."

"No, we get the shit we need for Anna and we figure out how and where for the explosives, and we go."

Bernie crosses his arms, "You two are like the same person, only you keep switching roles and moods."

I look at him to argue but a laugh bursts from my lips. It's so true.

Will shakes his head and finishes stuffing his face. I turn my back, looking out at the lights starting to glow brightly. I wonder where Leo is and if he's safe. I wonder if I would know in my heart, if he weren't.

We leave the apartment through the same creepy hallway, but this time it's lit and not scary. The parkade is, as well. The lights turn on as we walk.

"Motion sensors so the lights don't just stay on."

I smile and nod at the pride in his voice, "You all are clever."

He nudges me, "You don't impress easily do you?"

Will scoffs. I look back at him. He grins and walks up to open the door for me. I choose the other side of the truck and climb in, getting my own door. Bernie laughs at it all. Will scowls at me, "What's your deal?"

I shake my head and look at Bernie. I don't want to talk about it. Not in front of another person.

I still hate the parkade, but at least I can see where we are going. The lights turn on as we get to them and turn off as we leave. It is pretty genius.

We drive out onto the road.

"Where are the other cars?"

Bernie looks at me in the rearview, "Most people walk. There are buses that bring the doctors and nurses to and from the farms, but hardly anyone has a car."

I feel panic in my stomach, "Stop the truck."

He does. I jump out and start walking down the road.

"What are you doing, "You two are idiots. No one drives, but we're driving along drawing attention to ourselves."

Will catches up, "You might have mentioned that, Bernie."

He shrugs, "I drive everywhere."

I shoot him a glare, "try to fit in. Blend—like Star says."

He shrugs, "Okay, it's a long walk though."

I snort, "You have no idea what a long walk is."

Will laughs. We walk in silence, like the people we pass on the sidewalk. They give us a wide birth, probably thinking we are like the kids who travel in packs. We don't pass anyone with more than two people in their crowd.

"We should split up," I mutter.

"Bernie, you walk up ahead. Keep a good pace."

He speeds up as I stop and play with the laces in my boots. Will waits for me.

"What's up with you?" he asks.

I glance at Bernie, "This feels wrong."

He drops to his knee too, "What does? Us? I thought it felt pretty right."

"What? No, this. The near-empty streets, the way we got into the city so easy, and the way Bernie has zero survival skills. It feels wrong." I look at the way his lip curls and can't fight the smile that crosses my lips, "Me and you is the only thing that doesn't feel wrong. Beyond you acting like a girl from Granny's romance novels, that is."

He grabs my face and plants a gentle kiss on my lips, "I just want to be the person you want me to be. I want to pretend all the other things didn't happen."

I shake my head, "But they did and I can't stop myself from loving you through them, so I guess they don't matter much."

The grin I love and hate breaks out across his face, "What was that you just threw in there? You love me?"

I shove him lightly, "Shut up."

We start walking again. I look up at him, "You need to focus. The thing I LIKE about you is your common sense and survival skills." I make sure I emphasize like. "Don't make me regret it."

He shakes his head, "Yeah well, the thing I LIKE about you is the way you manage to get under my skin constantly. In good and bad ways."

I nudge him and notice we are the only animated people on the road. We walk past a lady who is old enough to be my mom. She gives me a weird look. I drop my gaze.

"We need to blend."

He nods, "I see that. It's like these people died inside. The infected have more emotions than these people."

We walk past a man carrying a paper bag. He smiles at me kindly. I smile back.

"How did they choose who got to be a city person and who didn't?" I mutter.

Will shakes his head, "I would guess the politicians, scientists, professors, artists, engineers, and doctors. People who mattered."

I look up at him, "It's gonna sound weird, but I like the borderlands better."

"Me too."

We pass by an alley and I see three young teenagers walking away from us. They walk with swagger and attitude, not like the other people here. I look down at the road we're walking on. It's smooth and flat, like the old roads were. Everything is tidy and clean. The buildings are made of metal and glass and they sparkle along with the night sky and the streetlights.

"I remember being in the city with my dad, and not being able to see the night sky, 'cause the lights were so bright," I say, looking up at the stars I can see.

"Yeah, the pollution too. There is no haze here. We lived just outside of Los Angeles. It was bad there. Mom went to work and got sick right away. Dad took us before the first tidal waves came. He had a bad feeling. We went to the desert and hung there for a while. Then we made our way north. He thought Canada was a good idea. But none of the cars worked near where we were. Someone had let off an EMP and killed the power. We hid at a house with a swimming pool for a while."

I watch Bernie saunter down the road and listen to Will's story.

We round a corner as he continues, "Dad didn't come back one day. It was late, dinnertime and we were starving. Anna was pretty young, but she had paid attention to the things he was always trying to teach us. We were close to starving, by the time we decided to move on; he wasn't coming back. We moved on to a new place and found some food in the cupboards. We ate too much and ran out again. We didn't have any common sense back then."

I snicker, "Jake still doesn't."

He laughs, "No, he doesn't. He was worse then though, believe it or not. We were close to the breeder farms, we just didn't know it. We'd made it all the way to Washington, close to Canada. Anna and Jake were inside of a house, raiding it. She was so tiny and yet able. More able than me or Jake. I heard the others outside. One of them heard a noise inside— Jake of course. So I ran, drawing them after me. I let them take me. I knew Jakey and Anna were basically going to die. I didn't think he'd even have enough sense to get them out of there. But we'd seen the others taking girls as young as Anna. So I figured their best shot was me getting chased. I got taken and when I escaped I made my way back to where they were last—they were gone though. I spent a long while going back over our steps, retracing them. I didn't think I would ever find them. So I went and made a burial for them and just tried to get past it."

We round another corner.

I look up, "You did the right thing. It's the things I would have done."

He shrugs, "When we found you and you knew where they were, I nearly died inside."

I nod, "I didn't think you really cared that much."

He looks down, "I'm not good at caring. I turned that all off a while back."

I feel the sad look taking over my face, "I was wrong. I see that now. You were willing to risk me to get Anna back. You cared about them."

Guilt creeps across his face, "When I found out what they had done to you and it was my fault, I never have felt that kind of rage."

I look down at his clenched fist and do something I don't do—ever. I take it in my hands, surrounding it with mine. It feels like his hand is throbbing with anger still. I have to fight to stay focused on why we're here and not think about the feelings his hands make me have.

Bernie glances back at us, as he makes a turn under a streetlight. He winks. I frown.

It takes us a few moments to get to the spot he went in. It's an alley and he's standing at the end of it in the dark.

"Medical research building," he whispers as we get there.

It's tall and shiny, like everything else.

"There's a back entrance. I always take it. My card will get me in. You want to come too or wait out here?"

I struggle to see his face in the dark, "We come."

He turns and walks closer to the building. He moves and the door opens. I see the card slider as we walk in. The lights turn on as we walk inside. They do the motion thing. I don't want to hurt his feelings, but it's annoying.

It looks like the breeder farm hallways when we get inside.

The lights exasperate the hell out of me, the entire way to the stairs. "We don't do elevators, only stairs in the city. It's seven flights."

I raise an eyebrow, "You sure like it here."

He sighs, "I did. I loved it. It was like almost being back to normal, only without the fashion and luxuries. But the basics are here. I just can't risk Star. When she's older we will come and live here, but she needs to get past the breeder age. If they find out what she is... well you know."

I nod. I do.

"Is it weird, she's your sister?" he asks as we climb the second set of stairs.

Will coughs nervously, "What?"

I see the look on his face and wrinkle my nose, "Oh my God—you had sex with her, didn't you?"

His eyes widen. Bernie turns and looks at him, "Not cool."

Will sputters, "No. I swear. It's not like that. It wasn't like that."

I'm disgusted, because I friggin' knew it and because I'm a notch on his god-dammed belt, like my sister. I blow past them both and continue to climb.

"Bern, I never slept with her. I swear to the gods. I never. You know me. She tried a few times, but I didn't. I couldn't. Not after... just not after."

I ignore his words. Their footsteps start again behind me.

"I trust you," Bernie mumbles.

I don't. I look back to see the guilty, red face and fight the sneer on my lips.

I am almost running the stairs, ignoring them and the wind I'm sucking by the time I reach the door with the seven on it. I fling it open and walk into a hallway like the farms. The whole place is like a replica.

Bernie opens the door, almost wheezing. I look back, "Did they only let one building designer live through it all? Why do all these look the same?"

He laughs, "Cost and ease. Whew. I haven't done those stairs in a while."

Will is huffing next to him. He gives me a pleading look. I give him a look. He gives it back.

Bernie grabs my hand, "Come on, scowly. You've been grumpy all day. It's not that bad here."

I look around. It's dark inside and no one is here, just like he said.

We walk down a hall into an open lab. It's huge. He walks to a room with a huge, red sign on it that says BIOHAZARD.

He winks at me and opens the door.

"You're immune aren't you?"

He nods, "Will stay out here. You're not."

He pulls me inside of the room. It's dark until we are inside, then the lights flash dimly and slowly grow in brightness. The lab is white and big. The wall where the door is, is all windows. I can see Will through it. He still looks pissed.

"Can he hear us?"

Bernie looks at Will and then me, "No."

"Do you really believe he didn't sleep with Star?"

He shakes his head, "No. She has been in love with him since he saved her. She was raped in the back of a truck at the farms." He shudders, "She doesn't really remember much, blocking it out, I guess. Anyway, she remembers Will. He came and saved her. He beat them to death with his bare hands. He broke several fingers and knuckles. It was horrid. He was covered in blood. I don't know what happened to him in the farm, but he was a savage when he left."

I look at the intensity in his blue eyes, "It's weird. He's the most gentle person in the world one minute and a total psycho the next."

He snorts, "Who isn't nowadays?" He sounds distracted. I look at the huge glass canisters he's touching.

"What's that?"

He looks back at me, "The vaccine. We need to give it to Will. You go do that and I'll get the cure."

I frown, "It's a real cure?"

He nods, "As long as it hasn't mutated again. It should work fine. The research is done in Spokane." His eyes flash when he says it. I grimace and take the needle he passes me. It's huge and filled with a pale-yellow, syrup-looking liquid.

"Shoot it into his arm. He's gonna get crazy sick for a couple hours and then be fine."

I give him a look as he passes me a packet.

He shakes his head, "I know. Not ideal, but it's our best hope."

"He's going to be sick as we flee the city with the stolen cure?"

He laughs, "You really are a true skeptic, aren't you?"

His flippant behavior drives me insane. I take a deep breath and walk to the door.

"Wipe him with the cloth in the packet and then stick him."

I nod and close the door. Will looks down on me, "You think I'm lying, don't you?"

I hold up the packet, "I need to wipe your arm. This is the vaccine." I tear the packet with my teeth and tug the wet wipe out. I always get excited when I find these. I wipe his arm in the thick spot and try not to think about anything but the wipe. My hand shakes with the huge needle in it. When I lift it, his eyes widen, "Really?"

I nod and look in his dark-blue eyes. I smile bitterly and slide the needle in slowly. He winces as I press the liquid in slowly.

I pull the needle out and toss it and the wipe in the garbage can, next to the desk beside us.

He grasps my hand, but I stop his kiss with my evil grin, "You're going to be horribly sick for a day or so."

He cocks an eyebrow, "What?"

"It makes you really sick." I can't help but smile when I say it.

He rolls his eyes, "Why, because Bernie said so? He gets a sliver and feels sick. I'll be fine."

I shrug, "Ok. He has the cure, I think."

Bernie walks out, holding a small cylinder. He looks sweaty and off, "We need to go now. This can only stay active for a short amount of time."

We follow him out of the lab and down the hall. I can't help but feel like it's all too easy.

"Doesn't anyone guard the lab?" I ask.

He nods, "They do, but they rarely come up the stairs. It's too bloody far to check every floor."

Will laughs, "That sounds dumb. They don't put in elevators, so then the guards don't want to climb the stairs?"

Bernie chuckles and starts down the stairs, "I'm not one of the engineers who decided this. I told them it was stupid, but they never listened to me."

"Have you stolen the cure before?" I ask, starting to feel weird.

He shakes his head, "Nope. I haven't ever used it either. I heard it only works if the person taking it hasn't got the fever bad yet. That takes five days to set in and get so high the brain damage happens."

We reach the bottom of the stairs and enter the hallway with the lights that turn off as we walk.

As we leave the building, he hands the cylinder to me, "I'll go get the truck. You wait here, okay?"

I want to say no. I don't trust him. It's sudden. I don't like that we've put so much faith in him. But I don't. I take it and wait for him to betray us. I don't have a choice. We can't walk down the street with a cylinder, not without people giving us a look.

I look at Will, "Starting to feel sick so soon?"

He nods and I fight the grin that wants to take over.

He grabs my arm, "What if he poisoned me?"

I sigh and point down the alley, "You are the one who said to trust him. You are the one who said he was going to help us. Is that possible?"

He takes deep breaths and then nods, "Yeah. It might be possible."

I growl, "For fuck's sake." I grab his arm and drag him down the alley. We cross the silent street and enter an alley across the way. I drag him behind another building and up another alley. We walk for a few minutes and then I hear it. I pass him the cylinder, "Don't drop this, I don't care if you're dying."

He scowls, "She's my sister too." I like that he said too.

I scoff and walk up to the corner of the building in front of us. A group of the weird, breeder kids are standing in front of something. In the dark, I can barely make them out. I squint and manage to count five or six.

"Shit," I whisper and turn back around to grab his empty hand, "We gotta go." I see a window on the ground level and try to open it, but it doesn't move.

I pull him down the alley farther. We reach a building with stairs. We climb a few flights until we can see the road we are on. I sit. He sits beside me. I can feel him starting to shake. I take the cylinder and put it beside me. I wipe away the sweat forming on his brow.

He lifts one corner of his lip, "I'm sorry."

I scowl, "For what?" I have a bad feeling he's about to confess to sleeping with Star, who is my sister.

He shakes his head slowly, "For trusting him."

I watch the road for the truck, "He might be on our side. He might truly be good."

He leans on me, "I doubt it. We aren't that lucky."

I laugh and then sigh, "I know." The hopelessness of it all is writhing around inside of me. Anna is infected; she is going to turn in a few days. I have the cure, if it's even the cure, and Will is possibly dying next to me. Maybe he's going to turn. Maybe it's all been a lie. I grip his hand.

He kisses my cheek, "Thank you."

I look at him and shake my head, "For what? Poisoning you?"

He kisses my lips softy, "Giving me a chance to be the person I would have been, before."

I see the sweet face and feel the soft lips, and I can't see him any other way any more. I can't see the man beating the other men to death, or the man who gripped me and shook me so hard, he left finger marks on me. I see the man I wanted him to be all along.

"Thank you for not ruining the chance I gave you," I whisper back. Our silence is broken by the sound of a truck. I see him stop at the end of the alley and get out. He scratches his head and looks around.

"He looks innocent to me," I mutter.

Will nods. I run down the stairs and down the alley to the end of the building. As I get to the end of the building, I see headlights. I freeze and press myself against the glass window. I wave back at Will. He does the same. A truck stops behind Bernie.

"Bernard!" a man's voice rings out into the dark.

Bernie turns and I see his face change. He looks scared, truly scared.

"Richard, what's up?" Bernie sounds nervous.

My heart is attempting to beat out of my chest, and my lungs are with my stomach in my throat.

I hear footsteps.

"Why were you in the lab this late? Michael sent me to find you, when he heard you were there."

Bernie shakes his head, "Friend got sick. Thought I would try to save her."

A man with dark hair and the same linen clothes as the rest of us, walks up to Bernie. There are other men with the man.

"What friend?"

Bernie shakes his head, "Girlfriend of mine."

Richard's hands go out, "Is she in the city?"

Bernie shakes his head, "No. She's at a friend's house. I came here to get the cure for her. I thought you wanted it tested on pure people, not wasted on the borderland trash."

Richard crosses his arms. I can't see him in the light from the trucks. He shakes his head, "I do. Why didn't you bring her here? Or Spokane?"

Bernie crosses his arms too, but he looks like he's hugging himself, "She's sick. I didn't want to risk anyone else."

"When was she bit?"

"Yesterday."

Richard nods, "Okay. Michael doesn't like people sneaking around his lab. You know that."

Bernie nods nervously, "I know. I'm sorry, Richard."

"The guards said you had some friends with you when you came through."

Bernie looks stunned. He swallows and I can tell he's lying from the distance I am. He licks his lips, "I did. A nurse and doctor from the breeder farms. One of the outlying ones, where they don't really come here much. It was one of the ones that was destroyed. They're staying at my place for a few weeks. I'm never there anyway."

"Get in the truck, they'll drive you to the girl."

Bernie hesitates and then walks toward Richard and the men, "She's a long ways off."

"Okay. The guys haven't been out of the city in a while. Michael will need a report on how things are out there, anyway."

Bernie nods once, "Okay."

Richard looks at him, "Where's the cure."

I want to smack myself in the head.

Bernie stops. He doesn't know what to do, neither do I.

One of the guards slams him against the truck, "Why are you lying?"

Bernie shakes his head, "I must have left it in the lab."

I take a deep breath and walk from the alley. One of the guards turns and looks at me.

I smile, "Good evening."

He frowns. The others look.

I wave, "Hey, Bernard."

He waves, looking lost.

The men all watch me walk up to them, "What's going on?" I ask casually.

Richard scowls, "This is none of your concern."

I clear my throat, "I'm staying with Bernard."

He raises an eyebrow, "You are the nurse he's got staying with him?" His eyes are dark in the dim light of the headlights.

I swallow and nod, "I am."

"What's your name?"

I panic, trying to remember the name on the card, "Lainy Swanson."

He looks me over once, "You look young. How old are you?"

"Twenty seven."

He arches an eyebrow, "And you're a nurse?"

I scowl, "I am."

"Your institution was attacked then? By the vigilante?"

I remember them calling me that on the back of the truck, during the flashy crow conversation. I nod, "It was."

He folds his arms, "What was she like?"

I glance at Bernie. His face is stricken with fear, "Me," I say. "She looked similar to me. Thin, mid-twenties, long hair, but mean. Really mean. She shot the doctors in the head in front of the children. She was horrid." I try to remember the last one we attacked.

He sighs, "Why are you here? Why aren't you helping with the other institutions?"

I rub my belly, "I'm married and we're trying to have a baby."

He looks at my stomach, "I see. You've been given permission?"

I nod once. He glances at Bernie and nods at the guard, "Let him go." He points at me, "Don't go with him to see the sick girl. Some of the mutations aren't up to date with our vaccines. Bernard doesn't know that. He doesn't work the labs." He sneers at Bernie and walks back to his truck. Bernie walks to the truck. I mutter, "You forgot the cure in the lab."

He looks at me and nods, "Be right back."

I widen my eyes and climb into the truck. My hands are shaking. I don't look back at the alley. I don't know what to do. The trucks behind us leave.

A knock at the window scares me. I jump and look to see Will. He's pouring sweat. I open the truck and pull him inside. He weighs a ton and squishes me into the backseat with him. Bernard comes back within minutes. He's huffing and holding another cylinder.

"Jesus, that was brilliant, Em."

I hold Will's burning face to my chest, "Hurry."

He turns the truck around and drives back to his apartment. He parks and leaves us in the dark of the parking spot. Will is shaking and heaving.

"Em, I'm gonna die."

I shake my head, "No. Bernard said it made him sick, like he was dying too."

He shakes his head, "Baby, I'm dying. I know it. I got this bad feeling."

I shake my head, "I had that feeling when I was in Spokane and you came for me. You, Anna, and Jake. You found me. I am here, you'll be okay."

All of the pieces of my heart feel like they're up in the air, hovering. And any second they're all gonna drop at once, and I have to try to catch them all before they break. I have a sick feeling, I won't get them all.

Bernard comes back in.

"Slide on the floor."

I frown, "What?"

"Will, lie down on the floor and you on top of him. They won't check me on the way out, they never do."

I push Will onto the floor and lie on top of him. Bernard covers us with something.

I whisper, "Am I squishing you?"

He shakes his head, "No."

I press my ear to his chest and listen to his racing heartbeat. He is dying, that's how it sounds.

Bernard drives and we hide. I feel the truck slow several times, it makes my stomach burn, but he always drives on again. I don't know how close we are to the guards and if we will get stopped. They'll see Will and shoot on site. I'll get discovered and dragged to my dad or worse, back to Spokane.

I'm about to throw the blanket back and savagely attack Bernie, when I feel the truck come to a complete stop. I hold my breath. Will is passed out.

I hear muffled voices and Bernie's nervous laugh. He needs to work on his inner calm.

The truck starts moving as he shouts, "See ya in a couple hours."

He presses hard on the gas and Will and I are shoved back against the seat in a jerk.

The blanket comes off, "Is he okay?"

I shake my head, "I don't know. He's sleeping."

"Wake him up."

I sit up and scowl, "He's sick. Let him sleep."

He shakes his head violently and drives like a psycho, "He's gonna be barfing in about ten minutes. Trust me. I've lived through this."

I close my eyes and sigh. I want to choke Bernie, but I don't. I slap Will across the face hard. His eyes shoot open. He sits up hard and fast, wrapping his huge hands around my throat. I break his grip. He sees it's me and gasps, "Em. I must have had a nightmare. You okay?"

I laugh, "No. Remind me never to wake you by hitting you again."

He wrinkles his nose, "You slapped me?"

I laugh, "I did."

"Why?"

I point at his belly, "That's about to get bad."

He burps, "Its bad already."

I shake my head, "Bad!"

He winces.

Bernie pulls the truck over when we near the spot we let Leo out. I whistle.

Will stumbles out and gags. He gives me a deadly look, "What did you do?"

I put my hands up, "Bernie. Not me."

Bernie rolls his eyes, "You're fine, princess. It lasts a few hours." He looks around, "Can Leo stay with him, while we go for Anna?"

I nod, "Yeah," and whistle again.

Will puts a hand out, "No. That damned wolf will eat me. No."

I laugh and whistle again. I hear a crack in the woods and turn to see his sloppy face as he leaps from the woods. I drop to my knees. He runs around me, sniffing and checking. He growls at Bernie and Will. I chuckle and let him nudge me a couple times. He wraps his paws around me and nuzzles me. I hug him back, "Hey, boy."

I scratch his ears, "You have fun in the woods?"

He makes his weird noises and nips at me. He sniffs me and sneezes. I laugh. He turns and looks at Will, growling again.

I grab his mane, "No."

He snarls once and then coughs. Will walks to the edge of the road and sits on a log just inside of the forest.

I walk to Will and kneel in front of him, "You okay?"

He shakes his head, "I'll be fine. If I'm not, you kill Bern for me, okay?"

I laugh and look at Bernie who rolls his eyes again.

I give Leo my severe look for when I want him to listen to my command; he cowers. I point at Will, "You keep him safe. I'll be back, okay?" I kneel again and lean into Leo's fur, "I like him. Please." I stand up and look at them both.

Leo growls.

Will looks like he might growl too.

I put my hands on my hips, "Make it work."

Leo looks at Will and lifts his lip. Will does the same. I clap, bringing their faces around to me, "BEHAVE!"

They both have the same look.

I turn and stalk back to the truck with Bernie. He looks back, "He's gonna eat him."

I shake my head, "No, it's an act for me."

He shakes his head, "No. Em, he's gonna eat Will."

I look back and notice Leo is in his stance for attack. I laugh and get into the truck. I shout out, "I mean it!"

They both look at me and then Will loses his breakfast all over the forest floor. Leo jumps back, horrified.

I laugh, "He's good."

Bernie starts the truck, "That's a big friggin' wolf."

Chapter Thirteen

We race inside with the cure. Anna is out completely, on the couch. Star looks like she's been crying and Jake looks sick.

"Where's Will?" he asks.

I ignore him and pull apart the cylinder as Bernie wipes her arm down. He puts a hand out. I pass him the huge needle. He injects it into her arm. He looks worried. That makes me sick.

"How long has she been like this?" he asks and puts the back of his hand on her forehead.

Star hugs herself, "Two days."

Jake grabs my arms hard, "Where's Will?"

I shake my head, snapping out of the million things I'm thinking that are not good. "He's back on the road puking. He's sick from the vaccine."

Jake scowls, "You left him?"

I nod, "He's with Leo."

Jake shakes me slightly, "Em, focus. Is he okay?"

I look away from Anna's sweaty face to him and nod, "He's fine." I frown, "Is your throat sore?"

He swallows and shakes his head, "It's fine."

Bernie arches an eyebrow, "The other one in the truck is still good."

I clench my jaw, "What if he's not sick?"

He shakes his head, "I don't know. Want to wait for him to get sicker?"

I grimace and process it. Star jumps up and grabs his arm, spinning him, "You're sick?"

He clears his throat, "No."

She puts her hand on his forehead and nods, "He's sick."

"Shit," I mutter and run back out to the truck. I grab a wipes packet and the cylinder and run back inside.

I tear the packet and wipe his arm down. I give him a grin, "This is gonna sting."

He furrows his dark brow, and as I slide the needle into his arm, he winces. I inject him slowly, like we were shown at camp.

I notice the way Star is gripping to him and smirk. His eyes dart back and forth between us. The blush on his cheeks and the worry on her face, makes me feel better about the choice I've made.

I love him but not in the right way. I want to suck him dry of the goodness inside of him. I want him to fill in the cracks inside of me, smooth out the edges. But what was he ever going to get from the deal? A surly, mean, cross girl who would never know how to love him the way he deserved. Star on the other hand, is light and flighty... like him. She finds joy and peace, even though her life has been hard. She smiles and jokes and wears too-short shorts in an innocent way.

I think Marshall and the others have always seen her as a joke, just like I did. But seeing her as my sister, even a half, is changing things about her... like I am giving her the benefit of the doubt.

Bernie stands and looks at us all, "This is not good." He presses his lips together, "How old is she?"

"Young, not old enough for this," Jake says and rubs the spot where I've taken the needle out.

Star kisses it better. He looks uncomfortable with her affection in front of me. I wink at him, "I'm glad you guys were here with her. Was she scared?"

He shakes his head, "You know what she's like... you, but chatty."

I scowl, "I'm way more chatty than I used to be."

He looks at Bernie, "Did she even talk once on the trip?"

Bernie shrugs, "She asked a couple questions."

Jake laughs, "Mission questions. She does that."

I sigh and squat next to Anna, "Is it too late?"

Bernie shakes his head, "I don't know. She's young; they always bounce back faster." He sounds defeated.

"Carry her to the bed for me?" I ask Jake. He nods and lifts her like she weighs nothing.

When he lays her down upstairs, I lie beside her and look at him, "I'm happy for you."

He frowns, "I just wish you..."

I put a hand up, "I'm happy for you."

He nods, "Okay." He smiles and makes everything better, if only a little.

I stroke her hair, "She's so sick. I haven't ever watched them change before."

He shakes his head, "It's bad, I think." He sits on the bed and puts his face in his hands, "I didn't know what to do. She just started to get sleepy and I let her. I should have kept her awake."

"No. She needs sleep."

He runs his hands through his hair, "This cure better work."

I yawn, "Yeah, I'm not gonna imagine the possibility of it not working. I don't think that's going to be good for me."

Bernie pops his head in, "I'm gassing up and we're heading back to the city first thing tomorrow morning. It's her best bet and we can't leave Will in the woods longer than a day. He has nothing."

I frown "You sure about taking her to the city?"

He nods, "She has the cure. The virus can't be given to anyone once the cure is in the system. It can still hurt her if it's done enough damage."

"Okay."

He nods at Jake, "You and Star can stay here. You're not going to get sick now and she's immune. You'll be fine here. My dry storage is filled with food. A year or two worth. So if anything happens, Star knows what to do. She knows where the food and hiding places are."

I feel a heavy sickness in my chest. Bernie leaves and Jake shakes his head, "You can't take her to the city. She'll end up in a breeder farm."

I shake my head, "She'll be lucky to live long enough for that."

His hands grab mine and cover them, "Don't leave."

I feel tears slip down my cheeks; I don't even know why. I don't wipe them away. If I acknowledge them, he'll see them and know I'm crying. I just stare down at our hands and wait for the heavy feeling in my chest to go away.

"We've been so lucky, ya know?" I mutter.

He squeezes, "Not really."

I laugh and look up. He sees the tears and just like Leo would, he pulls me into him and holds me. I lose it. I sob, "Will is in the w-w-woods with Leo and Anna is s-s-sick and it's all my f-f-fault. I had to go and k-k-kill my dad. We were all at the cabin. We were all s-s-safe there. I n-never even g-g-got to k-k-kill him. I nev-never even s-saw him."

He strokes my head, soothingly, "How fair is that though? We were safe. No one else was. Meg, Sarah, and Anna deserve to live in a world where they don't have to worry about breeder farms and creepy men. The world is fucked and it deserves a do over. We all do. It's not fair that people like your father get to run the world like that." He pulls me back and wipes my tears, "You were right. This is the right path. Anna is going to be okay. I know it."

I sniffle and shake my head, "If it was any of you putting us at this kind of risk, I'd kill you."

He laughs, "I know. But you're insane."

I snort and wipe my eyes. I lie back next to Anna and snuggle into her.

"How are you feeling?" I ask him.

He shrugs, "Sick, like a head cold. I haven't felt like this since the last time we slept together."

I hold Anna's burning body next to mine and close my eyes, "Can you stay?"

I feel him adjust on the bed, "Yup." I open one eye and see him lying next to us. He puts his hand over hers and squeezes. I close my eyes and try to imagine how it would have been if we'd just stayed in the damned mountains, at the cabin. I hate that I dragged them down the damned hill for my own revenge.

I fall asleep, bitter and pissy.

I wake to movement on the bed. I open my eyes to see her staring at me. I jump back, prepared for her to try to eat me. She grins. Her lips are pale but her blood-shot eyes aren't milky.

"Em," her voice is gravelly, like it's barely there. Jake is gone.

Tears spring from my eyes. I jump on her, hugging her tight to me.

"I'm sorry."

She shakes her head, "I'm an idiot."

I pull her back, "Your voice?"

She nods, "My throat still hurts. I don't think it's ever gonna be okay again. I coughed a lot of blood."

The hoarse sound of her voice made me want to clear my throat. I put a hand up, "Don't talk."

She smiles.

I kiss her clammy forehead.

She gives me a look.

I frown, "What?"

She looks around and whispers, "Star and Jake."

I nod and grin, "I know."

She grimaces, "You okay?"

My cheeks blush, "Yeah." I'm whispering back for whatever reason.

"Where's Will?"

I bite my lip. I don't want to tell her but I have to, "I left him with Leo."

She wrinkles her nose, "Yikes."

I nod, "Yeah. I didn't have a choice. He was puking everywhere and super sick, so we left him in the woods with Leo to guard him. We came here to get the cure to you."

Her eyes widen, "He's sick?"

I shake my head, "From the vaccine. He's not sick."

She looks worried, "Jake?"

"He's fine. He took the cure too. He was getting sick."

Her worried look doesn't leave. She whispers, "This is my fault. I wanted to act brave in front of Bernie. I wanted him to think I was strong like you. I tried to fight them, but too many came."

I roll my eyes, "I'm not strong or brave... I'm an idiot."

Tears, with a slight-pinkish hue to them, leak from her eyes leaving pink stains on her cheeks. I stroke her hair back, "Hey, I'm a mutant too. You're smarter than me. It could have happened to anyone."

She shakes her head, "I kinda like him."

I grimace, "He's like twenty-nine or some shit."

She laughs and it makes a squeak like the infected. A raspy squeak. My heart is literally tearing from my chest. She isn't going to make it. I know that.

I am useless to her, so I lay there and watch her eyes. The blue is so bright, compared to the pink blood-shot of the whites.

She smiles, "I like that he's smart and he cares about things we haven't had for a long time. He's like Jake. He can remember the taste of the burger he ate when he was fifteen. He can remember the smell in the wind when he was at the beach."

I smile through the tears, "Suntan lotion."

She beams, "Exactly what he said. You could smell the sun in the lotion. It was summer and popsicles and grass and staying up late. He remembers those things and I like that."

I point, "He's too old for you."

She shrugs, "I'm too old for me."

I sniffle and nod, "You are. You're older than both your brothers."

She laughs the squeaky wheeze again and closes her eyes. I panic when she does it, but I see her chest rising and falling in jerky breaths.

The room goes dark. I keep my hand on her stomach and stay awake. Bernie comes in and sits in the chair next to the bed. He reaches over and grabs a hand to hold.

"She's got no throat left and pink tears," I whisper.

He whispers back, "We'll take her to the city. Your dad has solutions to things. I've seen him bring them back further than this."

I scowl, "He just picks and chooses?"

"Pretty much."

I shake my head, "I don't care. She's worthy."

He sighs, "She's an amazing girl. She's so strong and kind of crazy. I should have protected her. I should have fought with her and I didn't. I tried to get her to run away. She wouldn't. Leo saved her and I hid."

I want to blame him but I can't. I know where the blame belongs, "This is my fault."

The sun rises as we talk. The room fills with pink light, like the tears she cried.

I see his face and sigh, "We should get going."

He stands and scoops her up. She sleeps still, snuggling into his arms.

I follow him from the room. When we get downstairs, we find Jake and Star sleeping on the couch, wrapped in each other.

Bernie glances back at me, "I told Star we would be back for them in a week or not at all."

My breath gets caught in my chest, like it's trapped in a sob. Jake's sleeping face is beautiful, as is hers. I want them to come. I don't want to leave them behind.

"What if the bad people come?" I ask.

He looks back at me again, "I have bunkers, where the food is stored. They won't ever find it; you could burn the house to the ground and not find it."

We leave the house for the truck, "Good to know."

The drive is silent. I wouldn't have noticed it before, but now that Jake has said something to me about it, I do. I am still wooden in so many ways. I still don't talk for no reason and it never bothered me before.

I look back at Anna in the backseat; she's sleeping peacefully. Her skin is normal colored again, not so pale.

"I think she's getting better," I mutter.

He glances at me, "She needs medical help still."

I nod, "I know."

He taps his fingers on the steering wheel, "You and Will... you are... uhm... together?"

I frown and nod again.

"And Jake and Star are obviously together. Is Anna..."

I see him look at Anna in the rearview and feel my insides churning, "She's seventeen."

He looks shocked, "Is that all?"

I bite my lip to stop myself from saying something that would be bad.

He sighs, "I figured twenty."

I purse my lips, "You like her?"

He nods, "I do. I admire her, but she's a child."

I furrow my brow, "You wouldn't want to be with her?"

He scoffs, "If she were a few years older, at the very least. I'm not a pervert."

A smile breaks across my lips, "I like you, Bernie."

He shrugs, "Okay. Thanks." He stops the truck as we near Will's spot in the woods.

I open the door and whistle. Leo comes running fast and then back into the woods. I know what that means. I look back, "You have weapons?"

He grins and gets out. He opens the back door and lifts the floor up. He hands me a shiny steel handgun. I almost hear angels sing as he passes it to me. I see him take one and scowl, "How good are you?"

He shrugs, "I'm alright."

I put my hand out. He makes a face, but I cock my eyebrow, "Will's possibly hurt. I'm better than alright. Stay here with her. Leave if you have to, just keep her safe."

He resigns and hands me the gun. I turn and follow Leo into the woods.

I hear the birds and insects. Everything is moving, as it should. We run over logs and bushes and suddenly the noises stop. Slowing my pace, I can hear ragged breaths. I wince and lift the guns.

I hear a high moan and close my eyes. He's turned. The vaccine never helped him, he's sick now instead. He's sick.

Leo stops and paces the spot where I am standing. He whines. I grimace, "Sorry, buddy."

He tilts his head, just as I slide against a tree and feel something land on my shoulder. I look up as slime falls from a branch. I move out of the way, to discover a puddle of slime on the ground. Will is in the tree, clinging to it. The slime is his vomit.

He looks rough but manages to point. I turn in time to see it. I fire. The gun jerks in my hand, causing me to miss. I fire a second time, dropping the infected man to the ground.

I look up at Will in the tree and shake my head, "You aren't one of them?"

He chuckles, "I'm gonna kill you and Bern when I get outta this tree, Em. Kill you."

That answers that. I look around the forest and realize how many there are.

"Oh shit," I mutter. The forest is filled. I am surrounded. I swallow and look down at Leo, "Stay low." He crouches and growls.

I nod and he's off. He takes the first one down, I shoot the ones coming for him. I hear something behind me. A tall man with bloody tears, and a shriek that could make my ears bleed like his are, stumbles at me. I shoot him between the eyes and then a shaggy-looking man behind him. Leo yelps. I shoot the one that has him on the ground. I run closer and shoot the one grabbing at his back legs. He snarls, taking a lady down.

"Behind you, Em!"

I look where Will is yelling and shoot almost point blank. The lady drops to the ground and I fire at the one behind her. A small child rushes at me with blood dripping from her lips. She froths the yellow foam. I don't like killing the small ones. I fire and look back at Leo. He takes a man down by biting his entire head off. The squishy crunching noise is nasty.

I don't have the second to focus in on it. I blast one rushing me, she jumps a log and I hit her mid-air. She drops, breaking the old, rotten log under her. There are seven left. I shoot five as Leo takes the other two. Not fearing them touching or biting or infecting me, changes the way I fight them. I would have run after dropping the closest ones.

I look up at Will in the tree and wince, "All night?"

He nods and throws up again.

"Anna is sick," I say it and leave it out there to hang with his heaving that's filled the whole forest. It's no wonder, really, that so many came.

He stops and glances up, "Did she get the cure?" he coughs.

I nod, "Not sure it's worked though. Jake got it too, but when we gave him the cure, he wasn't far along... She had the fever."

He closes his eyes and breathes deeply. I look at Leo who is eating one of them. I grimace. But he makes his sloppy-wolf face and chews away. I shudder, "You're riding in the back of the truck."

Will struggles, climbing down. He stands uneasily smacking his lips together.

He points, "I have never been this sick in my life."

"You stink."

He nods, "I know, baby."

I put his huge arm over my shoulder and start the hike out of the woods, "They're starting to pack like animals," I look at the dead.

"Yeah, it's weird. Six or seven was a lot before. Now you can find ten or twenty together," he mutters and struggles with the walk.

"You're cold now. The fever is gone."

He nods and spits on the ground, "Thank God."

Leo catches up and nudges against Will. I smile and walk to the truck.

Bernie is still there. He's holding a shotgun, shaking sort of, as he stands there.

"What the fuck?" he shouts at me.

I shake my head, "Infected. They treed him like a cougar running from wolves."

He looks around, "They gone?"

"Yup."

He takes Will for me. I stretch my arm and shoulder. He weighs a ton. I look down at Leo, "You go back to the house."

He whines. I drop to my knee and grimace at the greenish goo on his muzzle, "Jake needs you." He shakes his head and turns and runs into the woods.

"You're a stubborn brat!" I call back.

I sigh and climb into the truck. Will sits in the backseat looking like he might die any second. Anna is asleep across his lap.

Bernie gives me a look, "Thought you said you were a good shot?"

I glare at him, "I am."

He arches an eyebrow, "You fired like sixteen times."

I blink at him, "I only missed once."

His jaw drops, "There were that many?"

I shake my head, "Leo killed his share."

He moves back a bit, lifting both eyebrows, "Oh." He starts the truck and drives in silence.

We arrive at the guard gate. I tuck the guns that I'm not giving back and pull out my ID card.

The guard gives me a look. It's a different guy. He seems mellower than the first guy.

"How's it going, Bern?" They know each other.

Bernie nods, "Alright, Dan. I got a couple of sick people. They took the vaccine."

He makes a face and looks over my ID card, "I hated that stupid vaccine. I was sick for a week."

Will moans. Bernie passes Will's ID card. The guard doesn't even bat an eyelash at the fact Anna doesn't even have one.

"I'm bringing her in for Michael. She isn't doing so hot with it," Bernie says like he has done this before.

The guard nods, "Move ahead. They just need to make sure the virus isn't live. Take it easy, Bern."

"Will do, you too, Dan." Bernie puts the truck in drive and heads slowly to the next guard stop. We each give a saliva sample on the stick and are moved on.

"No live virus?" Bernie asks. The guy shakes his head, "Nope."

Bernie smiles and drives on. We don't go to his house. We stop in front of a building that looks shiny and pretty. A lady is walking past in the linen clothes. She glances our way, probably wondering about the truck.

"Can you find your way back to my place?" he asks.

I look around and shake my head, "No."

He sighs, "Will?"

"Yup," he croaks from the backseat.

Bernie gets out and opens the back door. He lifts her out, "I'm taking her in. Go hide at my place. If you hear anything, there is a spot in the bathroom where the tiles open. You'll be fine down there for a few days."

Will climbs out and grabs Bernie's arm, "You keep her safe or I will skin you alive."

Bernie nods, "I won't let them hurt her, I swear. The key on the truck that looks funny is the one for the apartment for when the power is out."

Will nods, but all I can think about is the fact he's going to see my dad. It feels weird for me that the man in the building who will fix Anna is my real father. The uncle I never knew.

Will gets in and drives away, as Bernie slides his card and walks into the shiny building.

My stomach is in my throat, "We should go back."

He ignores me and drives. I don't think he's doing well enough to be driving. It takes longer than it did for Bernie, but he finds it.

When he parks the truck he looks at me in the dark, "You gotta be calm, okay?"

I realize my breathing is a bit intense. I swallow and nod, "Ok."

He climbs out clumsily, almost falling onto the ground.

I hurry around the side of the truck, tucking my guns in the back of my pants. I help him up and open the back door. I lift the floor and grab the ammo from the small space and the shotgun from the floor.

He takes the shotgun and walks casually. If anyone sees the amount of firepower we have, we're dead.

He uses the key and opens the door. We walk into the hall, both looking for people. He gets to the door and opens it fast. We scramble inside and close it, locking it. We both lean our backs against the closed door, panting.

"I'm going to take a shower," he mutters and walks away.

I take deep breaths and nod. I reload the guns and refill the empty cartridges.

I feel like I'm having a heart attack. I need a shower too.

Chapter Fourteen

Six days pass in silence. We don't talk, mostly because neither of us needs to. We don't kiss or touch. We pace, take turns cooking and sleeping. The walls slowly creep in on me and I think we're avoiding each other.

My heart hurts.

He passes me a stale bun. I eat it like I'm one of the infected. I chew and swallow and ignore everything about it.

I reach down and lightly finger the gun in the back of my pants.

The sun sets and I shake my head, "I have to see."

He turns and grabs the shotgun from the wall where he has it resting, "Yeah."

"How are you feeling?"

He shrugs, "Normal."

He grabs the keys but I stop, "We're walking."

He nods, "I know but we have to lock this place up and I want to be able to get back in."

I sigh and walk to the door, "If we can't find them, I'm leaving here. I never want to come back."

Will grabs my hand, "What about your dad?"

I shake my head, "I'm an idiot. That was a childish, stupid plan. You were right—I should have formed a proper plan. I should have left Jake and Anna up the hill."

His eyes narrow, "This isn't your fault."

I shrug, "It doesn't matter now."

He leans over and kisses me. It's the first kiss since the day we had sex. It makes my belly heat up. He gently caresses his lips against mine and sucks my lower lip in. He pulls back smiling, "It matters. You can't take on that kind of guilt. You didn't do anything to deserve it. You wanted to stop the injustice. No one sees that as wrong."

I walk out the door, peeking both ways, "I spent so long not caring about any of it and anyone, I swear I don't know how to just do anything a little. And I can't seem to just care about the people with us."

He laughs, "You still kill pretty easily."

I look back at him as we make our way to the parkade, "Those people chose the wrong side. They chose to be on the side of the tormentors. It's like Anna said, they probably have families and loved ones, but they made the wrong choice. That's all I see."

He opens the door to the parkade. A man walks towards us. He smiles at me. I smile back. Will holds the door for him, holding the shotgun behind his back at a weird angle.

I turn my back too, hiding the guns stuffed down the back of my pants. He frowns and hurries inside.

We close the door and run for the truck.

We hide beside it for a minute, not talking but clearly thinking the same thing. Seconds later, a man comes out with a gun and a flashlight. He looks around and talks into a radio like in the old shows. I glance at Will. His jaw clenches.

"Should we go back and hide?" I ask, never imagining those words would leave my lips.

He steels his eyes, "No. We'll wait; they'll be gone soon enough."

I look around, "Do you think there are cameras that record, like in the old days?"

He smirks, "No. Too much power usage." He kisses my cheek, "You're cute."

I scowl. I don't know why he says that, but the way he does bugs me.

The man leaves and Will stands, but I grab his hand, "Wait."

He scowls, "Stop being so paranoid."

I shake my head, "I always wait. One more minute."

He crouches down again as a truck comes up the ramp and drives past us with a flashlight shining all about. We are standing at the front of the parked truck, hidden well. He looks at me, "Does that always happen?"

I shake my head, "No, but I learned that whenever you feel like it's safe, it's not."

We wait and leave after a few minutes. We run as quietly as we can to the street. It's dark so we creep through the alleys and hope no one sees his shotgun.

"Can you find the building?" I ask.

He nods, surveying the area, "Yeah."

He doesn't sound certain, but he ditches the shotgun behind one of the many gardens we see in the alleys. He grabs my hand and pulls me through to the road. We walk casually, wooden. My shirt is baggy enough to hide one gun but I give him the other. He tucks it the way mine is.

My skin is damp from nerves and fear.

"I hate it here," I whisper.

He smiles, "Me too."

Our hands brush against each other and words shoot from my mouth, "Why haven't you touched me all week while we've been hiding here?"

He looks down on me, "I felt gross. I didn't want to gross you out too."

I grin.

He looks confused but I smile. He was being considerate.

"You thought that I got what I wanted, so I didn't want it anymore?" he asks.

My smile fades and I feel like the horrid feeling in my stomach makes sense. I stop walking and look at him; suddenly I'm angry. I did think that. I was so worried, I never noticed what it was. I look at him, "Yeah."

He shakes his head, "Emma, I am never going to get tired of you. No amount of time spent or love given, will be enough. I feel like a bottomless pit when I'm with you. I just want more and more."

I frown, "What if it's 'cause I'm not enough?"

He laughs, "No, it's because you're addicting, and weird, and I can't put my finger on anything you think or feel or do. I want to solve you and have you figured out, and I don't think one life time will ever be enough."

I nod, "Okay." I start walking again.

"You have to tell me what that look is," he sighs.

I glance at him and shake my head, "I don't know. I just can't help but wonder if normal girls are easy to figure out, and fun to be with, and the reason I'm so confusing is 'cause I'm a mutant."

He stifles a laugh, "Mutant?"

I nod, "The doctor said I have mutant blood."

He laughs again, "Oh my God." He grabs my hand and kisses it, "You're going to get us killed. Mellow out. He probably said mutated."

I roll my eyes and jerk my hand free, "I don't mellow."

He nudges me, "I like that about you."

"You do?"

He smiles, "Of course I do. I never want you to change. I like the feisty, crazy girl you are. I don't like it when you savagely attack people, or make bad choices and put your life in danger, and scare the shit out of me. But I like that it's never dull and I never know what's going on in that brain of yours."

I shrug, "Probably a lot less than you think."

We round a corner and he points, "That's it."

I feel sick again. People are few and far between.

I pull out the card Bernie made from the one I had stolen and swipe it. It works. I glance up at Will. He shakes his head, "Feels like a trap."

"That, or we are just the most jaded people on earth."

He chuckles and holds the door. We walk inside and instantly the lights do the thing they were doing in the other building. I groan, "I hate these lights."

"Me too. Makes it hard to focus."

I look back at him, "Maybe that's the plan."

We walk into a reception area. A man walks out of a door and smiles at us, "Can I help you?"

I hold up my ID badge, "We are looking for a friend of ours, Bernard."

He nods and looks around, "Bernie. Of course."

I see a look in his eyes and punch hard. His head snaps back. Will grabs him and puts the chokehold on him. He passes out. Will carries him to a room and opens the door, placing him inside of it.

"Shit," I mutter.

"Yup.

We enter the door, peeking our heads in. It's a lab but none of the lights are on. No one is in there... If they are, they're not moving around. Will opens another door, "Stairs."

We climb them to the next floor, checking for lights until we reach the fifth floor. Lights in the far back corner of the huge, open floor, stop us both in our tracks.

"Can I help you?" a man asks.

I turn, swinging my gun hard and backhand him. Will grabs him, snapping his neck. He winces.

I shrug, "Wrong side."

His eyes flare, but he drags the body inside and hides it under a desk. We duck and creep through the desks and shelves, not that it matters. The lights come on over us as we walk. The closer we get, the less we see over top of the furniture. I sneak to a corner and peek. A man is reading and doing work at a desk. He's typing something but we can't see his face. He doesn't look up at the lights moving in the ceiling.

I frown, "Is that a computer?"

Will nods, Looks like one."

I stand up and tuck my gun again. Will undoes a button on my shirt. I swat at him but he puts a finger to his lips, "Trust me. Act dumb and tired from working all day. They are not expecting us. He didn't even bat an eyelash at us walking and making the lights come on."

I swallow and shake my head. He grabs my face, kissing me hard. When he lets go, I stumble back and out of the hiding spot. I smile at the man who glances up at me.

"Hi," I say. My lips are still shiny from the kiss.

He grins, "You all done for the night?"

I nod, "I am. I'm beat."

He sits back, folding his arms and grinning. "What section do you work in?"

I point back at the other desks, "I work up a floor. I was coming down and saw the lights. I didn't want to walk home alone.

Thought I would see... if you were leaving soon?"

He stands up from the chair and closes the computer. It's a folding one like Granny had.

"I was about to leave," his eyes settle on my chest. I feel bile rising. I can't do it. I can't let him ogle me. I feel the panic and hear the tearing. I tell myself it's only one man. I wipe my hands on my pants and smile.

He steps away from the desk, "I'm getting tired anyway. What's your name?"

I nod, "Lainy."

He grins, "What do you do?"

"Nurse."

He frowns, "In this building?"

I nod, "I'm here to deliver things to the farms." I have no idea what I'm saying.

He sighs, "I see." His face looks funny when I say the word farms.

"How are things there?" His eyes search mine.

I shake my head, "The vigilante killed a lot of people."

A smile plays on the man's lips. Will sneaks up behind him and grabs him by the throat, but I put my hands out, "Stop!"

Will holds him tight as he struggles. He is nothing compared to Will.

I have a feeling about him and ask, "Are you a rebel?"

His eyes flash.

I decide to just go with it. We can kill him if we have to. I sigh and say, "I'm the vigilante."

He claws at Will's arm. Will releases him and gives me a look.

He looks at me intently, "I'm friends with Marshall."

I roll my eyes, "Well, he's a bastard, so that's not a good thing."

The man puts a hand up, "I haven't spoken to him in months. Last I heard, a vigilante from his camps was taking down those disgusting farms."

He turns and faces Will and they both laugh and hug. I don't understand.

"Al, what the hell? How did you end up here?"

The man shakes his head, "It's the best way to sabotage, from inside."

"You two know each other?" I ask.

They nod together, "Allan here, used to work the farm I was at."

Al patted him on his back, "He was, by far, the worst inmate, ever."

Will's face grows serious, "My sister is here somewhere with Bernie."

Allan grimaces, "Bernie, that little shit? Oh God."

My stomach sinks.

Al walks away from us to the door, "Up two floors. You'll need weapons."

I pull my gun. He looks at me, "You really are the vigilante?"

I nod, "I guess. They call me that."

"The Phoenix girl?"

I scowl, "No. That flashy crow thing is not for me. I just want to stop them." I don't say my dad but Will does.

"Michael is her father."

Al winces, "Oh. I'm sorry."

I frown, "For what?"

He shakes his head, "Your father is a very bad man. Was he always evil?"

I shrug, "I think so. My mom ran with me when I was little." I lie and flash Will a look. I don't know this man. I don't want him to know I'm a Gen baby.

Will shakes his head. We enter the stairwell again. The dim lights are a welcome sight, compared to the constantly-changing ones in the labs.

We climb the stairs as Al whispers, "Bernie has been allowed to come and go. We all figure he has something Michael wants. He is allowed a truck and a house on the outside. No one is allowed that. He's up Michael's ass all the time. If he has your sister, she might be...gone."

I shudder and push harder up the stairs. "This level is guarded. It's Michael's personal lab."

I crack the door and peek. There are lights on in several areas. "At least four of them moving in there," I whisper.

"Go to the right... me and Al will go left," Will whispers.

I look back at him. His eyes tell me what I want to see; he's watching Allan just in case.

I sneak into the lab, hating the stupid flashing lights above me. Whoever thought of it, was an idiot.

I swerve to the right and watch. No one notices the lights coming on. I've noticed this about them all. They've gotten so accustomed to the lights that they don't pay attention to them. They move around, making the lights move with them, like spotlights.

I see the ceiling lighting up to the left where Al and Will are walking. I peek around a desk to see Bernie. He's bent over a book. I stand up and tuck the gun in my back pocket. I walk to him like I'm supposed to be here.

He looks up; his face loses all its color.

I know the look on my face is scary. I can feel the rage simmering under my skin. I have an urge to pull the gun and fire, but I don't. I watch his face.

He looks around, putting a hand up. I stop. He gets up, bringing the book with him. I stand next to a large shelf of books.

He whispers when he gets close, "What are you doing?"

I growl, "We want her now."

I see something on his face that I want to smash off of it. He swallows, "She is in the back lab, with your dad."

I grab his shirt, pulling his face down closer to mine, "I will kill you, without making a fucking sound. Do you understand me?"

He winces, "She was really sick. He saved her but it took a lot. She isn't ready to be moved."

My fingers slide up to his throat. I grip tightly, "I am stronger than I look."

He swallows, I feel the lump of fear in his throat, "I swear she is okay. I wouldn't do anything to hurt her."

My lip twitches, "We met Allan. He doesn't seem to think you're what you say you are."

He shakes his sweaty face, "I swear, Em. I won't let them hurt her." I hear men talking. I step back into the shadows of the bookshelf. Bernie stands there shaking. The fear on his face worsens.

A voice from my past fills the air around us, "Bern, what's the solution? None of us can get her to tell us anything."

Fear fills his voice, "Not sure. I still think the fever cooked her brain; she has damage we can't see."

The man I can't see makes a humming noise, "I guess. There is that possibility. Well, she's your friend. What's the decision?" he sounds exactly like my father did. I should jump out, I should attack, but I'm scared. I don't move. I freeze like I used to before. I want to sneak away like a coward.

Bernie winks at me with the eye the man can't see, "I think I'll end her. She's a veg."

"Do it fast. I have someone bringing up a guy who is infected and hasn't had a fever yet, at all. No fever and no sickness. He's been incubated for seven days and nothing. They found him on the road in, bite marks and all. You want in on this one?"

Bernie twitches his head, "No. I'm going to take her and bury her. I know where her family was buried."

"Okay. Goodnight."

Bernie nods, "Night, Michael."

My heartbeat picks up. His voice and way of speaking, is exactly the same as my dad's was. I'm frozen. I turn and watch the lights flash as the person walks to the door. Another set of lights do the same. They meet in the middle and leave together.

Bernie sighs, "We have to be fast. I've drugged the shit out of her. She can't talk anyway, but this is stopping her from using any of her muscles." He grins and wipes his face, "It's an old-fashioned date-rape drug."

I scowl.

He shrugs, "I never made it for that purpose. People took it to get high. I sold it in high school. It's how the CIA found me. I was in ninth grade, doing twelfth-grade courses and building a science lab in my basement."

He walks and I follow him. We meet up with Will and Al. Al gives Bernie a nod. They seem to dislike each other.

Will looks savage, "Where is she?"

Bernie shakes his head, "Calm down. You can spazz when we're out of the city." He scans a door and opens it. Anna is lying on the table in a white gown. Her legs and arms are tied to the table. She doesn't move at all.

I claw at the restraints. Will scoops her up, hugging her tightly to his body.

We turn and run from the room. I take his gun and move slightly, except of course for the lights. I look back at Bernie, "Stupid lights!"

He shakes his head and sighs. We get to the stairwell but Al points, "Let's take the ones on the other side. No one uses them."

We run after him and start down the stairs.

"I can't believe you've had her for a week. What the fuck, Bern?"

His voice is high pitch, "I had no choice." I think he's lying. I'm going to gut him when we are out of the city.

We enter a hall I never saw before. Al leads us. The lights flash above, making me agro. The warm summer air hits us like a wall, as we leave the building through a side door. Will breaks into a run through the alley. When he gets to a dark corner he stops. I'm surveying constantly.

"Al, go with Bernie and get the truck. We'll wait here," Will growls. He bends and looks at his sister, "What's wrong with her?"

Bernie shakes his head, "She's drugged. I secretly was drugging her. It comes across as brain damage but it's the drugs."

Will scowls, "They don't check for drugs in her blood."

He shakes his head, "Only the first day they have her. They ran it but her fever was still really high. I started drugging her as the fever broke."

Will nods, "Hurry up."

I brush her hair out of her face, "He said she can't talk at all."

Will frowns, "At all?"

I shake my head, "It probably destroyed her voice box, like it does to the infected."

He kisses her forehead, "I hope that's all that's wrong with her."

I look around, "Security is loose here."

He nods, "I know. They're cocky and relaxed. They think the walls and the guards keep them safe."

I tap my foot, "It would be easy to destroy it."

"Yup."

I squat next to him in the dark and wait.

When I hear a truck, I go look. Bernie grins at me from the driver's seat. Al hops out and opens the door. We climb in fast and head for the guards with Anna on the floor of the truck, under Will's and my feet.

Chapter Fifteen

On the tenth whistle, he comes running out of the woods. I put my hands on my hips and he drops the rabbit in his lips.

He jumps into the back of the truck. I climb back there and sit with my back against the back window. The wind in my hair and his fur in my fingers makes me feel like things might be all right again.

I'm scared that we'll get to Bernie's and Jake and Star will be dead or gone, taken. I'm scared a lot now. My 'us' is too big and I can't keep them all safe. I lean on Leo and remember how easy it was when he was my 'us'.

When we get there, my worst fears come true—Bernie's house is ransacked.

He drops to his knees when he sees it. Anna is still sleeping in the backseat of the truck. I run throughout the house. Every drawer is pulled, every bit of furniture is sliced and pulled apart. It looks like the raids that used to happen in the beginning, when people's houses still had things. It happens less now; everything has either been blown up or picked apart.

Bernie rocks back and forth. I see the millions of things floating by in his eyes. He looks at me and I see it. The blame.

"Where is the shelter?" I ask.

He wants to tell me to go screw myself—I see it in his eyes. Instead, he points at the kitchen, "The cupboard beside the fridge has a latch inside of it. It opens a door."

I run there. I open the cupboard and feel around. The latch is well hidden. I press it and release the cupboard. I run down the stairs. My throat pulsates like my heart is beating in there.

I bang on the steel door at the bottom, "Jake! Star!"

I bang and cry out again, "Guys! It's Emma!" Leo is next to me clawing at the door.

It opens with a hard bang and a loud creak. Jake looks confused, "Are they gone?"

I nod, "I guess. Who was it?"

He swallows, "Marshall." He hands me my bow.

"He's awake?"

Jake nods, "Yeah. And apparently he followed Star here once or twice. He knew exactly how to get here. He called for us all. He had military men with him."

Star looks scared, "Is my brother with you?"

I nod. She smiles, "Is Anna okay?"

I shake my head and turn and run up the stairs. Bernie is still crying about his house. He's annoying me to the point, I want to kill him. I grip my bow and storm to the truck.

Will is circling the house, "No one is here."

I look at the woods, "It's Marshall and the military."

Al shakes his head, "He would never."

I snarl, "NOT EVEN FOR A FREE PASS TO LIVE IN THE CITY WITH HIS DIABETES?"

He stops, "I don't know about that."

I stomp around, pacing, "What if he knows about my cabin? What if Sarah, Meg and Mary are in danger? What if he sold out everyone at the camps?" I point at Allan, "What if he told them, where we were going?"

Will grabs my arm, shaking me, "STOP! THAT DOESN'T EVEN MAKE SENSE!"

I jerk free, "YOU STOP! I'M NOT GOING BACK TO SPOKANE!"

"YOU DRIVE ME INSANE SOMETIMES!"

I glare at him, "LIKEWISE!"

He runs his hands through his hair roughly and takes deep breaths, "The camps are probably in danger. There isn't anything we can do about that. Not right now. The cabin is, more than likely, fine."

Leo is back and nudging me. He whines. I look at Anna sitting up in the backseat. She waves, but her eyes are almost dead inside. She looks sick still.

I jump at her. She wraps around me as Will wraps around us. Jake comes running out shouting, Anna!" He attacks too. I'm being squished into her. She shakes but no sounds come from her, not even the weird squeak.

She gives me a look.

I kiss her cheek, "I'm sorry." She shakes her head.

We all step back to give her air and Jake scoops her up. She hugs him tight, as silent tears slip down her cheeks. I can't believe she's alive. I don't even care how alive, which is selfish.

Leo jumps on Jake, wrapping his paws around her.

She struggles from Jake and lets Leo fully hug her.

"That's a very unique animal, Lainy."

I glance at Al and smile, "My name is Emma."

He frowns, "Oh."

Will gives me a shitty look. I return it, "What's the plan?"

He shakes his head. "I don't know. Do we risk going to the cabin, and leading them there, or do we head to a camp, and try to get as many people as we can? Or do we just take the city the way we are, with whatever bombs we can get Bernie to make?"

I scratch my head, "I don't know. But we can't stay here."

Will grins bitterly, "Guess it's the stars for us tonight?"

I nod and head inside to find salvageable items.

Bernie sits in the backseat with Leo and me as we drive away from his beautiful mansion.

I glance at him and shrug, "I know how your feel."

He gives me a blank stare.

I nod, "I do. I was once faced with a similar choice with them... I helped them and my whole world has fallen apart."

He sighs, "I guess you do then. At least everyone is still alive."

I look back through the window at the ghostly girl in the white nightgown, who used to be my best friend, and nod. It doesn't feel like she is though.

We drive to the base of the mountain where the farmhouse is, and start the hike into the woods. Bernie looks back at the truck and makes a moan.

Will pats him on the back.

Jake carries Anna.

I look out at the broken-down vehicles and rubble, "My dad is down there somewhere." The mountainside we are on, is the hill I ran. Flashes of the branches hitting me in the face and screams trapped in my throat fly through my mind.

I look at bones of the cars and turn away.

Will takes my hand in his, pulling me up the hill.

Gripping to him feels like he's an anchor for me, grounding me to this life. I should be grateful for this moment; Anna is alive, Jake is alive and giving Star his charming smile, and Will is holding my hand, giving me more than he can imagine. More than I ever imagined, I would have.

Leo gives me a look. I smirk and pass my gun to Will. I pull my quiver and bow and run up ahead with him. We move through the woods like always. Listening to the sounds of the creatures—the sounds they give for the warnings.

We make it to the meadow that is right below the farmhouse, and stop. I look around as Leo does his rounds. He circles back and I see his ears twitch. They don't go back. He doesn't look worried.

He looks content. He smells the familiarity of home and the peace that we have found in the hills surrounding us.

The others make their way to where I am sitting on a log, listening to the birds.

Will smiles, "You look familiar."

I frown at him, "What does that mean?"

He shakes his head, "I haven't seen this girl in a while. The girl who looks content."

I glance at Jake and smirk, "Your family has a way of taking away my peace."

Jake shakes his head, "You need to get over that."

I laugh, "no."

Star looks confused.

I give Bernie a smile, "Welcome to my world."

His lip twitches in disgust, "Where are we sleeping? When do we stop walking? My feet are killing me."

Will laughs, "You city folk have it pretty cushy."

Al gives him a look, "You liked it cushy, if I remember correctly."

Will's eyes sparkle, "That was a long time ago. I have preferred the company of nature over mankind for a while now."

I roll my eyes, "He still prefers the tent to the stars."

Anna holds herself and staggers to where I am sitting.

"How are you?"

She shakes her head.

"Dizzy still?" I ask.

She nods. She gives me a look and my heart breaks. I wrap an arm around her. Bernie's dark eyes look broken too.

Al looks confused.

We are a sad group of people. Star hands out food and water from the packs. I take a packaged bar from her. I haven't had packaged food in a while.

The crinkle of opening it makes me remember the snacks I used to have in my lunch at school.

Anna opens hers and takes a bite. She swallows and I can see it takes effort for her. I grab a drink and pass it to her. She smiles faintly.

I'm angry.

I realize it, as the light hits her blue eyes, and I still see the faint pink in the white. I'm savagely angry. I'm going to kill things in a rough, bad way. I can't let it go. My hands vibrate when I think about his voice. It was there. I had a gun and it was so close and I let it scare me. I am still the coward who turns her back.

I eat my bar and watch her, to make sure she doesn't choke. There will be vengeance. I decide this, in between bites and watching her swallow.

Chapter Sixteen

The farmhouse looks the same. Anna looks happy when she sees it. I walk past the old, brown bloodstain on the siding and smile. I never cleaned it off, because it reminded me of how close I came too many times.

I open the hatch and grin. I grab the pants, shirts and boots I have stored. I take them and walk to Anna. I grab her hand and pull her inside where Will has cleared.

We change in a musty bedroom. She is skin and bone.

I stomp my feet and grin, "The boots fit finally."

She laughs silently. She nods and stomps her feet. She gives me a thumbs up.

When we leave the room, Leo finds his way to her. He stays close. I noticed it on the way up the hill. He scouted ahead and circled back, rubbing against her dangling feet. She runs her hands into his fur.

I swallow the bad feelings and thoughts.

We settle in, with Anna sleeping on the couch and Jake and Star making dinner. I sit in the hayloft with the shotgun.

It starts to feel normal as the sun sets and I hear the crickets. There are more this summer than last. Everything is healing. It's taken the decade, he sad it would. The lack of rain and the dead zones changed the way nature worked.

But now in the dark of the night, I can hear the dry wheat sway back and forth, scratching against itself. I can hear the few crickets singing in the field.

I hear footsteps crunching on the gravel between the house and barn. I look to see Will crossing the space. He comes up the stairs almost silently.

"Hey."

I look over, "Hey."

He sits beside me, watching out over the dark fields.

"How's it going out here?" he asks.

I frown, "Fine."

He reaches over, taking my hand in his. He strokes the palm of my hand with his thumb. I swallow hard as he kneads.

He leans over, kissing my neck. My lips instantly part, making my breath join the sound of the quiet night.

He kisses gently and tugs at the buttons on my blouse. I want to protest but I don't. I let him unbutton my shirt. The way he touches me is soft, delicate. I recall him being rough with me earlier and pull away.

"I have to watch the field."

He whispers in my ear, "I want you."

I shake my head and jerk away. I start doing the buttons up again.

"What's wrong?"

I turn away slightly, "You were an asshole to me earlier and I forgot till now."

He chuckles quietly, "You can't be mad about something that happened earlier. That's against the rules."

I shrug, "I already told you, I don't need you, Will."

"But you want me."

I look back, "Not when you're a jerk. You shook me again. You said you wouldn't do that again."

He points, "You were gonna lose it and kill someone. I saw that look."

I sneer, "I was fine."

"Liar."

I don't care. I'm not letting him touch me.

"I'm sorry for shaking you."

I shrug, "You're sorry because you want sex."

He sighs and gets up, "I'm not going to get into this whole 'ugh me caveman' who only wants sex. If that's what you think of me, then I don't want to be around you." He leaves and I'm the bad guy, again.

I shake my head and hate how he manages to always make me the one who's to blame.

The night is silent. Leo comes up after a while and curls into me. Halfway through, Jake comes and takes over. I don't trust him with the watch, so I sleep in the hay as he holds the gun.

I lay close to him and Leo.

When the dawn comes Leo stirs, waking me. I look over at Jake passed out with the gun in his hands. I sigh and take it. I listen to the wind and look out over the field and grounds. There is nothing.

I tiptoe down the stars to the ground floor. I jump when I see Will leaning against the door to the barn.

He glances at me and smirks, "Have a good sleep?"

I whisper, "He was on duty, not me. It was my turn to sleep."

He nods, "Okay."

I frown and walk past him. He grabs my arms but this time it's gentle. He steps to me instead of dragging me to him. He looms over me and tilts my chin back, "I love you. I am sorry I hurt you. I get scared when you get that irrational look in your eyes."

My brow knits together and I want to deny the irrational, but I know there have been times I could have taken a different path. The doctor I shot for just touching the leg of the young girl, is first in my mind. He might have been soothing her. I know that, but at the time my brain was fired and in its cold zone.

"I am sorry," he says again and brushes his lips against mine softly.

I pull back, "Did you stay up all night or do we have to check the grounds?"

He laughs, "I know, I know, you love me too and you really can't wait to get my clothes off." He kisses me again, "I stayed up all night. Your watch and his." He grabs my hand and pulls me to the house. When he gets to the door he shouts up, "Wakey, wakey, Jakey the snakey."

Jake sits up fast. His hands are still shaped like they're holding the gun. He rubs his eyes, "What the heck? I wasn't sleeping."

We both laugh. Even Leo rolls his eyes.

Jake frowns, "Shit."

Will nods at him, "Keep watch this morning, okay?"

Jake nods and yawns.

Will pulls me inside, to the only empty bedroom, and closes the door.

He crawls into the bed and kicks his boots off. I climb into the bed with him and close my eyes. He makes our cocoon and we both fall asleep instantly.

I wake to the sound of the house. Jake is telling a story loudly and Star is giggling. Will doesn't open his eyes, but he kisses my forehead. I lean into the kiss and smile when I feel his fingers at the buttons on my shirt again.

This time I let him unbutton it all the way. His mouth leaves warm kisses the entire length of my torso. I slide my hands into his thick hair. I love the feel of him. He pulls his shirt off, pressing our naked skin against each other. I wrap my legs around his waist, holding on too tight.

He rolls so I am on top of him, my hair falls around us, like we're in our own cave. He tucks it behind my ears and looks at me, like it's the first time he's ever seen me before. I smile and lean forward to kiss him.

Chapter Seventeen

The hike to the cabin is intense; the incline is steeper. Bernie bitches the entire way about his blisters and Anna is too exhausted for us to hurry. Leo and I stay behind, guarding them—hoping nothing follows us into the hills.

They reach the cabin but we stay behind, to watch. I sit in a tree and Leo stays below. He paces and looks around at first, and then settles into his silent-wolf mode. It's creepy.

Nothing moves beyond the woodland creatures. The song of the forest is amazing and constant. In the middle of the night, I climb down, and we make the silent trip to the cabin—the long way. We pass the hole in the earth and I can't fight the smile. It's the hole that started it all.

Leo stalks silently.

When we reach the cabin, I see the glisten of his eyes in the moonlight. I speak in a low tone, "Hey."

I can hear the smile, even in his whisper, "Hey yourself."

When I reach him, he kisses me softly, "Anything?"

I shake my head.

He nods, "Good. Go get some sleep."

I pass him my bow and arrows.

He scoffs, "You might as well just bring them. I can't use them nearly as well."

I shrug and head inside. The couches and floors are filled with people. The cabin is busting at the seams. I don't even want to think about how the well water is going to take this level of consumption. I head into the room with beds, only to find mine has a sprawled-out eleven-year-old. I kick my boots off and climb into the bed next to her. She wraps around me, choking me with heat. I smile and close my eyes.

The sleep is familiar and relaxing. I haven't had many of them. The ones I did have were with Will. I open my eyes to Meg and Anna sleeping next to each other and Leo on the floor. Anna's hand is draped off the bed, touching his fur. He opens one yellow eye, watching me. I smile at him.

Anna wakes up and looks at me. She whispers, "You okay?"

I shake my head, "I will be. You?"

She shakes her head too, "No."

"What did they do to you for the week?"

Her eyes twitch, "Tests. Tons of tests."

"Did they hurt you?"

She shakes her head, "Bernie wouldn't let them hurt me."

I swallow, "Did they want to?"

She nods once slowly, "The head guy did. He wanted to do experiments. He wanted to try things that Bernie kept saying no to. Bernie lied and said I was his girlfriend. The head guy thought I was too young for him, but Bernie lied and said I was twenty-three."

"That's good."

She nods, "You and Will—all the way, huh?" She changes the subject. I don't blame her. I'm pretty sure that head guy was my real dad.

I smile, "All the way."

She shrugs, "I always was rooting for Jake."

"Me too."

She looks into my eyes, like she is trying to tell me something important, "You don't know where you'll find love, but it's almost always going to be, the last place you think it'll be."

I cock an eyebrow, "Did you read that somewhere?"

She beams, "I read it in one of your Granny's romance novels that were on the shelf you told me to start with."

I laugh quietly and whisper, "I meant the survival books."

She wrinkles her nose, "Those were boring."

I laugh again, I love you."

She rolls her eyes, "Even though my family ruins your life?"

I nod, "Even though."

She leans forward and whispers even quieter, "Weird about Star and Jake, huh?"

"Very weird. They suit each other though."

She gives me a funny look, "She said you guys are sisters."

I nod, "That is the weirdest part for me."

She winks, "I hope you guys fight for real. Two badass sisters with foul tempers and hardcore strength. No sissy slaps like back at Bernie's."

I laugh, "No way."

Anna climbs out of the bed, making Meg stir and moan. I climb out of the bed too. My feet are a bit sore from breaking in the new boots.

I follow her into the living room. Allan looks at me from in the front window, "Some cabin."

I watch his eyes follow Anna as she stretches, "Belonged to my Granny and Gramps and Dad. They bought it when I was a kid. Dad was always planning on coming here when the meltdown happened."

He looks out the window, "Seems like a smart idea. He must have known then?"

I nod, "I think he might have. He had a friend who worked for my other dad." I don't even want to attempt explaining them all. I don't honestly feel like I've ever had a proper explanation. I tug on my boots and head to the front door. I look back at Anna, "Make a huge pot of oats."

She nods.

Allan stands, "I can help her."

I shake my head, "No. You can come with me."

He looks confused but follows me out. I whistle for Leo.

He comes trotting out.

We walk into the front yard. As the door closes, I pick up my bow and quiver and tuck my knife into my boot.

"You really are the vigilante, aren't you?"

I look back, "Why do you keep saying that?" He gives me the creeps. I have given him the benefit of the doubt for Will's sake, but I don't like him.

His dark-brown eyes watch me, "No reason. Just amazing there is a vigilante who is a little girl like you."

I frown, "I'm not so little, trust me."

He follows me into the woods. Leo senses my shitty mood and stays close.

"How did you come across such a magnificent animal?"

I shrug and walk into the forest, "I don't know, luck I guess."

Leo lifts a lip. I snort, "He hates you."

He chuckles.

I turn around and face him, "Animals are a good judge of character."

His bushy, dark eyebrows lower, "What is that supposed to mean?"

I step towards him, "I see the way you eye up Anna."

He shrugs, "She's a beautiful girl."

My hand twitches with the want to choke the life out of him, "She's seventeen, so she's an actual girl."

He scowls, "Oh. I thought she was twenty-something."

Disgust creeps across my face "How old are you?"

"Thirty-eight."

He looks forty-five. His dark hair is greasy and thinning. His thin face is sweaty and wrinkled, like he was fat before and his skin hangs a bit from the weight loss.

I make sure we are eye to eye when I speak to him, "This is your warning. I kill perverts. I kill them every day of the week. Ones bigger than you and stronger than you and meaner than you. If I even suspect you're a pervert, I won't give you another warning. This is the one you get." I point back towards the cabin and use Will's words from the camp, "This isn't a democracy. I know it looks like one, but that's my cabin. I will kill you in a heartbeat."

He flinches and backs up, "Hey..."

"No. You don't talk. You just hear me." Leo steps towards him and growls.

He swallows and nods, "Okay." I see it in his dark eyes, he wants me dead. He wants my cabin and the people who are there. The people I call family.

Ron comes walking up, "Hey, Em." He smiles and waves.

I smile back, "Hey, Ron. Allan was just going to collect firewood. Why don't you escort him and show him the ropes?"

His smile grows, "Welcome, Allan. It's just this way." He points and starts walking.

I turn to see Leo nuzzled against Will, who is leaned against a tree.

He looks angry.

I point, "He..."

"I trust you. I trust your instincts. If you say he eyeballed Anna, I trust that."

I walk to him and let him wrap his arms around me "I just don't want to act like a crazy psycho. I feel like my feelings are all wrong. I thought that about Bernie, but he was kinda grossed out when I told him how old Anna was. He assumed she was closer to my age."

Will pulls me back, grinning like a fool, "You admit you were wrong about him?"

I sneer, "He's a whiny little bitch most of the time," I sigh, "But yeah, I was wrong. He isn't a pervert. Not all guys are perverts I guess."

Will nods towards Allan, "Allan's a lot older than Bernie is. He's old enough to be Anna's dad. Not cool." His eyes narrow.

I smirk, "You made me bring him up this damned hill. He knows the way to the cabin."

Will speaks over my head, "I don't think we have to worry about him going down the mountain, Em. He looks at my sister again and I'll snap his neck myself." I see the dangerous glint in his eyes and nod.

I look back at Allan and Ron rounding the corner to the woodpile. Ron and Bernie both have turned out to be nice guys. I look back at Will and smile.

Will looks down on me, "You let me handle it though, okay?"

I agree, "Okay."

His smile turns mocking, "Look at my girl getting all civilized."

I pull back and walk away, "Ass."

His tone reflects the smile on his face, "Whatever you kill, make sure it's big. I am starved."

I pull an arrow and head to the sweet spot.

Meg finds me alone, sitting on the hillside listening. I barely hear her sneaking up on me, "You're so quiet, Meg. You need to teach Jake to do that."

She rolls her eyes, chewing on a piece of grass and plops down where I'm sitting. "He ain't never gonna learn how to be quiet."

I snort, "Yeah, I guess not."

She nudges me, "You all right then?"

I shake my head, "I hardly know." I look at her dirty face and frown, "How are you dirty already, it's morning?"

She sticks her tongue out, "I was chopping firewood. I gotta do something with all my extra energy. Ron is gonna be the death of me. I think I'm almost a virgin again."

I growl, "Stop talking like that."

She grins, testing me, "Why? It shouldn't bother you that you're a virgin and I ain't."

My cheeks flare instantly and I lower my gaze.

I see her jaw drop, "Oh, no way. You did it? Which one of them hunky brothers got the golden goose outta ya?"

My nose wrinkles, "Stop being disgusting about it."

She laughs and lies back, "I bet it was Will. That's who I would want. He's a real man. He'll take care of ya. I think Jake might only ever take care of one thing. Not that it's a problem, but a girl's gotta eat too, ya know?"

I cover my face with my hands and moan. I want to choke her but I don't. I breathe deeply, "You know, I can go through a lot of shit and still it doesn't feel as disturbing as a conversation with you."

She snickers and chews the grass. I listen to the woods and

glance at her after a minute, "You okay to stay if we leave again?"

She nods, "I don't trust Mary with Sarah."

I nod, "Me either."

Meg taps her foot, "You hear that?"

I strain my ears and shake my head.

"That's Jake and that bitch, Star, fighting."

I nudge her, "She's my sister."

She scowls, "No way."

I nod once.

She grimaces, "Sorry."

I shake my head, "I don't know her. I know she's different. I wanna feel bad for her for what she's been through, but I feel like she brings it on. Being all flakey and shit. She makes men think things, ya know?"

Meg points her piece of grass at me, "No means no, Em. A girl could walk through these hills naked as the day she was born, and no man has the right to take nothing. There ain't no way to act that gets you that kinda attention."

I feel bad for saying it. "I know. I shouldn't have said that. She just annoys me. She acts so sweet and dumb and I think she's thinking things."

She smacks my arm, "No, you shouldn't say that or hate her. She's your kin. I'm sorry for what I said."

I sigh, "Don't be."

The ground cracks behind us. I see the little, blonde head and bright-blue eyes and smile instantly.

Sarah walks up and sits next to us. She leans into me, "I missed you guys."

Leo makes his way over and curls up next to her. She rubs her small hands into his thick fur.

"You okay?" I ask.

She nods, "Mary is kinda mean. She doesn't like me or Meg much."

I look at Meg who shrugs, "She ain't no meaner than my momma was."

I raise my eyebrows and look at Sarah. She nods and gives me a knowing look.

"Ill talk to her." I mutter.

Meg sighs, "Don't do that. It'll only make her meaner. If she gets outta hand I'll knock her around a little, when no one else is around."

I laugh. Sarah looks hopeful, "You should. Beat her little brat too."

Meg points her grass at me again, "That little bastard is evil. God forgive me for hating a child but that there is Satan reincarnated."

I laugh harder. Leo raises his head, giving us a look.

Meg nods at him, "Leo knows. That kid's a little shit."

Sarah sighs, "She got mad at me a couple days ago 'cause he hit me and I hit him back." I notice the way she is talking, is starting to sound like Meg. I take her hand in mine and squeeze, "She touches you again, you get Meg. This is our cabin, not hers. She's a guest."

Sarah gives me a smile and looks past me to Meg. Her smile turns to a slightly-evil grin. It looks like Meg's.

I sigh, "I gotta shoot something. You two gotta be quiet now, okay?"

Sarah stands and dusts her patchwork pants off, "I'm gonna go. I need a drink."

Meg gets up too, "Me too. See ya back there, golden goose." She nudges me and saunters off. I could swat her.

They leave and I get my wish, the one I've had for a long time. I pull an arrow and I take a deep breath, waiting for the sound I need to hear. Leo crouches low and pants softly. The wind is on my face, the air is fresh and clean and Leo is by my side.

I smile down at him and take in a slow, but deep lungful of the clean, forest air.

"If I die in this moment, Leo, it'll be okay," I mutter.

Leo half closes his yellow eyes. I crouch down with him and run my fingers through the fur on his head. We listen as birds chirp and squirrels fight.

It's silent bliss until I hear the sound I want. I stand slowly and pull back the arrow. I spot a huge, colorful male pheasant. Instantly, my leg burns where I got shot a few months before. I take deep slow breaths, sighting him in.

He moves through the woods slowly. I plan his next step and release. The arrow slices through the base of his throat. He thrashes and drops.

I walk over and grab him by the feet. Leo sniffs him. I step on the wings and pull the feet. His skin and wings suction from him. I gut his belly and cut his feet off. He's a big boy. I glance at the quill scars I still have on my hands and arms and chest. I shake my head and start back to the cabin. I leave the remains in the woods, like always.

Leo sniffs them but when he sees my face he stops and pounces about the forest after me. I get back to the cabin to find them laughing. The outdoor cookstove is going. Anna was smart enough not to cook in the cabin.

Jake sees the pheasant and grins, "You killed it with your bare hands?"

Will smiles, "You know her, she probably sweet talked it into coming to her."

I roll my eyes.

Star comes and takes it, "I'm pretty good at cooking them."

I nod and let her take it, "Okay." I see Meg eyeballing her and grin.

Star takes it inside to start prepping it. Meg glares at Jake, "Go help her find the pots and shit."

He jumps up, "When did you get all saucy?" I catch a glimpse of a slight limp as he walks inside. Whenever he gets up fast, it's there.

I shout after him, "She's in charge here, when I'm not here."

He looks at me from the door and grins, "She's exactly like you. You, she and Anna are like the same hateful girl."

I toss a stick at him as he ducks inside and closes the door.

Meg gives me a look.

I wash up with the bucket of water there and take a bowl of oats from Sarah who is helping Anna. I wink at Sarah. She tries to wink back but fails and blinks both eyes.

I point at her pants, "Who sewed those?"

She sighs, "Me. Meg is making me read everyday and do math and learn to sew. She made me chop wood the other day."

I nod, "Good."

Mary gives me a look. I point at Andy, "He should be doing the same. We learn faster than regular kids."

Mary smiles, "I have been teaching him things." She is getting on my last nerve.

I take my cereal and glance back at Anna who looks worn, but I think it's the best I've seen her look, "Thanks."

She nods at me.

I sit on the circle of log seats they've made outside, and blow on my spoonful. I catch a look from Allan. He looks down at his cereal when he sees me notice.

Will sits next to me, "You still want it, don't you? Your revenge," he says quietly.

I take the bite, "Yup. More than before."

"Should we go to the camp? Ask for help?" he asks.

I swallow and blow on the next bite, "They believe Marshall. They don't like me."

His eyes twinkle as he speaks, again in a hushed tone, "Yeah, but they love your sister, Star."

I sigh. He grins. He is loving the idea that I have to ask her for help, and that I have misjudged her and Bernie. I think he loves it when I'm wrong.

I glance at Allan, "He comes with us."

He nods, "Yup."

I catch Anna's eye on me. She is trying to tell me something with her stare, but I don't know what it is. I get up and carry my bowl over to her.

She whispers, "I'm coming with you."

I shake my head and whisper back, "You can't."

She laughs, "Why are you whispering?"

I shrug.

"I am coming with you."

I frown, "Why?"

Her eyes dart, "I want to see him die."

I scowl, "Who?"

She looks up at me and I see a fire in her eyes, like nothing I've seen before, "Marshall."

I don't want to argue with her. She looks scary. I just agree, "Fine, but we can't leave till you're healthy."

She nods, "Me, you, Bernie, and Will." She glances back at the house, "Jake stays with the kids."

I look around, "Star has to come. We need her to convince the camp to help. And I'm not leaving Allan here."

She looks at him and nods, "He's creepy."

"Yeah."

I look down at the cereal, "You better eat up. If you don't gain some strength back, you're not coming."

She raises her eyebrows defiantly, "We'll see."

Chapter Eighteen

She comes. As usual she is feisty and mean, even with only a whisper, and forces her way on it. Will doesn't argue with her since she got sick. He hates listening to her whisper/yell. I snicker watching the display. He feels bad and gives in.

The group of us walking to the retreat is bigger than it needs be. Bernie comes because Anna and Star are coming. Jake comes for the same reason. Allan comes because I don't want him alone with Mary and the kids. Leo stayed behind. Meg hugged him and squeezed him and begged him to stay. As much as I don't like leaving him behind, I'm glad he's with Mary and the kids.

He looked pissed and I don't imagine it will be long before I see his sloppy face again. He won't stay long at the cabin without me.

We get to the border where the guards are.

Will whistles and the guard whistles back.

"Hey, Will!" he shouts down.

Will waves, "Hey!"

I snarl. I'm still the savage they ran out of town, in my mind.

We get into the camp and immediately two things happen. Star gets hugs and I get scowls.

Jake nudges me, "You're like the evil stepsister."

I growl at him. He laughs and rubs my head.

One of the women comes to me smiling, "How are you, Em?"

I know she's one of the breeder moms. She is towing a little monster with her. He shrieks.

I smile weakly, "Good."

She looks over at Will, who is bossing everyone about, and blushes, "Has he settled with anyone? I heard he was single still and I knew you guys were friends."

I feel a blush creeping up my face. She is so beautiful and I would slap her normally just for saying it. But the screaming kid makes me shake my head and plant an evil smile on my face, "No. No and he loves kids."

Jake coughs.

She beams at us both, "Oh really? Do you think he remembers me?"

Jake nods, "He does. I'm sure he does."

Anna watches us with a horrified look on her face. The girl turns, "Thanks, Em."

I nod and fight the evil grin crossing my lips.

Anna pokes me. I give her a look, "Hey. He gets crabby sometimes. He deserves this."

She shakes her head and walks away. Jake laughs, "You do have a sense of humor."

I point at the girl walking up to Will, "You know he's going to think I'm gonna get all jealous too."

Jake stays close to me, as Will answers questions and greets people with Star.

"You know they really were made for each other," Jake says quietly.

Seeing the way she's soft and sweet and making everyone comfortable and he's gruff and firm but they respect him, makes me agree.

I look up into Jake's blue eyes and smile at the way they twinkle.

He smirks, "One day you'll see that me and you are the better fit."

I scowl, "You're with Star."

"No one is really with Star. It's like saying you're with Will. No one can own something that magnanimous."

I don't know what that word means. I almost wonder if he knows what he's saying.

"They're bigger than one person. Look at her, she's smiling and flirting and being friendly. She is making that whole group of people happy. She's like the Mother-somebody from before. The nun who went around and healed the sick and fed them and shit."

I shrug, "I don't know. I'm not Catholic."

He rolls his eyes, "Everyone knew who she was."

I start ignoring his talk and notice the faces of the people talking with Will. Their eyes dart at me. He crosses his arms. He's getting angry. His hands are in fists. Suddenly Star shows up and smiles and touches their hands and Will's. She shakes her head and they start seeing what she's saying.

"Do you think they're talking about me?" I ask nervously.

Jake nods, "Oh, hell yes." He watches too. Allan is gone. I cuss under my breath and look around for him.

Bernie is gone too.

I sigh and see Anna next to Will and Star. She has the same outgoing personality as Star, but the sense of Will.

I look at Jake, "We gotta find Bernie and Allan."

He points, "Bernie is over there. He's talking to a guy on the other side of Will. Looks like he's in on the cause."

He scans the tents and trees and points after a minute, "Allan is over there. He's chatting up a lady with a baby."

I stand on my tiptoes and watch him talking to her. She looks mid twenties.

Jake makes a face, "Ewww, he's trying to pick up. She has a baby. What the hell?"

I laugh and point to the path, "Wanna go swimming?"

He nods and we walk away. We get to the bottom of the path and the flat rock, and my stomach hurts like I'm doing something wrong. The guilty feeling is back. I look over at Jake taking his shirt off and shake off the feeling.

"Turn around." He does and I pull my pants, shirt and boots off and jump in, in my underwear. The water feels amazing.

The sun is setting but the heat of the day is still there. It never really goes away.

"The water is warmer," he says.

I ignore him and paddle about. The water is the cleanest feeling I get.

Jake splashes me. I splash him back.

He lunges at me and dunks me. I kick at him and scramble to swim away. He grabs my foot and drags me back.

I come up for air, to see Will standing on the flat rock. Jake dunks me again. The guilty feeling comes back instantly.

I kick Jake hard and come up for air. Jake comes up and wraps his arms around my bare chest. He drags me down into the water, growling like a bear. I see the water stir up and know Will has dove in. I come up for air. Jake is laughing. I look around, "Did Will get in?"

He wipes his face, "I didn't see him."

My breath feels too loud, like I should be still and wait for Will to surface. I don't see him though.

"Did he jump in?"

Jake shakes his head, "I didn't see him."

"I saw him at the shore and then the water stirred. Do you think he's holding his breath?" Panic starts to fill my voice.

"Not this long." We swim to the edge of the pool but there is nothing but our clothes and the flat rock.

I look at him, "Do you think he thought something?"

He frowns, "We were swimming. We weren't doing anything."

He's close to me, too close. I look down at my breasts and shake my head, "Look away. I'm going to get out."

He turns his face in the other direction. I climb out and pull on my shirt. The dark t-shirt covers me. When I pull my pants up, I see him watching. I point, "I said look away."

He laughs, "You took too long."

I narrow my gaze, "Hurry up. It's getting dark and the teenagers come to mess around when the sun goes down."

He shrugs, "Maybe I wanna mess around."

I throw my arms in the air, "What's your deal? You're messing around with Star already."

He laughs, "You don't even like her."

I shake my head, "That's not fair. I don't even know her. It doesn't matter, she's my sister and your brother and I are... well you know."

He splashes water at me, "What, Em? What are you two?"

"He's my boyfriend, I think."

He laughs, "I love how weird you are."

I turn and leave him there. I stomp up the path. I get halfway when Will walks down to meet me. He still looks angry. I swallow, "Hey."

He folds his arms across his huge chest, "You sent a lady with a baby to hit on me, so you could sneak off and skinny dip with my brother?"

My jaw drops. I realize how the two look like they could be related. A nervous giggle leaves my lips, "It's not what it looks like."

Jakes comes up the trail behind me. I could hear him from a mile. He stands too close, dripping wet still. Will's eyes lift to meet him directly behind me.

"What are you doing?" he asks Jake.

"Having a swim, trying to tempt your girlfriend to wrestle naked with me. You know, regular shit." The tone in Jake's voice is mocking. He's angry about something.

Will clenches his jaw, "Why don't you go see where your girlfriend is?"

"Why, you want to fuck her again?"

Will's face flinches. Jake nudges me as he walks past us. My heartbeat rages inside of me. I can see the truth on his face.

I take a step back.

He doesn't move.

"Oh my God," I feel instantly sick.

He shakes his head back and forth.

"When?"

He looks sick.

I feel hot tears flooding my eyes, "Oh God, it was since we met, wasn't it?"

I give him a wide birth but he grabs my arm, "Baby, it's not what you think."

I rip my arm from his grip but he grabs me hard. I slip, dropping my boots and bow and quiver. I drop to my knees in the dirt.

I see his hands shaking. He wants to grab me and shake me and make me listen but he doesn't. He drops to his knees too and starts picking up my stuff.

"It was when you were at the breeder farm," his voice is hollow.

I shake my head and plug my ears with my dirty fingers, "I don't want to know."

He grabs my hand roughly, "It was a mistake. I knew it then. I drank way too much. I thought you were gone forever. It was a mistake. I never imagined in a million years, you would get out. I knew you wouldn't leave without Anna. I've seen inside of those places. I knew what I was sending you there for. I let you go there so my baby sister wouldn't die alone."

I shake my hands from his, "But you lied."

When he talks it looks like his words taste bad, "I never wanted to do it. I was sleeping in my tent and she came. I never wanted her like that. I felt sick after what I'd seen done to her at the farms, and I did the same thing. I used her. I never loved her. It makes me sick."

"But you lied. You lied about having sex, with my sister." The words taste bad for me too.

He looks down, shaking his head, "I didn't think you'd understand."

I grab my quiver and bow and boots roughly, "Well I don't."

He looks up, "Babe, don't leave me. Please."

I scowl at him, "I need you to finish the job I have to do. I can't leave you. I have to kill Marshall and my dad." He swallows, looking hopeful, but I cut him off, "But me and you, that's over."

I stomp past him. He grabs at me. I pull an arrow, dropping the boots and quiver at the same moment. I pull back and release, grazing his shoulder with the tip. He cries out. I grab another arrow and run up the hill. He's up and after me; I turn and pull it back hard. He walks up to my arrow with blood dripping down his shoulder, "We aren't over."

I nod my head, "We are."

His blue eyes are ice, "Then release the arrow."

I shake my head, "Don't make me."

He leans into it farther. My arms and hands are burning. I release the tension, dropping my arm and the arrow down.

He leans into me more, "If you need time to get past this, fine. But

I'm not playing around. I love you. You have my whole heart."

I sigh, looking down, "Will, you don't have a heart. You're just like every other man out there, except Bernie and Jake. And I'm not even sure about Jake."

I turn away and walk up the hill with my bow. I don't even go back for my quiver and my boots.

I climb into the tent me and Anna used last time and curl into the blankets. She comes in a minute later and snuggles into me.

"You know now don't you?" she whispers into my face.

I nod sniffling.

"At least nobody died, Em."

I nod. She is so much like Bernie.

I snuggle into her and listen as the music starts up at the fire. I hear Jake and a girl singing. Anna starts snoring, which doesn't make much sense, since she can't make other noises.

Then I hear the sound of our tent zipper. I sit up, ready for a fight but it's just Will. He drops my boots and quiver and climbs in.

I shake my head and point at the door, "Go." I whisper.

"Hear me out, please."

"No."

He crawls to me, not listening at all. He lays down on my pillow, "I fucked up so bad. I know we weren't together at the time and you liked Jake a lot. I didn't think I stood a chance with you. I made such a mistake, kissing you in the woods that day, when we first met. I just had to. I don't know why. I came off as a smug ass. That's not me."

I shake my head, "I don't want to hear this."

"I liked you instantly. You know how they say love at first sight? I think I had that. There you were, with that big wolf, and that mean scowl, and a surly teenager. You were savage and crazy, but at the same time, the most loyal person I'd ever met. You were ready to die for the people you were looking for. And then, when you said you knew where my family was, I nearly kissed you then. You were ready to die for my family. I acted like a dick. I saw your face when you saw Jake, and I was pissed. I knew he'd gotten there before me and he was the better man. He deserved you and I didn't. I fucked up."

His words are nice; they make me feel something, but it isn't enough of a something. I shake my head, "I'm sorry, Will. I can't do this."

He sits up and pulls me down onto him. I struggle but he holds me there. The hot tears are there again. I sob into his shirt and hate myself for letting him touch me. When I feel his grip relax, I whisper, "I do love Jake. I always did." It's a lie but I need him to not want me. I need him to go away and leave me alone.

Instead, he wraps himself around me, "I know you're lying. I saw you swimming today. I saw you look scared, when you saw me. You were worried about what I thought, even though you sent that girl to hit on me."

I shake my head, "I'm sorry I shot you but I don't want you."

He kisses my forehead and gets up, "I want you enough for us both for right now. I came to tell you too, we have a good size group of us to go after Marshall. We leave tomorrow. Star made that possible. Don't hate her."

I shake my head, "She's my family. The only real one I have left. She never lied to me."

He looks at me, "You know that thing your dad was holding out to you, when he was dying and he told you to take it? Babe, that was his heart. He gave you his heart and his hope and his love. That's what was in his hand." He leans forward and grabs my hand, "Take mine too." He lets go of me and leaves the tent. The sound of the zipper hurts. I want him to stay.

I grip the pillow and try to make the hurting go away. Anna cracks an eye, "I'm your family, asshole."

I nod as a single tear drips down my face, "I know. Sorry. That was a shot at him, not you."

"I know... make him wait. He deserves to suffer before you forgive him."

I scowl at her, "What makes you think I'm gonna forgive him?"

She grins, "In Granny's romance novels they always forgive them, after a bad heartbreak like that."

I laugh bitterly, "I've created a monster. I never should have told you to read that damned bookcase."

She smirks, "How else am I going to learn about love?"

I roll my eyes, "Not from me, that's for damned sure. Did you read the *Outlander* book by the Gabaldon lady?"

She nods, "Yeah."

I sigh, "I wish Will was more like Jamie."

She sighs and whispers back, "I think we all wish men were like that."

I close my eyes and fight the dreams about tomorrow.

The End

Stay Tuned for information about the last of The Born Trilogy:

Reborn

ABOUT THE AUTHOR

Tara Brown is a Bestselling author who writes Fantasy, Science Fiction, Paranormal Romance and Contemporary Romance in New Adult, Young Adult and Adult fiction. She lives in Canada with her husband, two daughters and pets.

Other Books by this author

The Devil's Roses Series
Cursed
Bane
Hyde
Witch
Death

The Born Trilogy
Born
Born to Fight

The Blood Trail Chronicles
Vengeance

The Light Trilogy
The Light of the World
The Four Horsemen – coming soon

The Blackwater Witches Trilogy
Blackwater

The Lonely
The End of Me
My Side

Made in the USA
Lexington, KY
03 July 2013